VIOLENCE AGAINST CHILDREN

This body of research is dedicated to all children living in difficult circumstances.
It is further dedicated to my two children, Alexander and Megan,
by whose existence mine became further realised, and to my husband, Nico,
for enabling me to 'fly'.

I would like to acknowledge Nasser Mustapha of the University of the
West Indies (UWI), St. Augustine Campus; Mathijs Euwema, Director,
International Child Development Initiatives (ICDI), Leiden, The Netherlands;
and Huug Van Gompel of Garant Publishing, Belgium.

Every attempt has been made to ensure the accuracy and reliability of the information in this book.
Neither the author nor the publisher can be held responsible for any inconvenience
due to possible inaccuracies which readers may encounter in this book.

Rona Jualla van Oudenhoven

Violence Against Children
A Rights-Based Discourse

Antwerp-Apeldoorn

Rona Jualla van Oudenhoven
Violence Against Children
A Rights-Based Discourse
Antwerp – Apeldoorn
Garant
2016

210 blz. – 24 cm
ISBN 978-90-441-3359-2
D/2016/5779/43
NUR 752/740

© Rona Jualla van Oudenhoven & Garant Publishers

All rights protected. Other than exceptions specified by the copyright law, no part of this publication may be reproduced, stored or made public, in any way whatsoever, without the express, prior and written permission of the author and of the publisher.

Garant Publishers
Somersstraat 13-15, B-2018 Antwerpen
Koninginnelaan 96, NL-7315 EB Apeldoorn
www.garant-uitgevers.be   info@garant.be
www.garant-uitgevers.nl   info@garant-uitgevers.nl

Garant/Central Books
99, Wallis Road, London E9 5 LN, Great-Britain
www.centralbooks.com   bill@centralbooks.com

Garant/International Specialized Book Services (ISBS)
920 NE 58th Ave Suite 300, Portland, OR 9721311, USA
www.isbs.com   info@isbs.com, orders@isbs.com

Garant/University Book House
130, Planning Street Box 16983, Al Ain, UAE
www.universitybookhouse.com   bookhouse@emirates.net

Table of Contents

¶	List of Figures	8
¶	List of Tables	10
¶	Abstract	12

Part 1		13
1.0	**Introduction**	15
2.0	**The violence discourse**	19
2.1	Theoretical and Conceptual Framework	19
	2.1.1 Conceptualising Violence	20
	2.1.2 Structural Violence	22
	2.1.3 Cultural Violence	25
2.2	Violence, Colonialism and Development	27
	2.2.1 Structural Violence and Colonialism	27
	2.2.2 Structural Violence and Development	29
	2.2.3 Cultural Violence and Colonialism	31
2.3	Violence and Tolerance	33
2.4	Violence Typologies and Its Effects	35
	2.4.1 Effects of Violence on Children	35
	2.4.2 Typologies of Violence Worldwide	37
	2.4.3 Corporal Punishment	37
	2.4.4 Domestic Violence	40
	2.4.5 Media Violence	41
	2.4.6 Gender Violence	42
	2.4.7 Street Children	44
	2.4.8 Violence and Inequity	47
	2.4.9 Violence and Terrorism	48

3.0	**Talking rights**	**49**
3.1	Upholding the Rights Discourse	49
3.2	Violence and the Convention on the Rights of the Child (CRC)	50
3.3	Country Review: Bangladesh, Canada, Nicaragua, the Netherlands, T&T Bangladesh: A Violent Place, Particularly for Girls and Women	52 53
3.4	A Child Rights-Based Approach	67

Part 2   71

4.0	**The study**	**73**
4.1	Historical, International and Local Context	73
4.2	Objectives of the Study	78
4.3	Core Assumptions	79
4.4	The Instruments	80
4.5	Data Analysis and Limitations of the Study	83
5.0	**The findings**	**85**
5.1	Analysis of the Data	85
	5.1.1 Definition of Violence	86
	5.1.2 Most Common Forms of Violence	87
	4.1.3 Worst Forms of Violence	89
	5.1.4 The 'Causes' of Violence	90
	5.1.5 Sources of Information	92
	5.1.6 Is There a Difference between Violence against Girls and Violence against Boys?	93
	5.1.7 How Can We Protect Girls from Violence?	95
	5.1.8 How Can We Protect Boys from Violence?	95
	5.1.9 Do You Think Physical Punishment is Okay or Not Okay?	95
	5.1.10 What Would You Do If You Suspected an Incidence of Abuse or Domestic Violence?	97
	5.1.11 What Kind of Violence Do You See Street Children Faced With in T&T?	98
5.12	Who are the Main Perpetrators of Violence against Street Children?	101
	5.1.13 What Can Be Done To Lower the Violence against Street Children?	103
	5.1.14 What Situations Do You Think Help Lessen Violence?	104
	5.1.15 What Are Some Things That You Can Do As an Individual To Stop the Cycle of Violence against Children?	105
	5.1.16 What Could Be Done To Combat Violence?	106
	5.1.17 How Do People in T&T Look at Violence from an Historical and International Perspective?	108
	5.1.18 What Role Should the Government Play in Fighting VAC?	113

5.2	Testing the Hypotheses	113
5.3	Children Living in Institutions	123
5.4	Children: Violence, Fears and Happiness	140
6.0	**Recommendations**	**143**
6.1	Multi-angular Lens	144
6.2	Adopt a Rights-Based Approach to dealing with the situation of VAC	147
6.3	Including All Stakeholders in the Violence Discourse	149
6.4	Engage Antidotes to Violence	154
6.5	Explore Positive Deviance and its Relevance for Combating Violence against Children	163
6.6	Creating a VAC Epistemic Community	165
6.7	Conduct Research: What Can You Do to Stop the Cycle of Violence?	168
6.8	Being Visionary in Approach	172
7.0	**Conclusion**	**175**
¶	**References**	**179**
¶	**Appendices**	**197**

List of Figures

Figure 2.1	Galtung's Typology of Violence Source: Galtung (1969, 173)	21
Figure 2.2	Galtung's (1996) Triangular Model of Violence	25
Figure 3.1	Ratification Status of the Convention on the Rights of the Child	51
Figure 5.1	Response Percentage for Three Conceptual Dimensions of Violence	86
Figure 5.2	Response Percentage for Four Categories of Violence	86
Figure 5.3	Worst Forms of VAC Identified by Respondents	90
Figure 5.4	'No Difference' In Violence against Girls and Violence against Boys	94
Figure 5.5	Suggested Methods of Protecting Boys from Violence	96
Figure 5.6	Responses to Suspected Abuse or Domestic Violence	97
Figure 5.7	Kinds of Violence Most Frequently Encountered by Street Children	99
Figure 5.8	Main Perpetrators of Violence against Street Children	102
Figure 5.9	Ways of Reducing Violence against Street Children	103
Figure 5.10	T&T's Violence Ranking Compared with the Rest of the World.	108
Figure 5.11	Respondents' Tolerance of Violence	109
Figure 5.12	T&T 20 years ago, T&T now, T&T 20 years from now?	113
Figure 5.13	Relationship between Definition and Acceptance of Violence	117
Figure 5.14	Relationship between Definition and Tolerance of Violence	119
Figure 5.15	Relationship between Definition of Violence and Violence Intervention	122
Figure 5.16	Example of Violence: A Parent Hitting a Child for No Good Reason	123
Figure 5.17	Example of Violence: A Parent Hitting a Child for Misbehaving	124
Figure 5.18	Example of Violence: A Boy Hits a Girl	124
Figure 5.19	Example of Violence: A Girl Hits Boy	125
Figure 5.20	Example of Violence: A Husband/Boyfriend Hitting His Wife/ Girlfriend	125
Figure 5.21	Example of Violence: A Wife/Girlfriend Hitting Her Husband or Boyfriend	126
Figure 5.22	Example of Violence: A Child Not Being Allowed To Go to School and Have an Education	126
Figure 5.23	Example of Violence: A Child Not Getting Help in the Hospital	127
Figure 5.24	Example of Violence: Someone Shouting Bad and Hurtful Words at another Person	127
Figure 5.25	Example of Violence: Do You Think Physical Punishment Is Okay When a Child Does Wrong?	128
Figure 5.26	Example of Violence: Do You Think Physical Punishment Is Okay When An Adult Does Wrong?	129

Figure 5.27	Bad Forms of Punishment: Hitting With the Hands	129
Figure 5.28	Bad Forms of Punishment: Beating With a Stick or Strap	130
Figure 5.29	Bad Forms of Punishment: Locking Child in a Closet	130
Figure 5.30	Bad Forms of Punishment: Locking Child in a Room	131
Figure 5.31	Bad Forms of Punishment: Taking Away Food from the Child (No Lunch or Dinner)	131
Figure 5.32	Bad Forms of Punishment: Cursing the Child (Using Bad Words)	132
Figure 5.33	Bad Forms of Punishment: Tying Up the Child	132
Figure 5.34	Can You Name One (1) Right of the Child?	134
Figure 5.35	How Do You Feel About Violence?	136
Figure 5.36	Who Can Help Stop Violence?	137
Figure 5.37	Answers by Children <12 to the Question: 'Any Idea On How To Stop Violence Against Children?'	138
Figure 5.38	Ages of children	140
Figure 5.39	Child's Depiction of Happiness	141
Figure 5.40	Drawing by a Child Showing Happy Feeling	141
Figure 5.41	Child's Concept of Violence	142
Figure 5.42	Drawing Done by a Child to Show Violence	142
Figure 5.43	Violence Depicted In a Wall Painting	142

List of Tables

Table 2.1	Violence Typology According to Galtung	22
Table 2.2	Selected Countries and Their Positions on Corporal Punishment	38
Table 2.3	Policies on Corporal Punishment in the Caribbean Region	39
Table 2.4	Women's Attitudes towards Domestic Violence in Selected Countries	40
Table 3.1	Human Development Information on Bangladesh (UNICEF, 2013)	53
Table 3.2	Human Development Information on Canada (UNICEF 2013)	55
Table 3.3	Human Development Information on Nicaragua	57
Table 3.4	Human Development Information on The Netherlands	59
Table 3.5	Package of Children's Legislation Initiated in 2000	64
Table 4.1	Human Development Indices for Selected Countries	72
Table 4.2	Under-Five Mortality Rate for Selected Countries	73
Table 4.3	Global Peace Indicators for Selected Countries Neighbouring T&T	73
Table 4.4	Scores for 'Respect of Human Rights' (RHR), 'violent crime' (VC) and 'Perceived Criminality' (PC) of Selected Countries	74
Table 5.1	Categories and Number of Respondents	85
Table 5.2	Definitions of Violence against Children by Interviewees	87
Table 5.3	Most Common Forms of VAC Identified by Interviewees	88
Table 5.4	Types of Violence Most Frequently Encountered by Street Children	101
Table 5.5	Ways of Reducing Violence against Street Children	104
Table 5.6	T&T's Violence Ranking Compared with the Rest of the World	109
Table 5.7	Respondents' Tolerance of Violence	110
Table 5.8	T&T 20 years ago, T&T now, T&T 20 years from now?	112
Table 5.9	Example of Violence: A Parent Hitting a Child for No 'Good' Reason	123
Table 5.10	Example of Violence: A Parent Hitting a Child for Misbehaving	124
Table 5.11	Example of Violence: A Boy Hits a Girl	124
Table 5.12	Example of Violence: A Girl Hits Boy	125
Table 5.13	Example of Violence: A Husband/Boyfriend Hitting His Wife/ Girlfriend	125
Table 5.14	Example of Violence: A Wife/Girlfriend Hitting Her Husband or Boyfriend	126
Table 5.15	Example of Violence: A Child Not Being Allowed To Go to School and Have an Education	126
Table 5.16	Example of Violence: A Child Not Getting Help in the Hospital	127
Table 5.17	Example of Violence: Someone Shouting Bad and Hurtful Words at another Person	127

Table 5.18	Example of Violence: Do You Think Physical Punishment Is Okay When a Child Does Wrong?	128
Table 5.19	Example of Violence: Do You Think Physical Punishment Is Okay When An Adult Does Wrong?	128
Table 5.20	Bad Forms of Punishment: Hitting With the Hands	129
Table 5.21	Bad Forms of Punishment: Beating With a Stick or Strap	130
Table 5.22	Bad Forms of Punishment: Locking Child in a Closet	130
Table 5.23	Bad Forms of Punishment: Locking Child in a Room	131
Table 5.24	Bad Forms of Punishment: Taking Away Food from the Child (No Lunch or Dinner)	131
Table 5.25	Bad Forms of Punishment: Cursing the Child (Using Bad Words)	132
Table 5.26	Bad Forms of Punishment: Tying Up the Child	132
Table 5.27	Have You Ever Heard About the Rights of the Child?	133
Table 5.28	Do You Think That Children in T&T Have Rights?	133
Table 5.29	Rights of the Child Identified by the Children	133
Table 5.30	Have You Ever Experienced Any Violence in Your Life?	134
Table 5.31	Do You Think It Is Normal?	135
Table 5.32	Do You Think Some Children Never Experience Violence in Their Life?	135
Table 5.33	How Do You Feel About Violence?	135
Table 5.34	Answers by Children <12 to the Question: 'Who Can Help Stop Violence?	137
Table 5.35	Answers by Children <12: 'Any Idea On How To Stop Violence Against Children?	138
Table 5.36	Religion of Children	139
Table 5.37	Ages of Children	139
Table 5.38	Sex of Children	140
Table 6.1	Issues Deemed Suitable for the Positive Deviance Approach	164

Abstract

Violence against Children: A Rights-Based Discourse

This book is essentially a research paper that explores the situation of violence against children (VAC) in the Caribbean context against an international backdrop. It examines the different dimensions of violence (direct, cultural and structural) and involves a sociological exploration of the factors that contribute to the high tolerance of violence that exists in the Caribbean region, with particular attention to Trinidad and Tobago. A deconstruction of the violence concept and its epistemological implications allows for a defining, refining and re-defining of the phenomenon. The research examines the spheres of domestic violence, gender violence, violence against street children, and corporal punishment in great detail.

The research adopts a rights-based analysis of the issue of VAC and incorporates an international review; it also imports field research from Bangladesh, Canada, Nicaragua, and the Netherlands context to inform the study. It conducts an evaluation of T&T's[1] standing with respect to the implementation of the UN Convention on the Rights of the Child and puts forward sound recommendations for change. The multi-design approach uses qualitative and quantitative data analysis to assess the nation's knowledge, attitudes, perceptions and beliefs (KAPBs) on the issue of VAC.

The ultimate aim of the paper is for its utilisation by everyone, especially state policy makers, to promote a 'lowering' of the threshold of violence- tolerance, thereby fostering a more child-friendly society.

Keywords: children's rights; violence – tolerance; rights-based.

---

1. Throughout this text the labels 'Trinidad and Tobago' and 'T&T' will be used interchangeably.

Part 1

1.0 Introduction

This research work examines violence tolerance from the perspective of a historical colonial past and investigates its sustenance by contemporary factors, using a structural and post-structural analysis. The conceptual and theoretical discussion is anchored in the work of the Norwegian peace theorist, Johan Galtung, but also rooted in Critical and Structural theory, Marxism, Neo-Marxism and Postmodernism. The research adopts a rights-based approach to deal with the issue of VAC[1] and claims that "zero tolerance for violence is a matter of basic respect for human rights," Global AIDS Alliance (2006, 3).

The writer purports that an understanding of violence against children in a Caribbean context inevitably emanates from a critical grasp of the region's colonial history comprising periods of enslavement and indentureship and characterized by a culture of violence and tolerance. Violence has been built into the structures of the region (the legal, political, economic, and social structures) and has formed part of the fibre of these societies; violence ideology has been internalized and sanctioned as part of the culture. Morgan and Youssef (2006, 10) claim that "violence has been woven into the social fabric of modern Caribbean societies from their inception", while Sharpe (1996) notes that certainly Caribbean people have accepted harsh physical punishment of children as a cultural norm and even a historic legacy. Dependency theorists have long painted a violent parasitic picture of the region with a *metropolis-satellite* (Gunder Frank 1967)[2] model of development to explain its political and socio-economic dimensions, a historically *plantation-type society* (Beckford 1972)[3] characterized for the most part by *centre-periphery type economic dynamics* (Wallerstein 1998),[4] which inevitably construct systems that are structurally exploitative despite who

---

1. Throughout this text the labels 'violence against children' and 'VAC' will be used interchangeably.
2. Streefkerk notes that in Gunder Frank's 'metropole-satellite' theory it is further claimed that a temporary weakening of the ties between the metropole and the satellite would benefit the economic and industrial development of the satellite. Frank lists as examples of this the industrialization of Brazil, Mexico, Argentina, and India during the depression and the Second World War.
3. Beckford saw the plantation system as a total economic institution, where "the internal and external dimensions of the plantation system dominate the countries' economic, social and political structure and their relation with the rest of the world" (p.102).
4. Wallerstein divides the capitalist world-economy into core states, semi-peripheral, and peripheral areas. He notes that the peripheral areas are the least developed; they are exploited by the core for their cheap labour, raw materials, and agricultural production.

governs. The problematic for the region, and T&T society, is that these *structurally violent systems* (tolerance of injustice e.g. via the inaction of child-protection mechanisms and inequitable distribution of resources) create and support a *culture of violence* (daily perpetuation of violent acts) which leads to the continued existence of *direct violence* (e.g. child abuse).

At regional, national, community and domestic levels, awareness of children's rights is seldom developed as these are viewed as vague, intangible concepts that promote precociousness in children. This traditional view is held by many of the older generation's religious and community leaders; children are often treated as less important and powerless.[5] Children as powerful or children as right holders is still a very controversial issue, not only in T&T and the Caribbean, but in many regions of the world, as the mere concept challenges and threatens the status quo and the power relations and structures that have existed for too long. Yet, the ones to be listened to, should naturally be, children. The writer, along with many others in this fight against VAC, holds a view that runs contrary to popularly held notions that children "do not care about the future" or "are interested only in Facebook" or "have nothing to contribute or say".[6] They ought to be given the opportunity to be active agents and creators/shapers of their own lives and destinies. They are more than willing to embrace their roles; more willing than society has been keen to allow. It is not uncommon for state agencies, children's organizations, adults and the media to under-represent children, to portray them as victims and underplay their 'agency', treat them as objects rather than subjects, and dwell mostly on negative events and gender stereotypes.

This discourse embraces wider research and experiences on violence against children, and various forms of expertise and practices with the objective to review their suitability for the Trinidad and Tobago context as well as to validate the nation's own accomplishments and see how the Trinbagonian lessons could be of benefit to others. This involves what Santos (2005, 28) terms "the dialectics of the local and the global" and its inherent structuring problematic of balancing the subjects in the development environment so as to afford legitimacy to its claims. For too long, universalizing principles have hierarchically afforded local context an abysmal role in development knowledge: "the local is the subordinated counterpart of a reality or entity that has the capacity to designate itself as global" (Santos 2005, 20). Often a global perspective makes invisible not only actions on the ground, but also its own power source, contributing to normalization of the development establishment and its decision-making privilege (McMichael 2010b). The research liberates itself from this error and casts off a superimposed 'othering'[7] because of sheer virtue of global placement and proclaims its contextual significance, indeed, in a global perspective.

---

5. Policy Paper Child Rights, Plan Netherlands, Amsterdam (2006).
6. Director of Policy Development in a significant ministry in T&T, in discussion with the author August 2013.
7. The concept of 'other' is claimed by several writers. Friedrich Hegel introduced it as constituent in self-consciousness; it was formalized by Emmanuel Levinas and popularised by Edward Said. For Michel Foucault, 'othering' meant recognition of differences, usually with the incorrect implications of normal versus abnormal.

It is the personal experience of the writer that the know-how of Trinidad and Tobago makes sense in other settings, ranging from Bangladesh, Kenya, the Netherlands, Palestine, Pakistan, Thailand, Japan, and South Africa to Yakutia in Siberia, among others. Thus, small as T&T may be in land size and population, it is and should feel entitled and at ease when acting globally as its unique history, mixture of ethnic groups and customs, geographic location and problematic make it relevant to many.[8]

The research appropriates the universals of democracy, rights, citizenry and development as its method of analysis of violence and adopts a rights-based approach. It professes to be a unique and significant tool in addressing the alleviation of violence against children in the region; one that enriches the existing body of knowledge, gives additional voice to children and their issues, and allows for a multi-dimensional exploration of a very critical social ill.

---

8.  The 'first issue', 1 February, 2013, of the Canada Post stamp honouring T&T citizen Seraphim Fortes, illustrating the fact that a small twin island nation of Trinidad and Tobago with barely 1.3 million people can see its citizenry 'stamp' out a name for itself, so to speak, in almost any part of the world.

2.0 The violence discourse

2.1 Theoretical and Conceptual Framework

Critical theory forms the main theoretical framework of this research, right alongside Conflict theory.

> "Critical theory is essentially a pluralistic exercise and currently the dominant cultural paradigm in Western culture as it helps to foster debates between *multiple interpretations* and promoting *democratic pluralism.*" (Sim and Van Loon 2001, 5)

This allows for both a selective and 'magpie' approach to framing the debate on rights and violence. The writer endorses "this style of crossing theories such as Marxism with postmodernism, post colonialism with deconstruction, and feminism with poststructuralism" (Sim and Van Loon 2001, 6) to create a unique synthetic. The continued relevance of Marxism for the region lies in its colonial and post-colonial struggle for freedom, identity and survival, and is embodied in CLR James' (1947, 15-16) statement that "the dialectic is a theory of knowledge ... it is a theory of the nature of man" and his endless search for "some sort of completeness" and is further reinforced by the acceptance of the essentially universalising doctrine of Marxism as liberty, equality and self-determination, regardless of context. The reliance on post structuralism and postmodernism for analysis of the region seems only natural for, as Berkeley (2012) notes, one significant analytical tool emergent from Phillips' (2007) work on *Multiculturalism without Culture* is its implication of a useful framework of postmodern trajectory for analysing cultural and racial diversity in Caribbean societies such as Trinidad and Guyana. Berkeley (2012) supports Brathwaite's (1975) position on cultural pluralism in which he notes that multicultural societies can be studied in a postmodernist paradigm and argues that this would allow for a 'deconstruction of ethnic relations', with the result that people could be understood as individuals rather than belonging to groups that have been arbitrarily lumped together under grand or rather frivolous theorization.

2.1.1 Conceptualising Violence[1]

Conceptually, for many, 'violence' conjures up images of direct or physical force and violence discourse has for a long time been focused on personal violence, looking at violence and its physical and psychological effects, the effects of violence on the individual and society, violence versus the threat of violence, violence and wars, and violence whether intended or unintended. Johan Galtung (1930-), who founded peace research as an academic discipline, has taken the discourse further by having successfully explored the many faces of violence and created a flurry of discussions and debates on violence and its multifaceted dimensions. It is also his elaboration of violence and peace that proves very intriguing to this researcher as it pertains to the element of violence — tolerance.

> "I understand violence as the unavoidable impairment of fundamental human needs or, to put it in more gentle terms, the impairment of human life, which lowers the actual degree to which someone is able to meet their needs below that which would otherwise be possible. The threat of violence is also violence." (Quoted by Müller n.d, 1).

A consideration of the theoretical dimensions of violence extends the definition further than the previously held narrow concept to include the notion of violence as being a disparity between an individual's *actual* somatic and mental realizations and their *potential* realizations. Accordingly, violence is "defined as the cause of the difference between the potential and the actual" (Ibid). In today's society, according to this definition, violence is when a child dies from malnutrition because the resources exist to prevent such a situation; the situation is *avoidable*. Violence is when young girls are denied education simply because it is deemed as a right entitlement of the boy child; violence is the exploitation of boys and girls for labour by factory owners depriving them of their right to education and play.[2] Violence is forcing young girls into early marriages; statistics show that:

> "girls younger than 15 are five times more likely to die in childbirth than women in their 20s and that pregnancy is the leading cause of death worldwide for women ages 15 to 19".[3]

> "In other words, when the potential is higher than the actual is by definition avoidable and when it is avoidable, then violence is present." (Galtung 1969, 169):

> "Thus, the potential level of realization is that which is possible with a given level of insight and resources. If insight and/or resources are monopolized by a group or class or

---

1. This section draws on the initial research proposal for this research, 'A Culture of Violence: A Rights-Based Analysis of Child Abuse in Trinidad and Tobago'. Rona Jualla-Ali, 2007. Institute of Social Studies, The Hague, Netherlands.
2. Worldwide 126 million children work under hazardous conditions, often enduring beatings, humiliation and sexual violence by their employers, www.compassion.com/child-advocacy/find-your-voice/quick-facts/child labor/html, accessed 12 March 2013
3. www.icrw.org/child-marriage-facts-and-figures, accessed 29 September 2013.

are used for other purposes, then the actual level falls below the potential level, and violence is present in the system. In addition to these types of indirect violence there is also the direct violence where means of realization are not withheld, but directly destroyed." (Ibid: 169)

Another sphere of violence includes the distinction of harm as being inflicted on someone, by someone, the issue of subject/object presence. Does violence exist when no one is physically harmed? The literature deals with the threat of violence or the indirect threat of mental violence, for example, and acknowledges the element of intent in violence and the manifest or latent qualities that may be inherent in the act. Galtung (1969, 171) postulates that when there is an actor who commits violence then that is *personal violence*; where there is no such actor he claims that to be *structural violence*. In that instance "the violence is built into the structure and shows up as unequal power and consequently as unequal life chances" (Ibid, 172). Accordingly, he sees the object of personal violence perceives the violence, while the object of structural violence may be persuaded to not view an act as violent. Thus he proposes that personal violence is representative of change and dynamism whereas structural violence is silent. Personal violence can be acknowledged as violence whereas structural violence may be disguised as natural, normal behaviour. Figure 2.1 shows Galtung's initial typology of violence without the cultural component.

> "By making a fundamental distinction between personal and structural violence, it can be seen from two angles. Indeed, this is exactly the same as peace, which is understood as the absence of violence. A more expansive concept of violence leads to a more expansive understanding of peace: Peace defined as the absence of personal violence and the absence of structural violence. These two forms of peace are referred to as negative peace and positive peace." (Galtung 1969, 168)

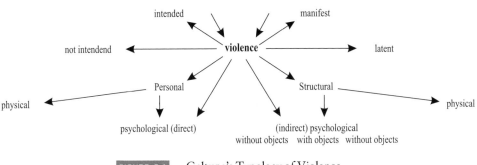

FIGURE 2.1 Galtung's Typology of Violence
Source: Galtung (1969, 173)

2.1.2 Structural Violence

Structural violence is a term introduced by Galtung (1969). He refers to a form of violence where the social structure or social institution harms people by preventing them from meeting their basic needs. He cites also elitism, ethnocentrism, classism, racism, sexism, adultism, nationalism, heterosexism and ageism as examples of structural violence. Galtung (1969) claims that structural violence and direct violence are interdependent and include such direct outcomes as domestic violence, racial violence, hate crimes, terrorism, genocide and war.

TABLE 2.1 Violence Typology According to Galtung

Violence typology	Need Groups			
Survival	Well-being	Identity/Purpose	Freedom	
(Negation: death)	(Negation: poverty, illness)	(Negation: alienation)	(Negation: oppression)	
Direct violence	Killing	Injury, siege, sanctions, poverty	De-socialization, re-socialization, Underclass	Repression, Imprisonment, expulsion, deportation
Structural violence	Exploitation A	Exploitation B	Penetration, segmentation	Marginalization, fragmentation

Source: Galtung (1993, 106)

> "... exploitation represents the main part of an archetypical violence structure. This means nothing more than a situation in which some people, namely the top dogs, draw substantially more profit from the interaction taking place within this structure than the others, the underdogs ... In reality, the underdogs might be disadvantaged to such a degree that they die (starve or waste away as a result of illness and disease): this is categorised as *exploitation A*. The second type of *exploitation (B)* means leaving the underdogs in a permanent involuntary state of poverty, which usually encompasses malnutrition and illness. All this happens within complex structures and at the end of long and ramified legislation chains and cycles ...

The best way to understand the next four terms is as a constituent part of the exploitation that is, strengthening components contained within the structure. Their function is to prevent awareness and mobilisation of this awareness which are two of the conditions needed to be successful in fighting exploitation. With the help of *penetration*, elements of the top dog ideology reaches the consciousness of the underdog; this penetration is linked to *segmentation*, which only allows the underdog a limited view of reality. The latter is the result of two processes, *marginalization and fragmentation*. This involves forcing the underdogs increasingly to the edge of society, condemning them as insignificant, dividing them and keeping them away from each other. These four terms actually describe forms of *structural violence*."[4] (Galtung 1993, 107)

Petra Kelly (cited at http://en.wikipedia.org/wiki/Structural_violence) described the millions of people — children and women foremost among them — dying from malnutrition and preventable diseases as victims of structural violence. This research has shown that updated statistics continue to reflect similar dreary events. However, commitment to the Millennium Development Goals (MDGs) has witnessed visible improvement in many countries, among them, those of the Caribbean and Latin America, with Africa and other war-torn regions having a long way to go.[5] Still, too many children live in poverty, die during birth or a few years later, do not go to school, and/or live out their childhood exposed to the most deplorable living conditions.

When talking about the health of subaltern or marginalized people, medical anthropologist. Farmer (quoted at http://en.wikipedia.org/wiki /Structural_violence) states that:

"… their sickness is a result of structural violence: neither culture nor pure individual will is at fault; rather, historically given (and often economically driven) processes and forces conspire to constrain individual agency. Structural violence is visited upon all those whose social status denies them access to the fruits of scientific and social progress!"

Many theories have postulated that structural violence is embedded in and sustained by the current world system, but is invisible to the naive onlooker. However, upon close examination, systemic or structural violence, for example, in the American health care system, becomes visible. In a study conducted by Moore et al. (1994), it was found that blacks had a significantly lesser chance of receiving treatment than whites. In the prisons in the United States the proportion of blacks to whites is proverbially highly skewed.

The prisons in Canada tell a similar story. Sapers (2013) notes that the trail of many social policies, which have marginalized one group of the population, defines *systemic discrimination;* he argues that there are slightly more than 3,400 aboriginal men and women who comprise a significant 23 per cent of the country's federal prison inmate population.[6] Thus, in federal prisons, nearly one in four is Métis, Inuit, or First Nations. Sapers (2013) also complains about the longer terms, and time spent in segregation and maximum security by

---

4. The emphasis (text in italics) is that of this researcher.
5. See /www.un.org/millenniumgoals/pdf/report-2013/2013_progress_english.pdf, accessed 4 October 2013.
6. Aboriginal people in Canada comprise just four per cent of the population.

aboriginal inmates; they are also less likely to be granted parole. Ryan (2013), looking at the situation in T&T, also notes an over-representation of young black males in the prison population.

Any theoretical discourse on exploitation, discrimination, systemic inequality and social change must begin with the father of revolutionary theory and structuralism, Karl Marx (1977),[7] who writes on the base-superstructure in his *Preface*:

> "In the social production of their existence, men inevitably enter into definite relations, which are independent of their will, namely [the] *relations of production* appropriate to a given stage in the development of their material forces of production. The totality of these *relations of production* constitutes the economic structure of *society*, the real foundation, on which arises a legal and political *superstructure*, and to which correspond definite forms of consciousness. The *mode of production* of material life conditions the general process of social, political, and intellectual life. It is not the *consciousness* of men that determines their existence, but their social existence that determines their consciousness." (Marx 1977)

The themes of violence and *systemic exploitation* recur in the works of Marx and Engels with a revolution only possible if first the proletarians (masses) remove their cloak of *false consciousness* (culture of tolerance). The similarities in Galtung's typology of violence[8] are seen here. Consciousness or awareness plays a huge role in revolutionary change in Marxist philosophy as it does in today's society, whether or not the recourse is violence.

> "The changes in the economic foundation lead, sooner or later, to the transformation of the whole, immense, superstructure. In studying such transformations, it is always necessary to distinguish between the material transformation of the economic conditions of production, which can be determined with the precision of natural science, and the legal, political, religious, artistic, or philosophic — in short, *ideological* forms in which men and women become conscious of this conflict and fight it out." (Marx 1977)

The ideological dimension necessary for initiating structural change is noted by Marx and this ideology comes from the cultural makeup of the group which is after all responsible for the transmission of dominant and mainstream ideology. Caribbean scholars Morgan and Youssef (2006) claim that:

> "Few among us appreciate as keenly as we might the ways in which our lives and circumstances are constrained, not just by the societies in which we live, but by the power structures which dominate those societies. "Implicit assumptions", which are handed to us

---

7. Originally published 1959.
8. Those themes of exploitation, penetration, segmentation, marginalization and fragmentation.

by the powers that be, constitute the "ideologies" by which we live, though we may think of these ideologies merely as commonsense realities ... We tell ourselves that we live in democracies and look to the "Third World" dictatorships as entities where governmental control is coercively maintained, convincing ourselves in so doing that we are not under constraint. In reality, however, as critical discourse analysis has shown us, each governing body "controls" us through the web of reality that it creates and recreates through language, and releases to us daily through the media." (4)

2.1.3 Cultural Violence

Some twenty plus years after the introduction of the concept of 'structural violence' Galtung (1990) developed his more multidimensional Triangular Model of Violence with the three dimensions of violence: *direct violence, structural violence* and *cultural violence*. He notes that it is when these three forms of violence are combined that violent behaviour in its multiple varieties becomes evident. He notes that there is a cultural imperative for violence built into the societal values or cultural values of a particular religion or nation (Ibid, 1990). He argues that *cultural violence* is connected to the cultural paradigms and guidelines which rule socially accepted behaviour, whether consciously (explicitly) or unconsciously (implicitly). Thus he argues, cultural violence supports and perpetuates violence through cultural guidelines materialized through religion, language, art, and the different manifestations of culture. Structural violence meanwhile pertains to the injustice within society that allows negative situations to persist. "Symbolic violence built into a culture does not kill or maim like direct violence or the violence built into the structure. However, it is used to legitimize either or both, as for instance in the theory of a Herrenvolk, or a superior race." (Galtung 1990, 292). A nation's denial of access to education to the girl child then is both cultural and structural violence; cultural, because it is sanctioned by the norms and value system of the people, and structural, because the laws of the land condone it. The study is premised on this model.

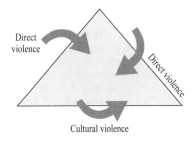

FIGURE 2.2 Galtung's (1996) Triangular Model of Violence

It is also premised on two underlying doctrines of Gandhism — *unity of life* and *unity of means and ends*. Galtung succeeded in including culture as a major focus of peace research.[9] Examples of cultural violence include the influence of religion and ideology, art and language, norms and practices. Some manifestations of culturally sanctioned (*tolerated and accepted*) systemic violent practices against children include genital mutilation,[10] forced early marriages, stoning to death of rape victims (McGreal (2008),[11] infanticide,[12] and child labour, among others. Lazaro (2013, 1) reports that "there are about 140 million girls who have and are to become child brides from 2011 to 2020". In Yemen, it was only in February 2009 when the law made 17 the legal age for marriage; but this was again changed when numerous lawmakers said that it was entirely 'un-Islamic'. In Nepal, young girls having their period are considered unclean and are not allowed to touch anything in the house; they have to stay in the 'goth', a hut outside their village, where they are vulnerable to acts of violence, including rape (Gaestel 2013). In some sub-Saharan countries children with albinism are killed as it is believed that their blood can bring good luck and fortune when used in potions (Laing 2010). *Bacha bazi,* or 'playing with boys', is an old accepted Afghan tradition of sexually abusing young boys, sometimes dressing them up like girls and making them perform for men in tea rooms and at weddings, or keeping them in the backroom of their shops (Londoño 2013). In some rural Indian villages, it is customary and even encouraged for young girls to move into prostitution, with older women passing on the trade and their knowledge to the young ones (Gaedtke and Parameswaran 2013). Child labour is still a widely tolerated form of violence; although its incidence is declining in Latin America and the Caribbean, the number of children aged 5-14 in economic activity is increasing in Sub-Saharan Africa, with still some 215 million child labourers worldwide (ILO 2010).

Sen (2006), economist and philosopher, examines the unfortunate connection between violence and one's tendency to identify with a single key trait — ethnicity, or religion, for example — to the exclusion of all others.[13] He argues that persons can often triumph over this tendency by replacing the commonly held, narrowly-defined, limited sense of identity, with a more complex understanding of ourselves.

---

9. http://jpr.sagepub.com/content/27/3/291.abstract, accessed 5 May 2007.
10. About 140 million girls and women worldwide are currently living with the consequences of FGM; it is mostly carried out on young girls sometime between infancy and age 15; In Africa an estimated 101 million girls 10 years old and above have undergone FGM; FGM is a violation of the human rights of girls and women, accessed 30 September, 2013, www.who.int/mediacentre/factsheets/fs241/en/.
11. An Islamist rebel administration in Somalia had a 13-year-old girl stoned to death for adultery after the child's father reported that three men had raped her.
12. A stone-hearted father threw his infant daughter into the Ravi River on Tuesday after his wife gave birth to another baby girl instead of a boy, Geo News reported. The one-and-a-half-year old infant drowned immediately after she was thrown into the muddy waters of the river, accessed 10 September, 2013, www.thenews.com.pk/article-117630-Heartless-father-drowns-daughter-in-Ravi-River.
13. See http://economistsview.typepad.com/economistsview/2006/05/amartya_sen_ide.html.

This offers an intriguing dimension to explore given the multicultural and multi-ethnic society that is Trinidad and Tobago. The contradiction is, or so it seems, that on the one hand Trinidad and Tobago enjoys a cultural capital that is overwhelmingly rich, especially considering the small size of its population and territory, and the fact that it is sea-locked, while, on the other hand, there are the phenomena of under-performance on critical human development indicators and massive and pervasive violence. How can this be? Perhaps the first observation that must be made is that the paradox is of well-educated people, long traditions of culture, arts and science can readily engage in deadly wars, devastation of cultural property and even genocide. The European wars that have been raging since the emergence of the Roman Empire bear testimony to this; the genocide in Srebrenica, Bosnia, where more than 8,000 Muslims were killed, took place only a few years ago (1996). The flattening of Grozny, Chechen Republic, Russia, occurred at the same time. Every day, in Fallusha, Iraq, children are born with massive birth defects as a result of radioactive weaponry used by the Americans in their wars. And there are so many eruptions of pure barbarism initiated by 'cultured' nations elsewhere on the globe. Colonialism is but one example.

2.2 Violence, Colonialism and Development

2.2.1 Structural Violence and Colonialism

In the Caribbean context, a colonial history marked by destructive direct violence for a prolonged period inevitably leads to the construction of structurally violent and oppressive systems (political, economic, social, educational, and religious). The ideological and cultural transmission that results equates a culture that is loaded with violent elements, a conflict culture of sorts, which has been disguised, camouflaged, and transformed over the decades into mainstream culture and dominant ideology. Thus, although slavery and indentureship and successive periods of colonial occupation in the Caribbean region ended, and although the nation of Trinidad and Tobago has been an independent country since 1962, the legacy of violence has proven to be a more difficult cloak to remove.

> "The decimation of indigenous tribes, successive waves of human migration, geographical displacement of populations, the institutionalized violence of African slavery and the only minimally less disruptive and brutal East Indian indentureship, have in the main produced the contemporary population of the Caribbean ... As Bendad (1997, 202-3) argues: 'Colonialism works through violence and violation ... In the colonial project, violence is not opposed to reason; rather, it completes colonist logic'." (Morgan and Youssef 2006, 10)

"Thus, colonialism is a violation of the sovereignty and liberty of people, and is a form of collective violence" (Dugassa 2008, 15). WHO (2002) defined collective violence as:

> "... the instrumental use of violence by people who identify themselves as members of a group — whether this group is transitory or has a more permanent identity — against another group or set of individuals, in order to achieve political, economic or social objectives." (2)

This definition includes social, political and economic violence. From the perspectives of indigenous scholars, collective violence includes cultural and environmental violence which is physical and psychological and involves deprivation and/or neglect. Chambliss (1996) testifies that colonialism is a political and economic system in which people who are technologically powerful conquer, then rule and settle in another country. Fanon (1965) says of colonialism, that it is not just a simple invasion of physical space but also social and psychological. He noted that colonialism is the sum of all colonial subject positions created by colonial discourses. The notion of a 'civilizing mission' has theorized and legalized repression of indigenous peoples worldwide. For Dei and Asgharzadeh (2001), colonialism is imposition.

Foucault (1980) on epistemological violence says that knowledge is a social construct and that knowledge and power reinforce one another. "Subjugated knowledges", he postulates, are used not merely to understand but to legitimize history and to maintain political power relations and social structures — thereby standing the violence triangle on the cultural dimension base. Epistemological assumptions, or assumptions about the validity of particular *knowledges*, are associated with the identification with, or exclusion of (including through violence), certain groups of people; through knowledge construction, power is exercised (Foucault 1980). Goldberg (1993) maintains that assumptions, values and goals about economy, culture and political social relations are the outcome of epistemological frameworks. In fact, Shiva (2002) observes that indigenous knowledge has been systematically invalidated by colonial epistemology. In an all-encompassing way, colonial and privileged knowledge frames everything within the dominant perspective (Brown 2003; Crichlow 2002). This means that anything outside the Eurocentric scope of knowledge is considered invalid and diseased or pathogenised, and is regulated to be disposed of or incinerated (Dugassa 2008). Knowledge that challenges the dominant paradigm and stands outside the social and political order is most often dismissed as deviant (Habermas 2003); sometimes such knowledge is even criminalized (Brock, Glasbeek, and Murdocca 2014). Another inheritance left by colonialism then is that of *symbolic violence*, which according to Bourdieu (1990, 125) occurs:

> "... when a society lacks both the literacy that would enable it to preserve and accumulate in objectified form the cultural resources inherited from the past, and also the educational

system that would give its agents the aptitudes and dispositions required for the symbolic re-appropriation of those resources."

The maintenance of hegemony was achieved by what Althusser (1971) refers to as Ideological State Apparatuses (ISAs) and Repressive State Apparatuses (RSAs), which were set up in order to establish the role of institutions in society. The education system is seen as the ISA responsible for the transmission of the doctrines and attitudes of submission and compliance and the division of labour responsible for the maintenance of the status quo. Mustapha (2002) notes that Trinidad and Tobago was already a very diverse society when it became independent, and that it carried with it the effects of exploitation, domination and subservience installed by the colonial powers. He acknowledges that there was an attempt by the government to bring into effect a nationalist education system allowing for freedom from colonial domination and that the:

> "... initial expansion has probably changed the boundaries of stratification and access to opportunity has shifted away from solely ascriptive criteria to achievement criteria. However, the society's inequalities are becoming institutionalised and are beginning to follow regular patterns from generation to generation." (146)

Inequity, whether real or perceived, is a major driving force of crime in the region as the 'have nots' derive a strong sense of justification in their quest to balance the nature of things. Corruption and greed in the system politic is reflective of this institutional violence. The ills and struggle of living with a colonial heritage linger on; it is for this state of affairs that Bolioli (1993) suggests that Trinbagonians define themselves by forging a future together; a future not marred by usury, (neo-) colonialism and exploitation.

2.2.2 Structural Violence and Development

Marx (1977) called "commodity fetishism" (market objectification) what Polanyi (1944) later referred to as an illusion of self-interest, drawing attention instead to the rise and regulation of the market ("double movement") animated by counter-movement politics. This dialectic informed much of contemporary social movement analysis leading many critics of the world order to centre their development theory debates on issues of dependency, unequal market forces, underdevelopment, de-centering, accumulation and exploitation of labour.

> "The principal concern has been with the uneven development of capitalism across time and space: the economic enrichment of some nations and regions at the expense of others, expressed in First/Third World, and North/South binaries. This has produced a critical structural perspective on capitalist development, nevertheless still within an economic discourse." (McMichael 2010a, 5)

Much of post-structural development theory contests the legitimacy of this discourse as a misrepresentation of non-European cultures and a discourse of control (Escobar 1995; Said 1978). Bose (1997) notes that the Caribbean region followed quickly on the heels of Asia and Africa to join the 'family of nations' in the quest for independence and nation state building in a post-colonial era. The implications of this union meant

> "... a superimposed monetized commerce as a stimulus and referent of modernization, and post-colonial states harnessed populations and natural resources to the task of economic growth as the guarantor of development (and their legitimacy)."[14]

Rist (1997, 79) says of these new states that "their rights to self-determination had been acquired in exchange for the right to self-definition" and, in many ways, this statement captures the deeper wounds inflicted by the economic violence that occurred as a result of these exploitative relationships. This is an interesting statement in light of Dodson's opinion, on the issue of collective rights, that self-determination can be likened to a river in which all other rights swim" (Dodson 1996). Conflict Theory, as developed by Karl Marx (mid 1880s), Critical Theory as introduced by the Frankfurt School (early 1900s), Plantation Theory (Beckford 1972; Best and Levitt 1975), Dependency Theory (Amin 1974; Dos Santos 1973; Gunder Frank 1967), Caribbean Dependency Theories (Craig 1982; Girvan 1971), World Systems Theory (Wallerstein 1974, 1998), and even Chaos Theory (Elliott and Kiel 1996), amongst others, have at different points in Caribbean history been adopted and adapted to explain and understand growth and development in Caribbean societies. More recently Democratic Theory has helped inspire a much needed attack upon dogmatism and self-righteousness that have accompanied Eurocentric analyses of the region for far too long. The criticisms of Democratic Theory for ignoring institutions in favour of "movements" or "the people" and becoming pragmatic seem, however, to be its very strength.

> Creative and critical thinkers, especially when they are politically active and have outspoken personalities receive a great deal of flak. Johan Galtung who falls under these three categories is no exception. Even if one only focuses on his scientific work, as this study does, it is not surprising to note how much has been said and written about his work, many attesting to its path-breaking significance in the field of peace research and violence epistemology; while others allow for further investigation and study into his scholarly arguments. Among the many comments and critiques, are those of Winter (2012), for example, who proposes an interesting reversal on Galtung's assumption of perpetuation of violence as a result of the invisibility of structural violence, and claims rather that the opposite holds true, that violence is rendered invisible precisely as a result

---

14. Bose (1997) observed of the Indian state: "Instead of the being used as an instrument of development, development became an instrument of the state's legitimacy" (cited in McMichael 2010a, 7).

of repetition. While, Biebricher and Johnson (2012) lash out at Galtung's definition of profound violence in structural terms of resource distribution as undermining the basic tenet of neoliberalism, that of the 'unencumbered individual'. In the main, however, his views are increasingly regarded not only as pertinent to the debate and practice on peace research, but also regarded as highly needed paradigm to make sense of a world that is for ever growing in complexity and contradictions. This statement is in line with Verobej's (2008) comments who painstakingly, point for point, debunks the extensive and rather hostile criticism produced by Coady in his 2008 text *Morality and Political Violence*. Verobej's conclusion is that [Galtung's] "notion of structural violence remains a fruitful tool for peace researchers within the twenty-first century".

2.2.3 Cultural Violence and Colonialism

"If we wish to conserve our social institutions, there is one method — let us colonize" (Cohen 1980, 82). He also states, "Colonialism were but pawns in the struggle among European nation states, imbued with nationalistic fervor" (Ibid, 6). It is important to note that colonial empires were strong hierarchical systems of rule that did not uniformly embrace cultural diversity but rather gave way for the exploitation of traditional heterogeneous cultures and which, by a policy of divide and conquer, managed to impose their own European culture on others through *acculturation*.[15] Therefore, not only was colonialism used for economic 'development', but it was a tool 'to civilize', a mechanism to pull the strings of the 'uncivilized' societies to exert power and control, and overall to create a European supremacy where Western values and institutions were imposed on colonized societies. The legacy of colonialism is entrenched violence in the histories of colonized societies.

> "Colonialism is not satisfied merely with holding a people in its grip and emptying the native's brain of all form and content. By a kind of perverted logic, it turns to the past of the oppressed people, disfigures, and destroys it. This work of devaluing pre-colonial history takes on a dialectical significance today." (Fanon 1965, 210)

Even if the *natives* (as per Fanon) rediscover their own historical legacies and use them in an attempt to break free of colonial and imperial domination, there may still be a tendency to be dependent on the colonizer. The expansion of population, trade, capital, and culture brought the colonies into some form of dependency on it — direct or indirect — noting as one of the most detrimental and violent effects of colonialism, its strangulation of traditional culture:

---

15. Braithwaite (1974, 11) says of acculturation and interculturation, "the former referring to the process of absorption of one culture by another; the latter to a more reciprocal activity, a process of intermixture and enrichment, each to each." In all fairness to the culture that exists now much retentions and syncretism can be noted.

"Colonial domination, because it is total and tends to oversimplify, very soon manages to disrupt in spectacular fashion the cultural life of a conquered people. This cultural obliteration is made possible not by the negation of national reality, but new legal relations introduced by the occupying power, by the banishment of the natives and their customs to outlying districts by colonial society, but expropriation, and by systematic enslaving of men and women." (Fanon 1965, 236)

At the height of colonial empire building, the British Empire was the largest in history and was the leader of global power.[16] The British empire was so extensive that "within a single generation Britain acquired an additional 4.7 million square miles of empire, with 88 million new subjects" and "by 1900, half a billion people outside Europe, one-third of humanity, lived under European rule" (Cohen 1980, 1). The British Empire created a paradigm that was not only imperialistic but Eurocentric in nature, characteristically political, economic, linguistic, social, and culturally domineering. The cultural legacy of European influence in T&T is vast in its entities, and can still be observed in language, religion, visual art and the arts, education, government, and architecture. However, many 'survivals', 'retentions' and 'syncretism' of transplanted ethnic groups are evident as these once-colonised nations forge nationalism through various forms of expression: calypso, steel pan, music, literature, sport, cuisine, science and technology, and popular culture.

Henry and Stone (1983, 95) attribute utmost significance to culture in their socio-historical analysis of the Caribbean, postulating that "flight or movement away from oneself and one's situation and toward identification with the colonizer, is the distortion that colonization imposes". They claim that the resultant effect in the region at the time was cultural underdevelopment as a result of 'cultural colonization,' which occurred in two phases; first the phase of *de-culturization* of the colonized, followed by phase II or the *re-socialization* (into the culture of the colonizers) through education and religion. Phase I saw the colonized possessing a hybrid, dialect culture, while Phase II resulted in a situation of assimilation and, in a way, a cultural separation of sorts with a dependency on the colonizers. 'Cultural decolonization' occurred massively in the 1980s in an attempt to undo the imposed cultural dependency and move in the direction of the promotion of a 'national culture'. To a certain extent this was successful but not in its entirety, for what existed in the region was still a dependent culture and this was exemplified in its economic, social, cultural, and political institutions, in what became known as neocolonialism of Caribbean culture and identity. Models of 'plantation society' (Beckford 1972; Best 1968) highlighted the failure of the attempts at the development of a national culture.

---

16. In comparison to the Spanish, Portuguese, Russian, Danish, Swedish, Dutch, French, German, Italian, American, Belgian empires which began in 1402 (Spanish Empire) and ended in 1999 (Portuguese Empire).

2.3 Violence and Tolerance

A BBC News headline recently read "Violent crime down by 17% in Scotland". This good news was accompanied by the observation that "sexual offences increased by 10%", which implicitly fails to consider rape as a violent crime (BBC News 2012).

For Smith (1965), a plural society exists when groups that practise different basic institutions live side by side under a common government. Smith (1965, 9) claims that before decolonization, Belize, Suriname, Guyana and Trinidad were all models of complex pluralities, divided "into exclusive segments by culture, race, religion, language, social institutions, education, ecology, and in some cases by party organization". He claims that changes occurred after decolonisation and universal suffrage. The Caribbean region consists of different territories which differ in size, available resources, complexity and ethnicity; it is a major multicultural melting pot. Craig (1982, 143) notes, "We live, therefore within a complex, creative interplay of overlapping diasporas and intertwining roots." Thus the issues of tolerance and culture in addressing violence are critical. One cannot examine culture and tolerance in a vacuum, especially in these times when society and the world itself have become a global village — and a transcultural one at that. The process of transculturation represents a complex mixture with the onus placed on a varied dialogical process (Bakhtin 1984).

> "To express the highly varied phenomena that ... come about ... as a result of the extremely complex transmutations of culture ... real history is the history of its intermeshed transculturations." (Ortiz 1995, 98)

Tolerance, which is one of the nation's watchwords, may seem necessary in a multicultural racially-mixed society like Trinidad and Tobago. Pianalto (2010, 13) says, "it is often necessary for us to get along and better understand each other." He continues: "from a liberal perspective and point of view of the law, we must tolerate things we deeply find wrong, as in the case of abortion or gay marriages for some orthodox people". In the main in T&T, according to Kerrigan (2012), getting along with each other is not so difficult; he quotes the anthropologist Daniel Crowley: "the various groups in Trinidad and Tobago know something of the other groups and many members are as proficient in the cultural activities of other groups as their own". Berggren and Nilsson (2013, 177) have shown that "tolerance has the potential to affect both economic growth and well-being". In trying to discern its determinants they investigated whether the degree to which economic institutions and policies are market oriented is related to different measures of tolerance and found that:

> "Cross-sectional and first-difference regression analysis of up to 69 countries revealed that economic freedom is positively related to tolerance towards homosexuals, especially in the longer run, while tolerance towards people of a different race and a willingness to teach

kids tolerance are not strongly affected by how free markets are. Through instrumental variables and first-difference results they also found indications of a causal relationship between greater tolerance and the quality of the legal system."

Pianalto (2010, 13) suggests that:

"... Tolerance refers to a particular attitude of restraint towards beliefs or practices which we find disagreeable, while toleration only requires *acting* with restraint even if our attitude wants us to act against a situation or condition."

Reardon (1997, 1) notes that living with diversity is one of the greatest challenges facing societies today, where cultures increasingly intermingle. She acknowledges that teaching the skills of "learning to live together is an educational priority". She claims that:

"... tolerance is integral and essential to the realization of human rights and the achievement of peace. In its most simple and fundamental form, tolerance is according others the right to have their persons and identities respected."

And she notes that the element of democracy is interlocked with *peace, human rights* and *tolerance.* The achievement of these four values in the world society would constitute the basis of a 'culture of peace':

"... any culture is fundamentally the result of learning. Education is the learning that is planned and guided by cultural values. A culture of peace thus requires an education planned and guided by the values of peace, human rights, democracy and, at its very core, tolerance." (Reardon 1997, 1)

In looking at 'who can help to educate for tolerance,' she identified key players in the process — community leaders, school authorities, parents, social workers, and community personnel. LeBaron and Carstarphen (1997) call for cultural sensitivity and the recognition of cultural patterns and individual identities when dealing with mediation and conflict analysis in multicultural settings. They define multiculturalism as the philosophy and practice of honouring cultural differences through developing systems that institutionalize pluralism. What determines what is to be tolerated? A nation's tolerance of violence in the form of corporal punishment, for example, is visible in every sphere of the violence matrix. Corporal punishment that is used in the home and school setting which involves physical harm inflicted by a person on another is *direct violence*; this is also a form of *structural violence* because it is condoned by the lack of legislature to prevent the phenomenon from occurring, and it is indicative of *cultural violence* because members of society and the society itself sanction and enforce the act of violence.

2.4 Violence Typologies and Its Effects

Against the backdrop of multiple portrayals, descriptions and definitions of violence, and informed by many, some of whom are included in this text, the definition of violence used here is this: *Violence is any expression of human-engendered action that leads to an infringement of a person's inalienable rights.*

Expression: this can manifest itself in many and diverse forms.

Human-engendered action: this, too, can take on a wide range of appearances, among others, as described by Galtung (1996) in his direct, cultural and structural triad. It excludes violent instances caused by nature, unless this is the result of neglect or mismanagement, as is increasingly the case with the devastating impact of climate change, especially on vulnerable people.

Inalienable rights: these refer, in particular, to those enshrined in the Universal Declaration of Human Rights, and the UN Convention on the Rights of the Child.

2.4.1 Effects of Violence on Children

All forms of VAC are harmful to children, however, Lampinen and Sexton-Radek (2010) claim that family violence in the form of direct or vicarious domestic violence, media such as television, movies, and video games, and community and school-based violence are the most critical for their impact on children and adolescents. Responses to violence and trauma by children are dependent on a host of factors, such as genetic, neuropsychological, temperamental, cognitive, perceptual, and social factors. Perry (2002b) described how certain patterns of brain activation related to the 'fight-flight' response can alter brain growth and development, resulting in changes to physiological, emotional, cognitive, and social functioning. Rossman and Ho (2000) note that there tends to be a slower rate of information processing and decision-making in children who have been chronically exposed to violence, possibly due to decreased attention and concentration. Erikson (1950) suggests that exposure to trauma interferes with the child's development of trust and later behaviours lead to the building of autonomy and independence in the childhood and of identity in adolescence. Some studies (Cicchetti and Toth 1995; Perry 2002a) have concluded that infants and toddlers, who are the direct victims of violence or witnesses of violence show increased irritability and over-arousal, immature behaviour, sleep disturbances, emotional distress, fears of being alone, and regression in toileting and language. The importance of a 'good childhood' is being acknowledged and promoted as critical to a child's well-being and healthy development. It is also progressively recognized that a 'toxic' environment, particularly exposure to violence and the absence of care and protection leads to such mishaps as:

> "… low educational attainment, economic dependency, increased violence, crime, substance misuse, and depression, and a greater risk of non-communicable diseases, such as obesity, cardiovascular disease, and diabetes." (Chan 2013, 151)

Physical abuse is often the most visible expression of violence and has been, probably for that reason, extensively studied. A quick Internet search on the effects of physical abuse on children provides a consistent picture. Young victims may suffer from any one or all of the following behavioural disorders: damaged self-esteem, uncertainty, impaired cognitive skills, low thresholds of frustration, reduced capacity of 'perspective taking', difficulty with relating to peers and adults, and when older, an increased tendency to abuse drugs and alcohol, and to maltreat their own children. They also tend to be cruel with animals (Currie 2006). An older study (Cicchetti and Carlson 1989) summarizes the effects as follows:

> "The human costs are a litany of psychological tragedies. Maltreated children suffer from poor peer relations, cognitive deficits and low self-esteem among other problems; moreover, they tend to be more aggressive than their peers, as well as having behaviour problems and psychopathology. The emotional damage … may last a life time." (8)

Things haven't changed much since 1989, as Thompson and Tabone (2010), among a growing number of investigators, attest in their review of recent research findings. Sexual abuse causes everlasting wounds in victims and here as well the literature is abundant and still expanding, but also emitting the same disturbing message: victims can show any or all of the following symptoms and probably more: fear, anxiety, depression, anger and hostility, aggression, and sexually inappropriate behaviour. The longer-term effects may be equally bleak and include poor self-esteem, destructive behaviour, and re-victimization, feelings of isolation and of being unjustly treated. These effects seem to be universal as they are reported from all corners of the world (Pereda et al. 2009). Child negligence is by far one of the most common expressions of violence and, according to the USA National Scientific Council on the Developing Child (2012, 4), "the significant absence of basic, serve and return interaction can produce serious physiological disruptions that lead to lifelong problems in learning, behaviour and health". The Council further mentions that negligence could lead to impairment of the immune system, abnormal physical development, diminishing of executive functions, diminished capacity to cope with adversity, diminished electric activity in the brain, and greater risk of emotional and relational problems later in life.

2.4.2 Typologies of Violence Worldwide

Trinidad and Tobago is fortunate in the sense that certain forms of violence against children do not feature, such as the use of children as suicide bombers (Farmer 2012), female genital mutilation (WHO 2013), extreme forms of child labour as defined by ILO (1999), (female) infanticide (Fuse and Crenshaw 2006), flogging a girl for being raped,[17] or firing a bullet through a girl's head[18] because she goes to school. Violence against children has many expressions, and it seems that there is one conclusion possible: violence is a major and long-lasting stressor.

An innovative school of thought which attempts to explain the persistence of violence, and which is counter-intuitive to most proponent theories, is that of Pinker (2011). He states that the frequent, ubiquitous and horrible cruelties, brutalities and torture inflicted on criminals, slaves, servants, underlings, women and children are indeed largely a thing of the past. Backed by data drawn from many disciplines, he demonstrates that recent times show a decline in violence that holds for the family, neighbourhoods, between tribes and between states. People living now are less likely to meet a violent death, or to suffer from violence or cruelty at the hands of others than people living in any previous century. Factors related to this remarkable decline are better government, greater prosperity, health, education, trade and improvements in the status of women and an increased capacity to reason. Also, rising literacy rates and the fact that people read more and have more access to information — and in the meantime become more intelligent — are strong positive forces. As a result people are getting better at 'perspective taking' and at 'doing unto others as you would have them doing unto you'. The universal acceptance of human rights, especially those formulated for women, children and those embroiled in warfare, also counts heavily toward pushing the curve downwards (Pinker 2011). What then about all those reports that give the impression that the world is only getting worse, meaner, harsher and more corrupt? One reason put forward in the text is that, in this ever inter-connected and globalised world, where virtually everybody has access to and can be reached by everything and everybody, things cannot be hidden anymore and are broadcasted worldwide. This goes, as may be expected, for news and events that stir up emotions, scare, surprise and shock.

2.4.3 Corporal Punishment

In this text it would be interesting to test Pinker's study as it applies to corporal punishment and compare current data with that of some time ago. Teachers in Matagalpa, Nicaragua, felt

---

17. See: www.aljazeera.com/news/asia/2013/02/20132281222225801223.html.
18. Malala Yousufzai, the Pakistani 15-year-old girl became a symbol of youth resistance to the Taliban in 2012 as she was shot in the head on her way to school, and survived.

so, in their words "we, and our teachers, used to beat our children as a disciplinary measure, but not now any more. Besides, the children know it is against the rights of the child."[19]

Table 2.2, seems to corroborate Pinker's assertion as there is indeed a steady and unmistakable increase in the number of countries that have put a total ban on corporal punishment. The contents of the table is rather disheartening and yet there is every reason to believe that, as a whole, the Caribbean region, with Trinidad and Tobago in the vanguard, will follow the world trend. As of February 2013, no Caribbean state had prohibited corporal punishment in all settings, as table 2.3 shows.[20] While this text is being drafted, the Sindh Assembly (Pakistan) is debating whether to ask the federal government to repeal the anachronistic *Section 89* of the Pakistan Penal Code, which allows guardians and other people having lawful charge of children to punish them "in good faith for their benefit". The Sindh Assembly wants the law to be repealed because it is being misused by teachers to physically abuse children (*Express Tribune* 2013). But they are not the only government; sometimes in groups (as is the case with EU countries), sometimes step-by-step (as is happening with states in the USA), countries are moving towards total bans on corporal punishment in all settings.

TABLE 2.2 Selected Countries and Their Positions on Corporal Punishment

States that have completely prohibited corporal punishment of children by law in chronological order[22]		
Sweden (1979)	Ukraine (2004)	Republic of Moldova (2008)
Finland (1983)	Romania (2004)	Luxembourg (2008)
Norway (1987)	Hungary (2005)	Liechtenstein (2008)
Austria (1989)	Greece (2006)	Poland (2010)
Cyprus (1994)	Netherlands (2007)	Pakistan (2010)
Denmark (1997)	New Zealand (2007)	Tunisia (2010)
Latvia (1998)	Portugal (2007)	Kenya (2010)
Croatia (1999)	Uruguay (2007)	Congo, Republic of (2010)
Bulgaria (2000)	Venezuela (2007)	Albania (2010)
Israel (2000)	Spain (2007)	South Sudan (2011)
Germany (2000)	Togo (2007)	Estonia (2011)
Iceland (2003)	Costa Rica (2008)	Trinidad and Tobago (????)

---

19. Personal communication, Matagalpa, October 2007.
20. The websites 'www.endcorporalpunishment.org' and 'www.corpun.com' are highly informative sources.
21. 'Global Progress'. Global Initiative to End All Corporal Punishment of Children (2012), accessed 15 June 2012; see: www.endcorporalpunishment.org.

| TABLE 2.3 | Policies on Corporal Punishment in the Caribbean Region |

Progress towards prohibiting all corporal punishment in Caribbean states[23]					
			Prohibited in penal system		
States	Prohibited in the home	Prohibited in schools	As sentence for crime	As disciplinary measure	Prohibited in alternative care settings
Antigua and Barbuda	No	No	No	No	No
Bahamas	No	No	No	Yes	Some
Barbados	No	No	No	No	Some
Belize	No	Yes	Yes	Some	Some
Dominica	No	No	No	Yes	Some
Grenada	No	No	No	Yes	Some
Guyana	No	No	Some	Some	Some
Haiti	No	Yes	Yes	Yes	Yes
Jamaica	No	Some	Yes	Yes	Yes
St Kitts and Nevis	No	No	No	No	No
St Lucia	No	No	Yes	No	No
St Vincent and the Grenadines	No	No	No	No	No
Suriname	No	No	Yes	Yes	No
Trinidad and Tobago	No	No	No	No	No

In Japan there has been an alarming rise in the number of reports of corporal punishment of school children at the hands of their teachers, according to a survey by the education ministry. The rise in recorded cases has been attributed to an increase in reporting, which follows the highly publicised case of a high school student who committed suicide in December 2012 after his sports teacher hit him on repeated occasions.[23] Meanwhile in Germany, where corporal punishment of children is banned in all settings including the home, a new survey shows that one in four children say their parents smack them. Nine hundred schoolchildren aged between six and 16 from low to high-income families were interviewed as part of the 'Violence 2013' study, which found that corporal punishment was more common against

---

22. Information taken from www.endcorporalpunishment.org/pages/resources/downloads.html on 3 March 2013.
23. www.japantoday.com/category/national/view/student-commits-suicide-after-being-beaten-by-school-basketball-coach.

younger children.[24] 'Global progress towards prohibiting all corporal punishment, July 2011' prepared by the Global Initiative to End All Corporal Punishment of Children[25] contains a compilation of the countries of the world and their stances on corporal punishment in homes, schools, the penal system and alternative care settings.

2.4.4 Domestic Violence

The statistics on child protection also include a subscale on attitudes towards *domestic violence*, which lists the percentage of women 15–49 years old who consider it all right for a husband to hit or beat his wife for at least one of the specified reasons. Women were asked whether a husband is justified in hitting or beating his wife under a series of circumstances such as when she burns food, argues with him, goes out without telling him, neglects the children or refuses sexual relations. For Trinidad and Tobago this percentage was 8. Table 2.4 gives figures for a few other countries. Faulk (1974), in his research on men convicted of wife abuse, showed that the majority of them were suffering from mental illness, while (Pahl 1985) attempts to explain violence in terms of deviant or pathological personalities.

TABLE 2.4 Women's Attitudes towards Domestic Violence in Selected Countries

Percentage of women who believe that it is okay for husbands to hit their wives	
Country	Percentage
Ukraine	5
Suriname	13
Trinidad and Tobago	8
Turkey	38
Sierra Leone	85

Straus, Gelles, and Steinmetz (1980) claim that the family may be a training ground for violence but, for a fuller explanation, they recommend looking to wider society. The social-structural approach locates the cause of domestic violence not on the individual, but on the whole social situation. Pahl (1985), argues that the legitimisation of violence by the wider society is woven into culture at every level, from popular sayings to the level of legislation. Many societal jokes about domestic abuse show how much it is culturally legitimised and prolonged. He notes that any explanation of wife assault needs to be located in the

---

24. www.endcorporalpunishment.org/pages/docs/states-reports/GermanyAcc.docx.
25. www.endcorporalpunishment.org.

broader social context of the structural and ideological forces which shape the relationship between men and women both within marriage and in society at large. O'Connor (2013) noted that, even when there are no physical scars, aggression between siblings can inflict psychological wounds as damaging as the anguish caused by bullies at school or on the playground and found that those who were attacked, threatened or intimidated by a sibling had increased levels of depression, anger and anxiety. Domestic violence is by no means a universally accepted social ill. Take, for example, Saudi Arabia, where 91 per cent of girls think wife beating is justified compared to Serbia where only 2 per cent of girls think it defensible (UNICEF 2013).

Domestic violence in T&T and in wider Caribbean seems to take on a grim face as the number of murders has increased over the last decade. The true face may even look murkier as much of the violence acted out in families remains hidden and unreported (Rawlins 2000), while calls on the governments to act are also growing louder (Martin 2012). A victim of domestic abuse stated:

> "The judicial system in Trinidad & Tobago is plagued with overcrowding, lack of privacy, bureaucracy and insufficient human resources to effectively deal with all the issues brought before it."[26]

It appears that the passing of The Domestic Violence Bill, 1999, an act to provide greater protection for victims of domestic violence, is mere rhetoric.

2.4.5 Media Violence

The media it may appear, exhibits a high tolerance of violence as is exemplified by its 'glamorization and sensationalization' of violence in its reporting of the news.

> "There is sufficient evidence to suggest that the repeated depiction of violence behaviour desensitises individuals and creates a climate within which violence is seen as normal rather than aberrational social behaviour."

And:

> "Even to suggest some limited restrictions on press freedom, however, raises fundamental questions of constitutional human rights ... The repression of violence, whether criminal or political, national or institutional, has been a relatively low priority of most governments." (Quainton 1983, 62-63)

---

26. Voices of Advocates Part 1: Domestic Violence (Trinidad &Tobago), accessed March 19th, 2013 www.womendeliver.org/updates/entry/voices-of-advocates-part-1-domestic-violence-trinidad-tobago.

This certainly is the case in Trinidad and Tobago on both counts as violence continues to be captured on the front pages of the daily newspapers in full form or 'bacchanalia'.

Television violence in the form of movies and advertisements are also of great concern regarding the effects of these on not only children and young adults, but the populace at large. Bushman (1998) reported that viewers' memory for advertisements was impaired by adjacent violent movie content as compared with nonviolent program environment. This effect has also been observed by other researchers (Prasad and Smith 1994; Shen and Prinsen 1999). Thus, it does not matter how many positive messages are sent out during the advertisements, if the main program is heavily laden on violent content; all messages will fail to have the desired impact. Hopf, Huber, and Wei (2008), in a two-year longitudinal study, concluded that children exposed to chronic media violence (films, TV, and video games) develop "long-term aggressive emotions" such as frustration, rage, humiliation, blame, sadistic pleasure, and hate early on in their development. Pollack (1998), notes that feelings of inadequacy, shame, and powerlessness emerge from males who are victims of or witnesses to chronic violence. It is interesting to note that violence as a form of communication is now a new framework of analysis where treating acts of terrorism, for example, as 'senseless violence', now allows for it to be viewed instead as a kind of violent language (De Graaf Schmid and De Graaf 1982). Against this backdrop it comes as no surprise that the T&T Association of Psychologists warns against the negative effects of violence in the media on people, including children (The Guardian 2012).

Chadee and Ditton (2005) shed a different light on the discussion on 'media and violence'; first they state that current research does *not* see a link between media-generated violence as making people more violent, but does influence people's attitudes as to how perpetrators of violence should be dealt with (Surette, Chadee et al. 2011).

2.4.6 Gender Violence

At its most basic and obvious level, violence is an act that is carried out with the intention or perceived intention of physically hurting another person (Gelles and Straus 1979). The gender dimension amplifies the definition to include violent acts perpetrated on women because they are women. For example, being female subjects a woman to rape, female circumcision/genital mutilation, female infanticide, and sex-related crimes. Dunkle et al. (2004) and Russo and Pirlott (2006), drawing on international data, come to the same view: women, of whatever nation, bear most of the burden when there are risks around and they point out how strongly factors such as gender, sexuality, power, and intimate violence are interwoven.

In some Asian societies, for instance, because of her dependence on a man, a woman is vulnerable to specific domestic violence, such as dowry murder and sati, and the reason relates to society's concept of woman as property of the man (Jilani 1992). Gendered violence also relates a great deal to society's construction of both female and male sexuality. Jilani (1992) writes of Pakistan that the argument that violence is cultural or personal is erroneous, since in Pakistan she claims, the issue is more political and results from the structural pattern of control and dominance of the social institutions that exist. She argues that perpetual fear of violence in the home, at work, and in the streets is an obstacle to social participation and a hindrance to women's development but, at the same time, she acknowledges that the issue of violence against women is becoming a global human rights concern. An eight-year old Yemeni child bride recently died on her wedding night from internal haemorrhaging: "many poor families in Yemen marry off young daughters to save on the costs of bringing up a child and earn extra money from the dowry given to a girl" (Ghobari and Davenport 2013).

The Maldivian government will appeal against a court decision to publicly flog a 15-year-old rape victim convicted of having premarital sex.[27] Social media is proving to be an effective tool in the fight against violence. It is clear that the cultural factor plays a significant role in gender violence, for what is considered 'violence' is highly debatable under cultural norms and practices. Interestingly these traditions are then translated into often legal and state-sanctioned systems, such as marriages, education acts, societal laws or accepted medical practice. The cultural and structural violence is also manifested in the form of indirect violence against women that plagues many societies daily, for example, the fact that the HIV/AIDS infection rate is going up in Uganda mainly because more Ugandans (mostly men) are having multiple sex partners (Heuler 2013).

Italy's lower chamber of parliament has ratified a European treaty to protect women and girls from gender violence, as the latest victim — a 15-year-old girl stabbed 20 times and burnt alive. The UN Special Rapporteur on violence against women, Rashida Manjoo, said 78 per cent of all cases of violence against women in Italy are domestic in nature, with gender stereotypes "deeply rooted".[28] A 23-year-old Indian student was fatally gang-raped inside a bus in the capital, Delhi, on December 2012. Her father says:

> "That is what poverty does to you … makes you think about money all the time. Think about whether you have enough money in your pocket to take your daughter's body home … We just want to keep her memory alive as long as it's possible. I know one day people will forget her. But they will remember her death led to changes — changes in the anti-rape laws, change in consciousness."[29]

---

27. www.aljazeera.com/programmes/witness/2012/11/2012117113043777660.html.
28. www.crin.org/resources/infodetail.asp?id=31025, accessed 20 September 2013.
29. www.bbc.co.uk/news/world-asia-india-25344403, accessed 17 December 2013.

It must be acknowledged that internationally, regionally and locally great strides are being made in society by our women and young girls despite many of the obstacles faced. A case in point: "A Saudi woman has made history by reaching the summit of the world's highest mountain: Raha Moharrak 25 years, not only became the first Saudi woman to attempt the climb but also the youngest Arab to make it to the top of Everest."[30] And there are many more such acts of girls and women that challenge the traditional views on what they can and should do. In a similar vein, the decision by the House of Representatives to give final approval to a renewal of the 'Violence Against Women Act', should be seen as yet another expression of a worldwide emerging wish to combat this form of violence. The Act also holds for gay, bisexual or transgender victims of domestic abuse, as well as gives the right to American Indian women who are violated on reservations by non-Indians to take their cases to tribal courts; until now courts did not have jurisdiction over assailants who did not live on tribal land (Parker 2013).

Loubon (2013) sums up the situation in Trinidad and Tobago: "Gender-based violence figures alarming," says the Minister of Gender, Clifton De Couteau. Dobash et al. (1992), Dobash and Dobash (2000), and Nazroo (1995) proposed that 'overwhelmingly' it is men who use violence against women partners and not the 'obverse'. Responses serve to reflect public and institutional perceptions of violence and in that manner act as a barometer of public or professional concern about the problem (Dobash and Dobash 2000). In recent times society has also embraced the reality that men are also victims of gendered violence in the form of spousal abuse and acts of discrimination. The readings on the barometer seem to be changing however as 'over the past decades a growing number of studies have been released that support the contention that females perpetrate violence at rates equal, or similar, to males' (for reviews, see Dutton and Nicholls 2005; Fiebert 2007; Straus 1999). When gender differences and the personality profiles of a group of women and men who were arrested for domestic abuse were analysed, the personality profile most frequently demonstrated by women was different from both the personality profile demonstrated by men and male batterer personality traits. Simmons et al. (2005) showed that women demonstrated elevated histrionic, narcissistic, and compulsive personality traits when compared to the matched sample of men while the men demonstrated higher dependent personality traits than the women in the study.

2.4.7 Street Children

In almost any nation, boys and girls (usually more boys than girls) live 'on' and 'off' the streets or wastelands, trying to make a living; their relationships with their families vary

---

30. The performance van Raha Mobarak can be watched on 'Youtube": www.youtube.com/watch?v=hgZIIBr98Ac.

from strong and supportive to abusive and not-present.[31] Worldwide figures are hard to get, but their numbers run into the millions and, in most cities and towns around the world, they can be spotted. It is well documented that they run extremely high risks to their well-being and healthy development, to use an understatement. Rather than treating them as victims whose rights are trampled on, many see them as criminals and there are instances of 'clean-up squads,' supported by local businesses or even the police. At the same time, there is a plethora of international and national agencies and groups, supported by an ever growing amount of knowledge and experience, which have as their main mission to help these children and prevent others from starting a life on the streets.[32]

An indication of the government's lack of commitment and follow-up, or so it seems, is that there are no reliable data on the number of children living on and off the streets (Kong Soo 2013). Most of these children are indeed very streetwise and know when and how to disappear and become invisible, but in a country like Trinidad and Tobago, given its small population, and where 'everybody knows everybody', this situation could be better managed. The street dwellers are few and far between to come into contact with for they are fearful of being incarcerated in children's institutions where they report gross ill-treatment, preferring a life on the streets to institutionalization.[33] A first approach, therefore, would be to put names and numbers to these children. Although there are no precise figures, the feeling is that they are increasing and that more of them — with boys and girls trafficked into the country active in the sex industry and contracting HIV.[34] Indeed, the government has not yet formulated a policy — read set of measures — regarding street children (Theodore et al. 2012); one would think, though, that the Children's Act Chap. 46:01 would also apply to these boys and girls. UNICEF's *Situation Analysis of Children and Women in Trinidad and Tobago* (UNICEF 2010) and summarized by Theodore et al. (2012; quoted references are listed in UNICEF 2010):

— Approximately 300 homeless youth in the vicinity of Port of Spain in 2003;
— Approximately 154 street children in Port of Spain and about 54 in institutions in the same area in 2004 (Health Economics Unit 2005);
— Average age of the Trinidadian street child is between 10 and 16 years (Julien 2008);
— Average age is between 7 and 14 years (Marshall 2003);
— The typical street child is male (Marshall 2003).

---

31. It is common to make the distinction between children who spend most of the daytime roaming the streets, but have a fixed abode — family, shelter — to go to at night, and those who also spend the nights outside. Then, there are also complete families who live on and off the streets, without a fixed abode (see Appendix V).
32. One of the most useful databases on street children is provided by the Consortium for Street Children (CSC), a worldwide network organisation (see www.streetchildren.org.uk).
33. Research conducted on socially displaced people in T&T by the researcher in the capacity of Senior Research Specialist in the Ministry of Social Development (2006).
34. www.humanium.org/en/trinidad-and-tobago/, accessed 28 December 2013.

The authors also provide a brief overview of the responses about which there is an international consensus:
— The provision of physical accommodation for street children alongside psychological and rehabilitative care;
— The ability of such centres to provide much needed data to guide policy and allow for more targeted social programming;
— The reintegration of street children with their families and the provision of a broader care and support network;
— A focus on children's educational needs in the areas of vocational and life skills training;
— The development of a cadre of qualified and trained personnel to treat with street children;
— The provision of primary medical care; and
— An appreciation of the voices of street children with a view toward designing the best programmes and facilities to assist them.

The fact that street children are a worldwide phenomenon is not a sufficient cause for exoneration. This research points to additional measures that are needed to keep children off the streets and within their families. These will be more preventative in nature, more directed to supporting vulnerable families and calling on all segments of society.

> "It is extremely dangerous for them out there. Street children are exposed to abuse. We've had instances of boys who were involved in prostitution, with older boys pimping out the younger boys. There's the ever-present danger of physical and sexual abuse, the risk of contracting STDs and Aids, of drugs. We have a case of one of our wards who is a full-fledged addict and was being indoctrinated into a life of crime."
>
> Director, Credo-Sophia House, Port-of-Spain

All children are intuitively, but also by right, worthy of well-being and a fulfilling life. The *Times of India* states that in 2010, 5,484 street children were raped and 1,408 others killed in the country (Saxena 2011), while on the other side of the globe, writing about the situation in Honduras, CRIN, the authoritative and impartial Child Rights International Network, reports: "In fact, since 1997, more than 6,000 young people have been killed in the country, and security officials were suspected in more than a third of these murders".[35] These are only two arbitrary illustrations of the disregard societies harbour for their disenfranchised; the examples could be endlessly multiplied with examples from, indeed, many, many other countries.

---

35. www.crin.org/violence/search/closeup.asp?infoID=28824, accessed 22 June, 2012.

2.4.8 Violence and Inequity

The world is becoming more unequal and unfair and the gap between rich and poor wider; this phenomenon seems to be happening everywhere and in every sphere of life and threatens the economic future of many nations as well as their stability (Stiglitz 2012). There is another major concern, though; it more and more appears that early exposure to inequality has ill effects on the poor and the rich alike, and may result, even later in life, in both physical and psychological complaints such as life expectancy, cardiovascular disease, cognition and academic achievement.

For the discussion on early child development, the publication by Keating and Hertzman (1999), *Developmental Health and the Wealth of Nations*, is of singular significance. Its main message, and those in increasing number being conveyed in new research, is that the growing income gap in societies is associated with the health of its people. The wider the gap — or steeper the gradient — the unhealthier the citizens are. Nations with a 'steep gradient', that is with wide differences, endure an overall lower level of both physical and mental health than those with a flat gradient. Most remarkable, in this respect, is that the upper 20 percent of people in the UK, where the gradient is steep, are worse off than the lowest 20 percent in Sweden, where the gradient is closer to being horizontal. Even more remarkable is that exposure to societal inequality may not only upset the well-being of the young boy or girl, but also surfaces when they are of a fully mature age (Keating and Hertzman 1999). Structural and cultural violence gain special traction here as these dimensions of violence are borne out of systemic inequity and cultural hegemony.

The implications of inequality and societal injustice as a result of corruption and nepotism in the T&T context are significant. Bribery and corruption at high levels are likely to have a devastating effect on people, especially the young for whom fairness and honesty are key values: *"El que no tranza, no avanza"* or 'He who doesn't cheat, does not go ahead' (Zabludovsky 2013), remains unchallenged. The same seems to be happening in Brazil where, in 2013, massive protests erupted against a corrupt congress (Romero and Neuman 2013) or in Canada where a leading educator was accused of being a child pornographer (Pagliaro 2013). Heeraman (2013) writes:

> "Some known problems which significantly contributed to corruption in Trinidad and Tobago (T & T). They were unbridled political power, failing institutions such as the police service, lack of powerful legislation protecting and financially rewarding whistleblowers, a significant deficiency in national competitiveness and a relatively ineffective audit process."

A nation can only begin to stem the tide of violence if it prioritizes it on its national agenda and that can only happen when it starts to display a high degree of maturity, transparency, accountability, responsibility and integrity.

2.4.9 Violence and Terrorism

Violentology (Barker 2003) is the scientific study of violence, violent behaviour, terrorism, civil and military disorder, and the victims and perpetrators of these events. In these times, it would be remiss if the taboo issue of terrorism is not mentioned. Vertigans (2011, 2) defines terrorism as "the targeted and intentional use of violence for political purposes through actions that can range in intended impact from intimidation to loss of life." He contends that:

> "History can also be the source to which direct reference is made in the application of violence ... There is some support to suggest that the extent to which violence can be drawn from collective memories influences the nature and duration of the terror struggles." (24)

The implications for T&T society are cautionary, for, if not addressed, the existing conditions of corruption, injustice and increasing inequity may continue to proliferate, causing the nation to both implode and explode. This claim is supported by Quainton (1983, 58):

> "The sources of violence in our world will not only be political. Population pressures, competition for scarce resources, and income disequilibria are certain to provide the breeding ground for future violence and terrorism."

Crenshaw (1983, 2) states that the value of the normative approach to the dysfunction of a problem — in this instance, terrorism:

> "... is that it confronts squarely a critical problem in the analysis of terrorism, and indeed any form of political violence: the issue of legitimacy. Terrorists of the left deny the legitimacy of the State and claim that the use of violence against it is morally justified. Terrorists of the right deny the legitimacy of opposition and hold that violence in the service of order is sanctioned by the values of the status quo".

Quainton (1983, 54) notes that the tactics and weaponry may vary but that terrorism as "systematic violence is always used as an instrument of social and political change". The deliberation over the legitimacy of violence persists but governments have become less tolerant of terrorist violence, or so it seems.

3.0 Talking rights

Bangladesh, Canada, Nicaragua, the Netherlands, Trinidad and Tobago

3.1 Upholding the Rights Discourse

Society revolves around the *discursive*. This paper recognises discourse as action, as a '*practical, social* and *cultural* phenomenon' (Van Dijk 1997). Local discourse and context are recognised and interpreted as functional parts of global contexts and vice versa, establishing ideology as the link between discourse and society, often responsible for the reproduction of power and domination. Targeted change therefore has to embrace this element. It may mean, first and foremost, the adoption of a premise or a word or a doctrine or a philosophy that would start the wheel of change in motion. 'Rights' as discourse has to become the language of the streets; it has to be internalised as the modus operandi and it has to 'emerge' from the populace.[1] The influence of societal structures on ideology ought not to neglect the reverse. Gramsci (1971) identifies the existence of a 'political society' and a 'civil society' with the former being "the domain of coercion, the latter being the domain of 'hegemony'". He notes that at the same time, both elements establish and enforce the value system (Morera 1990). Althusser (1971) viewed:

> "... ideologies not as a nebulous realm of ideas but as tied to material practices embedded in the social institution ... the central effect ... as positioning people in particular ways as 'social subjects'." (261)

> "Michel Foucault's work on discourse was explicitly directed against Marxism and theories of ideology ... For Foucault, discourses are knowledge systems of the human sciences (medicine, economics, linguistics, etc.) that inform the social and governmental 'technologies' which constitute power in modern society." (261)

---

1. Reference is made here to the concept of 'emergence' as the first step in the process of "*collective definition*" of a social problem (Blumer 1979).

Frankfurt School philosophers maintain that cultural products are more autonomous expressions of contradictions within the social whole than mere 'epiphenomena of economy'.

> "According to Habermas,[2] a critical science has to be self-reflexive and it must consider the historical context in which linguistic and social interactions take place." (Althusser (1971, 261)

People can only make sense of the salience of discourse in contemporary social processes and power relations by recognising that discourse not only constitutes society and culture, but is also being constituted by them (Fairclough and Wodak 2007). Discourses are connected to each other; they involve an understanding of the rules. Discourse is not produced without context and cannot be understood without taking the context into consideration (Duranti and Goodwin 1992). Context then always includes intertextuality and sociocultural knowledge. A rights-based approach has to be cognisant of the subtle nuances of cultural interplay in shaping the mind-set of a people as, in the end, it may prove to be the most critical tool for change. While the paper adopts a macro structural and post-structural analysis, it simultaneously embraces micro interpretivistic and phenomenological doctrines, since it professes to be multi-angular in its spectrum of study. For, while Marxism is sometimes accused of being a *grand narrative* by the poststructuralists and postmodernists, guilty of 'discursive totalities' and 'universals', its survival in modern society as a theory of change may well mean the 'relocating of revolutionary activity to the domain of language'. Marxism has always been a theory of change and a revolutionary philosophy and it has always espoused ideological change in the form of heightened consciousness as a means of achieving social change, therefore never negating the profound effect of culture — and by its natural extension, language as expression — on ideological formations.

3.2 Violence and the Convention on the Rights of the Child (CRC)

The Convention on the Rights of the Child (CRC) is a human rights treaty setting out the civil, political, economic, social, health and cultural rights of children. It is the first legally binding international instrument to incorporate the full range of children's rights, and it is a contemporary and formidable document that may well be one of the 'greatest inventions of

---

2. Gramsci (1971) refers to the work of Jürgen Habermas in *Erkenntnis und Interesse* [1968] (*Knowledge and Human Interests*), examining critical theory in literary studies as a form of hermeneutics, i.e. knowledge via interpretation to understand the meaning of human texts and symbolic expressions.

modern times'³ and the most powerful weapon in the fight against VAC. Nations that ratify this convention are bound to it by international law and compliance is monitored by the UN Committee on the Rights of the Child. "The Convention sets out these rights in 54 articles and two optional protocols Convention inherent to the human dignity and harmonious development of every child."⁴ It is understood that, by agreeing to undertake the obligations of the Convention (by ratifying or acceding to it), national governments commit themselves to protecting and ensuring children's rights, to be held accountable for this commitment before the international community, and are obliged to develop and undertake all actions and policies in the light of the best interests of the child.

The child right's treaty was adopted by the UN General Assembly on 20 November 1989 and has been ratified by 195 countries, including all members of the United Nations, and recently in 2015, the newly established South Sudan. This makes it the most widely ratified international human rights treaty in history. Although the United States government signed the Convention on 16 February 1995 and played an integral role in the drafting of the document, it remains the only country that has not ratified it. This is due to the fact that both death sentences and life imprisonment for children are forbidden by the Convention, but are still legal in some US states.

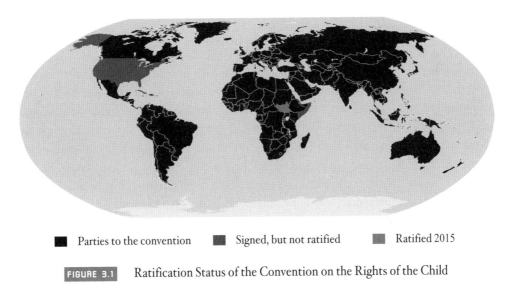

FIGURE 3.1   Ratification Status of the Convention on the Rights of the Child

Two optional protocols were adopted by the UN General Assembly on 25 May 2000:
1. *Optional Protocol on the Involvement of Children in Armed Conflict*, which requires governments to ensure that children under the age of eighteen are not recruited compulsorily

---

3. These words may sound cliché and over-zealous but this researcher is still hopeful.
4. See www.unicef.org/crc/ for articles and laws.

into their armed forces, and calls on governments to do everything feasible to ensure that members of their armed forces who are under eighteen years of age do not take part in hostilities. This protocol entered into force on 12 July 2002; currently, 151 states are party to the protocol and another 20 states have signed but not ratified it.
2. *Optional Protocol on the Sale of Children, Child Prostitution and Child Pornography,* which requires states to prohibit the sale of children, child prostitution and child pornography. It entered into force on 18 January 2002; currently, 163 states are party to the protocol and another 13 states have signed but not ratified it.

A third was adopted in December 2011and opened for signature on 28 February 2012.
3. *Optional Protocol to the Convention on the Rights of the Child on a Communications Procedure,* which would allow children or their representatives to file individual complaints for violation of the rights of children. The protocol currently has 36 signatures and six ratifications; it will enter into force on the tenth ratification.

3.3 Country Review: Bangladesh, Canada, Nicaragua, the Netherlands, T&T

What follows are 'vignettes' on four countries that, each in their own way, differ in many aspects from Trinidad and Tobago, and yet harbour experiences and expertise that are relevant for T&T and, at the same time, could benefit from knowledge and understandings originating in T&T. The information was gathered in various ways; the researcher had the opportunity of working with both governmental and non-governmental organisations concerned with children's and youth issues, met with a range of people and participated in their activities. In addition questionnaires were given to mixed groups of twenty to thirty people and their replies analysed. They are, by no means, representative of the views of the nationals of these countries. The short descriptions are neither exhaustive nor do they function as comparative accounts. They only serve to widen the discussion and lift it to a global level. As argued earlier, it is by participating in regional and international debates that Trinidad and Tobago stands to benefit as it will, in a natural fashion, adopt new ideas and see their own efforts validated. It may also lead to innovative forms of collaboration, which may, often via a serendipitous route, strengthen programme activities, attract support, create awareness, leverage funds and generate new knowledge.

Bangladesh: A Violent Place, Particularly for Girls and Women

TABLE 3.1 Human Development Information on Bangladesh (UNICEF, 2013)

Human Development Index	U5MR	Adult literacy rate	Life expectancy	GNI USD	Population (000)
146	139	57	69	770	150,495

"Bangladesh ratified the Convention on the Rights of the Child (CRC) in August 1990, marking children's rights to life, survival and development on the national agenda. Despite this, outdated legislation, inadequate policies and poor services continue to jeopardize the rights of children".[5]

The following is its Reservation:

"[The Government of Bangladesh] ratifies the Convention with a reservation to article 14, Paragraph 1: "Also article 21 would apply subject to the existing laws and practices in Bangladesh."

Discussions on violence with NGO staff, parents, and young boys and girls *in situ* showed that experience in the small island nation of Trinidad and Tobago with slightly over one million people was relevant for this country with a population close to 160 million. At the same time, valuable lessons were learnt. To gain a more structured perspective on how ordinary Bangladeshi think and feel about violence against children, focus groups sessions were held with three groups of Bangladeshi respondents (all respondents totalled 32), consisting of housewives, teachers, NGO staff, journalists and children (11-18years).

The discussion on violence struck a chord as almost all participants felt that the country had become more violent over the last decade and that tolerance of violence had dramatically increased, with very few people standing up against it. The common perception was that girls and women appeared to suffer most from violence; as instances of rape, torture related to dowry, forced child marriages were raised as major concerns. 'Eve teasing', harassing girls and women was common and actually seen as the most common form of violence; in fact, the shared opinion was that the female segment of the population had to cope with more violence than their male counterparts.

---

5. http://www.unicef.org/bangladesh/children_4878.html, accessed May 2, 2012.

Violence was mainly defined in its 'direct' expressions such as biting, teasing, beating, acid throwing and mental and physical maltreatment or torture. Yet, a few people also mentioned disregarding human and children's rights. Sexual violence, especially meted out to girls and women, was seen as most common, largely explained by the fact that 'sex', 'sexuality', 'sexual rights' and 'reproductive health' were issues hardly discussed in the nation, and if they were, were discussed in an unwholesome and incomplete manner. Herein, lies also the solution, as better education, awareness raising and skills training are listed as routes to a less violent society.

The country was hopeful about the future, as they were showing that, with fewer resources than their 'richer' neighbours India and Pakistan, they had outperformed them in the fields of health, child survival and women's education (The Economist 3 November 2012); they also think, that violence will decrease over the coming years. There is a unanimous view that the right kind of laws are largely in place, but that they are poorly implemented; respect for human and children's rights is also seen as critical.

In 2010, it was suddenly announced that the government, acting on an order from the High Court, had banned corporal punishment in all schools, a move that seems to have the support of a large section of the population; only a few of the respondents were in favour of corporal punishment, and that only in special circumstances: "if they are out of control of their parents" and "if somebody is involved in sexual violence".

Like everywhere else, children living on and off the streets have a tough life, to use an understatement. In addition to the regular exploiters, such as gangsters, corrupt shopkeepers or taxi or rickshaw drivers, the 'elite' was also singled out as abusing and taking advantage of them.

The lessons learnt? Foremost, perhaps, is that sharing experiences with each other is very motivating, as it helps to validate the work one is doing. The closer one moves to the grassroots, bits of concrete advice on 'how-to-go-about-things' are being jointly generated, almost naturally. There is another crucial phenomenon, as both countries are in many aspects divergent, expressions of violence against children are also dissimilar and just for this reason one can find solutions from each other's experience. For example, field games (sports) are a new and rather audacious pastime for girls in Bangladesh, and not so in Trinidad and Tobago. By showing that, as is the case in T&T, that nothing untoward happens to girls engaged in sport, rather the contrary, Bangladeshi girls and, for sure, boys and men, feel more reassured. There are also lessons for T&T to take from Bangladesh, the most important, perhaps, is to do more with the maximisation of the limited financial resources that a country has available to it.

Canada: A Developed Country in Development?

TABLE 3.2 Human Development Information on Canada (UNICEF 2013)

Human Development Index	U5MR	Adult literacy rate	Life expectancy	GNI USD	Population (000)
11	8	100	81	46,560	34,350

Canada became a signatory to the Convention on 28 May 1990 and ratified it in 1991. Prior to ratifying the treaty, Canada's laws were either largely or entirely in conformity with the treaty. Youth criminal laws in Canada underwent major changes resulting in the Youth Criminal Justice Act (YCJA) which went into effect on 1 April 2003. The Act specifically references Canada's different commitments under the Convention. The convention was influential in the following administrative law decision of Baker v. Canada (Minister of Citizenship and Immigration).

Reservations:[6]

"(i) Article 21
With a view to ensuring full respect for the purposes and intent of article 20 (3) and article 30 of the Convention, the Government of Canada reserves the right not to apply the provisions of article 21 to the extent that they may be inconsistent with customary forms of care among aboriginal peoples in Canada.

"(ii) Article 37(c)
The Government of Canada accepts the general principles of article 37 (c) of the Convention, but reserves the right not to detain children separately from adults where this is not appropriate or feasible.

Statement of understanding:

"Article 30
It is the understanding of the Government of Canada that, in matters relating to aboriginal peoples of Canada, the fulfilment of its responsibilities under article 4 of the Convention must take into account the provisions of article 30. In particular, in assessing what measures are appropriate to implement the rights recognized in the Convention for aboriginal children, due regard must be paid to not denying their right, in community with other

---

6. https://treaties.un.org/Pages/ViewDetails.aspx?mtdsg_no=IV-11&chapter=4&lang=en, accessed July 12, 2013.

members of their group, to enjoy their own culture, to profess and practice their own religion and to use their own language."

There are many ways to introduce the second largest country, with fewer than 35 million people of whom 4% are indigenous and that seems to be politically, socially, geographically, economically, culturally and demographically constant in the making. Typical also for the country, is the changing demographics; in Toronto, more than 50 percent are first generation immigrants. Canada, with its 100,000 people hailing from T&T, occupies a special place in the hearts of most Trinbagonians. The steady influx of qualified immigrants explains the country's wealth to a large extent (BBC 2013 website: Canada).

When a mixed group (gender-, age- professional wise) of some 30 plus Canadians were asked to share their views on a range of violence issues, they showed a fair grasp of understanding the situation in their country.

Striking is, given the underdog position of the First Nation people, that they tended to define violence in *direct* terms, and overlook its structural and cultural components. Bullying and domestic violence were seen as most common, as was the violence portrayed via the media. Sexual abuse of children and, notably, the stripping of self-esteem featured high among their concerns, with multiple causes bringing this about — substance abuse, stress, adverse early sexual experience, media exposure, lack of self-esteem, and poverty among them. It is remarkable that the increasing 'multi-ethnicity' of the society was not mentioned. There was also a strong belief that Canada was less violent than other countries, and that Canadians "don't tolerate violence", but there was also an undertow in their views that "sooo much goes on behind closed doors" and "sooo much goes unreported". One child reported that the worst form of violence was "the violence of a parent against a child".

The government was allocated a significant role in combating VAC: support education and disseminate educational messages, finance interventions that protect and shelter children and introduce stricter and "harsher" laws to punish and deter perpetrators. However, when the 'Spanking Law' was discussed nationwide, the voices in favour and against were almost evenly split — a majority approved of corporal punishment. The same division was noticeable among the interviewees: a good number saw nothing wrong in "slapping the child on the wrist" or in a "kick on the bottom" as long as it did not "harm" the boy or girl; others saw it as very wrong indeed. Given these divided opinions the Law remains on the books.[7] There is a consensus that any form of VAC should be reported, but there also appears to be a deep sense of *personal responsibility* transpiring in the answers to the question "What are

---

7. The Law reads: Every schoolteacher, parent or person standing in the place of a parent is justified in using force by way of correction toward a pupil or child, as the case may be, who is under his care, if the force does not exceed what is reasonable under the circumstances (Section 43 of the Criminal Code(1), Barnett, 2008).

some things that you can do as an individual to stop the cycle of violence against children?" Witness the following statements:
— "Educate our own kids so they have a strong sense of social and moral justice; create leaders for their generation";
— "Donate to local courses";
— "Be a block parent or have introductory neighbourhood gatherings (Meet and Greet at schools)";
— "Lobby for adequate social programs to prevent violence and situations where individuals feel powerless and hopeless and thus may resort to violence";
— "Violence is not something to joke or laugh about ... the only thing that is right to do, is report the violence, and then give moral support to the person who is being abused";
— As a teacher, "I continue to take workshops and ... they [the students] confide in me";
— "Teach your children that it is wrong to ... harm somebody that isn't as prepared as you";
— "Become a social worker and going out and talking with them"; and
— "Treat them as I would like to be treated".

In this sense, the lesson learnt from the Canadians is that of social and personal responsibility and holding each other accountable. This conforms to the principles upon which the country's Confederation[8] is based: *peace, order and good governance.* While it is apparent from discussions with educators, policy makers and 'regular folk' in Canada, that T&T can add to the body of knowledge and practice on multiculturalism, in light of Canada's migration thrust over the past few decades.

Nicaragua: A Rights-Based Approach to VAC?

TABLE 3.3   Human Development Information on Nicaragua

Human Development Index	U5MR	Adult literacy Rate	Life expectancy	GNI USD	Population (000)
129	66	78	74	1170	5.870

Source: (UNICEF, 2013)

Nicaragua ratified the Convention on the Rights of the Child in 1990 and has a good legal framework, but very often laws are not enforced and plans and policies lack funds for implementation.

---

8.   http://en.wikipedia.org/wiki/Peace,_order,_and_good_government, accessed September 21. 2013.

> "Poverty in the country limits the fulfillment of children's rights to an adequate standard of living, health, growth and development. A persistent culture of violence affects children's rights to freedoms from violence, abuse and maltreatment."[9]

In Nicaragua[10] it is almost impossible to meet a person who is not aware of his/her rights. This applies to boys and girls, men and women, the poor and the rich, to those who live in the towns and rural villages; they all are aware of their fundamental entitlements. "There is no way, that I can do otherwise as the children will immediately tell me that I'm violating their rights", reported a teacher of 10-year-old children of a special education school in Matagalpa, "when I was in school, the teacher would beat us and nobody would complain, not the parents, not the children, not my colleagues; things are so much different now".[11] When asked — and this is significant — corporal punishment had been banned in his school, at least. The belief in a rights-based approach to solving the nation's ills, including violence against children and women, rang strongly in the replies that forty-six people — teachers, parents, students, NGO staff — gave to the questionnaires they were given. It therefore does not come as a surprise that a good number of respondents defined violence in terms of "abuso de derechos". Noteworthy is that Nicaraguan adolescents see lack of communication and love between parents and their children and the use of violence as a means to stay 'on top' of their children, as the main causes of violence; they see their rights trampled by an abuse of power.

Among the individual replies there were some interesting remarks: three people included 'violence against animals' as relevant. The respondents also felt that NGOs had an important role to play; not only could they serve particular audiences, such as teachers, women's and parents' groups, but also challenge and cooperate with the government in defining and implementing policy. Perhaps it is for these reasons that, compared to neighbouring countries such as Honduras, El Salvador and Guatemala[12] where violence is rampant, Nicaragua is relatively peaceful. Things could be better, according to a frequently-noted observation when the law was not so poorly implemented.

There was also frequent mention made of 'machismo' as a cause of violence, especially against women and within the family; but they also qualified 'machismo' as being brought about by poverty, poor education, and being abused as children as well as being linked to a lack of self-esteem. In this view, 'machismo' had drifted away from notions such as being 'tough', 'chivalrous', obliging or just 'manly'. To deal with the often-encountered

---

9. http://resourcecentre.savethechildren.se/start/countries/nicaragua, accessed June 11, 2013.
10. The researcher carried out action research and worked with NGO staff on VAC during two sessions, in October 2007 and February 2013.
11. Personal communication, Matagalpa, October, 2007.
12. See: http://en.wikipedia.org/wiki/List_of_countries_by_intentional_homicide_rate_by_decade, accessed, 3 March, 2013.

'machismo' in the male-oriented *Policía Nacional*, the Policía Nacional increased the number of women to some 50% of its workforce, and changed its policies from a reactive to a preventive approach to VAC, also with notable beneficial effects (Cordero Ardila, Gurdián Alfaro and López Hurtado 2006).

The experience of Nicaragua is important as it shows that if a populace, children included, are aware of their position of 'rights holders', local and national authorities will be forced to act as 'duty bearers'. It also demonstrates that NGOs and government can both collaborate and challenge each other at the same time. It also tells that poverty is not an excuse for violence. Their colleagues from Trinidad and Tobago and the wider region could be particularly useful by validating the Nicaraguan efforts and including them in the wider debate on VAC. T&T as a nation can benefit from the Nicaragua context the adoption of a more "*revolutionary*" spirit to becoming more political in the sense of advocating and fighting for change.

The Netherlands:[13] A Less Violent Society?

TABLE 3.4 Human Development Information on The Netherlands

Human Development Index	U5MR	Adult literacy rate	Life expectancy	GNI USD	Population (000)
4	4	100	81	49.730	16.665

Source: (UNICEF, 2013)

The CRC was signed by the Netherlands on 26 January, 1990 and ratified on 6 February 1995. The Reservations of the Netherlands on the CRC can also be accessed.[14] Three are noted hereunder:

> "*Article 26:* The Kingdom of the Netherlands accepts the provisions of article 26 of the Convention with the reservation that these provisions shall not imply an independent entitlement of children to social security, including social insurance.
>
> "*Article 37:* The Kingdom of the Netherlands accepts the provisions of article 37 (c) of the Convention with the reservation that these provisions shall not prevent the application

---

13. This researcher has spent significant blocks of time in the Netherlands since 2007 and met with a range of people, both informally and professionally. Her professional involvement with International Child Development Initiatives, The Netherlands (ICDI) facilitated interactions with persons and organisations working with children in difficult circumstances.
14. https://treaties.un.org/Pages/ViewDetails.aspx?mtdsg_no=IV-11&chapter=4&lang=en, accessed 18 June 2012.

of adult penal law to children of sixteen years and older, provided that certain criteria laid down by law have been met.

"Article 40: The Kingdom of the Netherlands accepts the provisions of article 40 of the Convention with the reservation that cases involving minor offences may be tried without the presence of legal assistance and that with respect to such offences the position remains that no provision is made in all cases for a review of the facts or of any measures imposed as a consequence.»

The Netherlands is also known to be a 'post-modern' society (Fokkema and Grijzenhout 2004) and, as such, may present a collective view on violence commensurate with post-modern values and attitudes. To this end, approximately thirty questionnaires were handed over to colleagues of colleagues, this so as to ensure anonymity. The respondents were a mixed and interesting group of NGO staff, nurses, educators, and programme managers.

The definition of violence in its direct forms was given. However, there was that sense that with respect to violence, much of it had been attended to; that the Netherlands as a society had dealt with and continued to deal with infrastructural violence, so to speak. A trend that was clearly visible was that none of the respondents — unlike those elsewhere — complained about the existing laws not being properly enforced. There was not this notion of vulnerability that was evident in some countries. This of course, poses the risk down the road of complacency but this is speculation.

People seemed quite happy with the status quo and did not seem to see violence against children as a major national issue. One respondent saw somebody calling "a shit" as the worst form of violence; while another replied that it was "teasing"; yet another appeared more concerned and saw "death" as the extreme expression of violence against children. One person wondered whether violence against children happened at all. This is remarkable, as every week one child dies from being physically abused; the actual number is estimated as being much higher. Usually, the media gives a great deal of attention to these cases (Heck 2012). Some argued that there should more stringent laws and harsher forms of punishment.

When asked about the root causes of violence against children, the most common reply was that something wrong must have happened with the perpetrators when they were young. They, and all other wrongdoers acted the way they did because they "feel impotent", they "don't know what to do otherwise". Thus "awareness- raising", "good education", and "talks" were seen as the best remedies, actions to be individually initiated as well as by schools and the government. There was also complete unanimity that, when confronted with VAC, "one should speak out" and also that the Netherlands as a nation, 'stands up against violence'. Although any form of corporal punishment, also within the family, is prohibited, and well-engrained in any educationally-oriented syllabus, there was an unmistakable undercurrent that a pedagogical "slap on the buttocks" would not do any harm to the child.

In the main, people accepted that violence against children should be fought against, but there was an acknowledgement that child abuse, neglect, street children and related phenomena would always be around, whatever measures are being taken. This is in a way indicative of the society's postmodern acceptance of the violence phenomena. Against this backdrop the generally-shared view was that the best approach to violence was to make the children 'weerbaar' (defensible) by providing them with better education and above all with 'skills training', which included not only becoming street-wise about issues such as sex and sexuality, but also self-defence proficiency.

The most important lesson 'taken' from the Netherlands was that when a nation upholds its laws, implements and enforces these, and shows respect for the rights of all its citizens, the society as a whole stands to benefit. The Dutch, in their turn, seemed to understand that a Caribbean outlook on human development that rebelled against being 'othered' also made deep sense in their country, which increasingly sees more ethnic groups and cultural expressions within its borders.

Trinidad and Tobago: A Too Tolerant A Society?

Trinidad and Tobago signed the CRC on 30 September 1990 and ratified it on 5 December 1991. In so doing, it became part of a worldwide community of nations in formally endorsing this, by all accounts revolutionary, document. *Inter alia,* it defines states as 'duty bearers' and the children as 'rights holders'. In essence, this means that any child whose entitlements are not being honoured can legally challenge the government. The first two optional protocols have been ratified by more than 150 states, including Trinidad and Tobago. The third optional protocol is under review in Trinidad and Tobago.

Governments are supposed to report on the situation of the rights of children, every five years, to the Committee on the Rights of the Child, based within the office of the UN High Commissioner of Human Rights in Geneva. The Committee consists of 18 independent international experts of high standing. It is also customary that the NGO community in each country submit their own report, simultaneously but independently of their government's document. The Committee examines each report and raises concerns or makes recommendations to the state party and the reports are published on their website. The Committee's most recent report on Trinidad and Tobago dates from 2006 (Office of the High Commissioner on Human Rights 2006).

A somewhat parallel procedure takes place within the framework of the UN Human Rights Council, also based in the office of the High Commissioner on Human Rights. It is an inter-governmental body consisting of the Council comprising 47 United Nations member states, which are elected by the UN General Assembly. The Council is responsible for strengthening the promotion and protection of human rights worldwide and for addressing situations of human rights violations. It works all year round. It submits recommendations to governments and international bodies.[15] The human rights record of Trinidad and Tobago was last reviewed in December 2011.[16] Close reading of the ensuing report reveals also many pointers relevant to the situation of children. Both documents are detailed in their analyses and supply, observations and a host of recommendations that reveal the nation's unimpressive track record in children's and human rights. In fact, the two documents should be mandatory reading for those professionally engaged in protecting and improving the well-being of all Trinbagonians. Also striking is the fact that the lists of areas for concern and recommendations by both committees are very long; in the case of the CRC the number is close to 160, while that of the Human Rights Council comes near to 90!

A small, but pertinent, selection of the CRC Committee's recommendation reads as follows:

— Prioritize budgetary allocations to ensure the implementation of the rights of children to the maximum extent of available resources;
— Include human rights education in the official curriculum, at all levels of education;
— Develop initiatives with journalists and the media to disseminate widely the principles of the Convention and to promote a respectful treatment of children by the media;
— Amend legislation so that the principle of respect for the views of the child is recognized and respected, inter alia, within custody disputes and other legal matters affecting children;
— Expressly prohibit by law corporal punishment in all settings and ensure the implementation of the law;
— Take measures to ensure as far as possible the maintenance of children born out of wedlock by their parents, particularly their fathers;
— Adopt a comprehensive programme to coordinate the efforts and policies of different ministries and departments on foster care;
— Allocate adequate resources to strengthen services for children with disabilities, support their families and train professionals in the field;
— Take measures to increase school attendance and reduce the dropout and repetition rates, involving children and adolescents in these programmes;
— Establish an adequate mechanism to receive complaints from street children about cases of abuse and violence; and
— Undertake a comprehensive study to examine the sexual exploitation of children, gathering accurate data on its prevalence.

---

15. For details on the working of both Committees, see: www.ohchr.org.
16. General Assembly (2011), Report of the Working Group on the Universal Periodic Review: Trinidad and Tobago, Human Rights Council, Nineteenth session, Agenda, item 6, Universal Periodic Review, 14 December.

Going beyond these recommendations and adopting a 'meta vision', the overall conclusion is that Trinidad and Tobago is making progress, albeit slowly, but that this progress is not commensurate with the resources available to the country. It is also generally observed that, even when the right laws are there, enforcement of these is deficient and partial. The recommendations are also not spectacularly new. In fact, they are remarkably in line with those presented by the collective of interviewees in this study and can readily be picked up in editorials in the country's national newspapers. The next report on children's rights by the Government of Trinidad and Tobago was due in 2011. In lieu of this report, the 2010 Situational *Analysis of Children and Women in Trinidad and Tobago* by UNICEF could serve as a judgement on the government's accomplishment in implementing the CRC. If one reads between the lines, it confirms the observation that, in spite of its impressive resources and its slate of adequate laws and measures dedicated to the health and betterment of children and women, the country underperforms in the field of child and family protection. In, particular, infant mortality rates, incidents of school violence in secondary schools, numbers of street children, and violence against women are unconscionably high.

The knowledge to act is available in Trinidad and Tobago, as is made clear in, among others, the 'Strategic Plan 2012-2014' by the Children's Authority. This Plan is firmly rooted in the UN's Declaration of Human Rights and the CRC and offers measurable markers of progress. The status of the current legislation, pertinent to the rights of children, forms the basis of this Plan, the full details of which are presented below.

The *Draft Strategic Plan 2012-2014* of the Children's Authority[17] — the nation's child protection agency — provides a good example of how Trinidad and Tobago can and should move towards a *child-friendly society*. Its philosophy is profoundly rooted in the CRC and also recognises the need for involvement of all stakeholders — they mention the media, among the more obvious parties, but they leave out children and young people as 'experience specialists' and 'religious leaders'. The list of objectively verifiable indicators (OVIs) is meaningful, and measurable, with timed objectives developed in close consultation with people who matter — children and regional specialists included. The objectives are related to information gathering, assessment, training, quality control and inter-agency cooperation; action research is not specifically mentioned. In the main, the Plan conveys an air of 'we can do' and could serve as a format for a nationwide comprehensive and inclusive *child policy*.

---

17. http://ttchildren.org, accessed 8 December, 2012.

TABLE 3.5 Package of Children's Legislation Initiated in 2000

Title	Purpose	Status
Children's Authority, Act Chapter 46:10	Will establish a Children's Authority to act as the guardian of the children in T&T.	Partially proclaimed. Only certain sections are in force.
Children's Community Residences, Foster Care and Nurseries Act 65 of 2000	Will make provision for the monitoring, licensing and regulation of Community Residences, Foster Homes and Nurseries in T&T.	Not yet proclaimed — Includes areas of responsibility for the Authority.
International Child Abduction Act Chapter 12:08	Provides for the application in Trinidad & Tobago of The Hague Convention on Civil Aspects of International Child Abduction.	In force. Under this Act, the Civil Child Abduction Authority is the Central Authority for T&T. It is located within the Ministry of the Attorney-General.
Adoption of Children Act 67 of 2000 Adoption of Children (Amendment) Bill, 2007	Will replace present legislation regulating the adoption of children. The 2007 Bill proposes further amendment to the 2000 Act, to inter alia, replace the Adoption Board with the Children's Authority.	Not yet proclaimed — previous legislation continues to be in force. To be brought to Parliament.
Status of Children (Amendment) Bill, 2009	Would facilitate the replacement of blood tests by the introduction of DNA analysis to ascertain parentage and possibly for other civil law purposes.	Should be re-laid in Parliament.
Family Court Bill, 2009	Would vest jurisdiction for all family matters and juvenile matters in a Division of the High Court to be called the Family Court	Awaiting amendment before re-introduction in Parliament.
Children Act No. 12 of 2012	Makes provision for the increased protection of children against sexual conduct, facilitates more adequate treatment of children who are victims of abuse and deals more comprehensively with child offenders.	Not yet proclaimed — Requires systems and administrative infra-structure to be in place.
Trafficking in Persons Act No. 14 of 2011	An Act to give effect to the United Nations Protocol to prevent, suppress and punish trafficking in persons, especially women and children — the United Nations Convention against transnational organized crime.	In force: Requires the Authority to liaise with the Counter-Trafficking Unit to provide services to victims who are children.

Source: Children's Authority of Trinidad & Tobago (2013)

As the *Strategic Plan* is basically a child protection document and concerned with children who actually need external support, its recommendations deal, naturally, with the problematic of these boys and girls. To widen the canvas, the researcher interviewed relevant persons strategically placed in the following ministries: People and Social Development, Education, Public Administration, National Security, Planning, Health, Community Development, Gender, Youth Affairs and Child Development. Interviews were conducted with senior personnel in these ministries.[18] Interviews were also conducted with key players in the National Plan of Action Committee and the Children's Authority. To this end, a special evaluation tool was developed to conduct in-depth interviews (see Appendix IV).

The discussions revealed the following:
— To the best of knowledge, plans were being made to address the situation of VAC in Trinidad and Tobago; reference was made to the NPA and the developments made via the establishment of the Children's Authority as the department/body responsible for the implementation and systematic monitoring of the CRC;
— Some of the hiccups faced by the Children's Authority included the fact that it was "newly established"; "the length of time everything takes to get done"; and the fact that there are "too many channels to go through for approval";
— No major new law reforms in recent years; reformation of the Equal Opportunities Act — it mentions discrimination but not persons with disabilities;
— There is ample inclusion and involvement of civil society in the discourse on VAC; much collaborative work is done with NGOs and FBOs; not enough collaboration with the ministries and the university;
— Children need to be included more; they are not included in public consultations, nor is there a *children's council* to glean the views and opinions of children; there are no independent institutions for children's rights developed — no children's ombudsman, or child rights commissioners;
— "The political system will always influence the way things get done in the country";
— "Things are still not as they ought to be"; "much is yet to be done"; "sometimes the law hinders rather than helps the process"; "Too many meetings and not enough action";
— Introduction of guidance counsellors in schools is a step in the right direction; need for training, as many of the guidance officers are degree-holders but not trained in psychology or children's issues;
— Need for reformation in teachers' attitude to children; need to be more child friendly; need for revision of the curriculum — too stressful on children;

---

18. These ministries were selected because of ease of access by the researcher who had worked intimately with members of staff from the various ministries/departments and also because of their relevance with respect to child protection.

— The budget could be better allocated — little priority is placed on addressing VAC; monies are allocated but the trickle-down process plays a part — less funds should be spent on grand buildings, offices, conferences and more injected into the communities;
— Need for a Children's Registry — has been in the pipeline for too long;
— There is not enough systematic monitoring conducted through research and evaluation;
— There is an effort at information dissemination and educating the public and creating a more aware T&T;
— There is a need for training on children's rights; need for training of teachers on CRC; need to inform and educate children in schools about their rights;
— Children with disabilities are seldom included in the discussion on VAC — they are a disenfranchised group as are children infected and affected with HIV Aids — infrastructural changes to buildings, centres and schools ought to be addressed; lack of facilities for physiotherapy; not all bad — buses to transport these kids are now available, better schooling options, inclusive education is not on the agenda;
— Need to implement a national policy on persons with disabilities –approved since 2005;
— Lack of legislation; state has a huge role to play in VAC; judicial reviews and reformation of the penal laws; juvenile detention laws needs to be addressed;
— Parents need to be made more involved in the decision- and policy-making process in collaboration with the state; parents need to be educated about the rights of the child;
— In T&T children are not encouraged to be a part of the discourse on children's issues; adults tend to "impose thinking" on them; need for a 'Youth Board';
— Lacking specialist to deal with various children's issues/problems — in the health and education sectors for example (special needs children);
— Early intervention is necessary in all cases — in schools re: discipline issues; in hospitals re: diagnosis and follow-up; in neo and post-natal care; in early detection of problems;
— Need for specialist training; incentives to be given by governments to encourage careers in particular fields of specialist education and medicine (speech pathologists, physiotherapists); need to have salaries commensurate to attract and keep qualified professionals;
— Facilities in hospitals need be improved to retain a dedicated staff; doctors need to be trained in how to interact with children, parents and clients on a whole; "young doctors seem to be in the profession now for the financial rewards and this is not good";
— UNICEF does a good job in collaborating and coordinating efforts; still a need for more assistance.

3.4 A Child Rights-Based Approach

The United Nation's Secretary General's Study on Violence against Children 2006:

> "Much violence against children remains hidden because of *fear, societal acceptance* and *lack of reporting mechanisms*. The emerging picture is one in which some violence is expected and isolated, and the majority of violent acts experienced by children are perpetuated by people who are part of their lives: parents, schoolmates, teachers, employers, boyfriends or girlfriends, spouses and partners."

The report goes on to state that:

> "research points to the fact that the high level of violence in the Caribbean region is related to a combination of *extreme economic* and *social inequalities*, the *predominant culture of 'machismo'* which characterizes the region, as well as the *weaknesses in implementation of the existing legal protection mechanism.*" (Cited in Robinson, Schmid and Paul-McLean 2007, 2)

The Study adopts the definition of the child as contained in *Article 1* of the Convention on the Rights of the Child (CRC) "every human being below the age of 18 years unless, under the law applicable to the child, majority is attained earlier." The definition of violence is that of *Article 19* of the CRC: "*all forms of physical or mental violence, injury and abuse, neglect or negligent treatment, maltreatment or exploitation, including sexual abuse.*" Here 'violence' is defined as 'violence'! This provision tells states parties to take "all appropriate legislative, administrative, social and educational measures to protect the child from all forms of physical or mental violence … while in the care of parent(s), legal guardian(s), or any other person who has the care of the child." Other articles entitle children to physical and personal integrity, and establish high standards for protection. *Article 34* makes it mandatory for state parties to protect children from all forms of sexual exploitation and sexual abuse. *Article 37* prohibits torture or other cruel, inhuman or degrading treatment or punishment, as well as capital punishment and life imprisonment without possibility of release. It reads that "every child deprived of liberty shall be treated with humanity and respect for the inherent dignity of the human person, and in a manner which takes into account the needs of persons of his or her age." *Article 40* states that children who come into conflict with the law should be "treated in a manner consistent with the promotion of the child's sense of dignity and worth". *Articles 14, 16, 17, 37* and *40* for example, that pertain to freedom of thought and expression, right to privacy, access to information and the media, detention and punishment and juvenile delinquency, may certainly evoke rebuttals in many traditional circles.[19]

---

19. "Fact Sheet: A Summary of the Rights under the Convention on the rights of the Child," UNICEF, no date, accessed 29 December, 2012, www.unicef.org/crc/files/Rights_overview.pdf.

A child rights-based approach to development does not inherently mean that things will change overnight but it does establish a set of clear guidelines, goals and standards to measure progress that is outlined in an internationally agreed framework, gleans commitments from governments, civil society organizations, communities, families and children, and recognizes an established monitoring system that ensures transparency and accountability to the task at hand, providing a good, safe and just life for our world's children. With its adoption children are no longer seen as recipients of services, but as subjects of rights and participants in actions affecting them. In addition, duty bearers — local and national governments — are held to their obligations to do all that is needed in the best interest of the child.[20] This message forms the essence of this work and dictates the shape, form and outcome of this research.

The basic elements of any rights-based approach are:[21]
— Addressing the accountability of duty bearers (with reference to the CRC);
— Enhancing empowerment of the right holders through a participative approach and active involvement;
— Conducting interventions that directly address violations of rights;
— Having in place operational processes based on rights programming principles that guide and shape the development interventions (referring to e.g. conducting a situation analysis, and monitoring and evaluating of achievement in child rights and protection).

A Rights-Based Approach to Education: An Example

A rights-based approach establishes certain basic entitlements — such as education and freedom of expression — as a human right and a child's right. Education, for example, was formally recognized as a human right since the adoption of the Universal Declaration of Human Rights in 1948. This translates to not only access to educational provision, but also the obligation to eliminate discrimination at all levels of the educational system, to set minimum standards and to improve quality. A rights-based approach to education deems education as necessary for the fulfilment of any other civil, political, economic or social right. The Millennium Declaration commits many countries to ensuring that all girls and boys complete primary education and to the elimination of gender discrimination in educational access. Human and children's rights are mainstreamed into the policies and programmes of many countries and this leads to a conceptual, analytical and methodological framework for identifying, planning, designing and monitoring development activities based on international children's rights standards.

---

20. Policy Paper Child Rights PLAN Netherlands (April 2006, 10).
21. Ibid., 14.

The following elements are necessary, specific and unique to a rights-based approach and can be used for policy and programming in the education sector:
— *Situation assessment and analysis* to identify the claims of human rights in education and the corresponding obligations of governments, as well as the immediate, underlying and structural causes of the non-realization of rights;
— *Programme planning, design and implementation*. Programming is informed by the recommendations of international human rights bodies and mechanisms;
— *Assessing capacity for implementation*. Programmes assess the capacity of individuals to claim their rights and of governments to fulfil their obligations. Strategies are then developed to build those capacities;
— *Monitoring and evaluation*. Programmes monitor and evaluate both the outcomes and processes, guided by human rights standards and principles.

A Rights-Based Approach to Education: Benefits

— *Promotes social cohesion, integration and stability:* A rights-based curriculum includes a focus on respect for families and the values of society and thus promotes understanding of other cultures and peoples, contributing to intercultural dialogue and respect;
— *Builds respect for peace and non-violent conflict resolution*: Schools and communities are required to create learning environments that eliminate all forms of physical, sexual or humiliating punishment by teachers and challenge all forms of bullying and aggression among students;
— *Contributes to positive social transformation*: A rights-based approach empowers children and other stakeholders. It fosters social transformation towards rights-respecting societies and social justice;
— *Is more cost-effective and sustainable*: In the long term building inclusive, participatory and accountable education systems will serve to improve educational outcomes. Poor performance and high drop-out rates are facilitated by school violence and abuse, discriminatory attitudes, an irrelevant curriculum and poor teaching quality;
— *Produces better outcomes for economic development*: A rights-based approach to education can be entirely consistent with the broader agenda of a country's plan for economic and social progress.

Part 2

4.0 The study

4.1 Historical, International and Local Context

For Trinidad and Tobago, the concepts 'violence' and 'international' are almost Siamese twins. Perhaps the earliest settlers, the Ortoiroid, arrived in Trinidad and Tobago from north-eastern South America without strife in 4000 BC, but after that, violence became a principal social ingredient as wave after wave of 'occupants' made their way onto the islands, first the Saladoid, then the Barrancoid and the Arauquinoid, to be followed by the Arawaks, the Caribs, and then, starting with Columbus on Tuesday 31st of July 1498 on his third voyage, came the massive influx of Europeans: the Spanish, Dutch, Courlanders, French and British, and in their wake the subjugated peoples from the British colonies and, later, literally from all corners of the world. And it is no exaggeration to say that much of T&T's history is written in a concoction of sweat and blood. The indigenous population mostly destroyed, the Caribbean later comprised the European plantation owners and the African slaves who worked on the sugar plantations. Adamson (1972) notes that in May 1838, 396 East-Indian immigrants set foot in Trinidad and they kept on coming until 1917, followed by the Chinese and the Syrians. Brereton (1996) relates how the dismal outcome of this economic exploitation and betrayal of indentured immigrants, was the creation of a plantation dependence with large numbers of unskilled labourers in the Caribbean.

The adjective 'international' is apposite for the influx of marauding and subdued people *into* the country, for there are very few families, if any, who do not have family abroad and are in close contact with them. Approximately a quarter of a million people from the Caribbean settled permanently in Britain between 1955 and 1962 after the Second World War. Thus, Great Britain alone counts over 24,000 T&T-born citizens,[1] while in Canada the number exceeds 100,000,[2] with more than 250,000 Trinidadians living in USA.[3] One may, therefore,

---

1. Accessed 9 October 2012, www.investt.co.tt/blog/investt-blog/2012/september/uk-trinidad-trade-we-make-good-company.
2. Accessed 8 May 2012, www.mnialive.com/global-connect/canada/2381-an-estimated-100-000-trinidadians-now-live-in-toronto-canada.html.
3. Accessed 25 February 2013, http://en.wikipedia.org/wiki/Trinidadian_and_Tobagonian_American.

expect that the discussion on violence against children in Trinidad and Tobago is framed within an international perspective, especially as that provided by the United Nations and international human development agencies. It dares to suggest that T&T has something to offer to the international community, more than its calypso, carnival and cricket; that is not to say that it dismisses these achievements as irrelevant, for it will be shown in this research that culture embodied in music, dance and visual arts, as well as sports, are potentially strong *antidotes to violence*. The notion of culture and its role in violence becomes very relevant. The inherent, whether formed or forming, culture of the region needs to be contextually sifted through if one is to search for the elements of culture that shape or define violence. It is customary to use UN-generated indicators to obtain an impression of the health and wealth of nations. Rather than looking at Gross National Income (GNI), the Human Development Index (HDI), which is a composite of educational attainment, longevity and GNI, is applied. The 2010 issue of the Human Development Report, which publishes statistics on all countries, recognizes four categories: Very High Development, High Development, Medium Development and Low Development. Rankings run from 1 (Norway) to 169 (Zimbabwe). T&T finds itself in the High Income Development rubric with a ranking of 59. Table 1.1 gives the scores for some pertinent countries (UNDP 2010). The 2013 Human Development Report — *The Rise of the South: Human Progress in a Diverse World* — examines the profound shift in global dynamics driven by the fast-rising new powers of the developing world and its long-term implications for human development.[4]

TABLE 4.1   Human Development Indices for Selected Countries

Ranking of Trinidad and Tobago : 59							
Very High Development		High Development		Medium Development		Low Development	
Country	Rank	Country	Rank	Country	Rank	Country	Rank
UK	26	Venezuela	75	Suriname	94	Haiti	145
Barbados	42	Jamaica	80	Guyana	104		

Source: UNDP (2010)

Data provided by UNICEF is more relevant for children as it includes such indicators as nutrition, health, HIV/AIDS, education, demographic indicators, economic indicators, women, child protection, under-five mortality rankings (U5MR) and, importantly, the rate of progress. Usually, U5MR is taken as the 'hardest' indicator of a child's well-being, and by proxy, that of a nation. Here the ranking runs from 1 (Afghanistan) to 188 (Sweden).

---

4. Accessed December 2013, www.undp.org/content/undp/en/home/librarypage/hdr/human-development-report-2013/.

| TABLE 4.2 | Under-Five Mortality Rate for Selected Countries |

U5MR for Trinidad and Tobago: 77			
Country	Ranking	Country	Ranking
Haiti	48	Grenada	120
Guyana	54	Saint Lucia	130
Suriname	91	Cuba	158

Source: UNICEF (2011)

It is difficult to interpret these data as socio-economic and cultural contexts vary from country to country. Perhaps one thing could be said with certainty: looking at the example of Cuba, with a score of 158 but also with its relative isolation and limited resources, the U5MR of 77 of Trinidad and Tobago is unjustifiably low. Vision of Humanity, an Australian organization that promotes study, advocacy and action on peace, presented an annual Global Peace Index, which scores from 1 (New Zealand) to 149 (Iraq), with Trinidad and Tobago having a GPI of 59. Other regional countries' GPIs are given in table 1.3.

| TABLE 4.3 | Global Peace Indicators for Selected Countries Neighbouring T&T |

GPI for Trinidad and Tobago: 59			
Country	Ranking	Country	Ranking
Cuba	72	Grenada	120
Guyana	91	Haiti	141
Jamaica	91	Venezuela	138

Source: Vision of Humanity, accessed 12 December 2012, www.visionofhumanity.org/#/page/indexes/global-peace-index.

The GPI is made up of 23 sub-indicators, namely: level of organized conflict, armed services personnel, weapons imports, military expenditure, number of conflicts fought, jailed population, deaths from conflict (internal), potential for terrorist acts, level of violent crime, political instability, military capability/sophistication, disrespect for human rights, number of homicides, UN peacekeeping funding, number of heavy weapons, number of displaced people, neighbouring country relations, weapons exports, deaths from conflict (external), violent demonstrations, access to weapons, perceived criminality in society, and security officers and police. Each of these can be rated on a five-point scale (good = 1, bad = 5). Three of these subscales seem of particular interest; they are *respect for human rights, level of violent crime* and *perceived criminality*. The country's scores are as follows: 2.5 for respect for human rights, 5 for violent crime and 3 for perceived criminality. Grenada and Jamaica, like Trinidad and Tobago, have fairly high levels of violent crime while scoring low on perceived criminality. This speaks volumes for our threshold of violence tolerance.

TABLE 4.4 Scores for 'Respect of Human Rights' (RHR), 'Violent Crime' (VC) and 'Perceived Criminality' (PC) of Selected Countries

Scores for Trinidad and Tobago are respectively 2.5, 5 and 3							
Country	RHR	VC	PC	Country	RHR	VC	PC
Cuba	3	1	2	Grenada	2	4	2
Guyana	2	3	3	Haiti	2.5	4	4
Jamaica	3.5	5	3	Venezuela	3.5	4	4

Source: Vision of Humanity, www.visionofhumanity.org/#/page/indexes/global-peace-index.

The 2005 landmark study, *Violence against Children in the Caribbean Region, Regional Assessment,* prepared for the *United Nations World Report on Violence against Children* or named after its chief responsible officer, Sérgio Pinheiro, the 'Pinheiro report', lists the most important studies on violence against children in Trinidad and Tobago, and by framing it within a Caribbean context adds an extra dimension to the understanding of VAC (UNICEF 2005). Many countries share similar historical backgrounds, compounded by the ill effects of poverty, globalization and narco-trafficking. The report highlights that many initiatives are being taken to combat violence against children but notes that emotional abuse and neglect are still not given the attention they need as compared to physical and sexual abuse of children.

The World Bank (UNODC/World Bank 2007) deplores the high rate of murders in the Caribbean, the highest — 30 per 100,000 inhabitants — in the world, with a peak in Jamaica, but with Trinidad and Tobago catching up. As to the causes of this high level of violence, it comes to similar conclusions as mentioned above, but also lists youth unemployment, large-scale migration, a weak education system, ineffective policing, easy access to weapons, drug and alcohol use, and the presence of organized gangs as contributory factors. It also notes that youth are disproportionately represented in the ranks of both victims and perpetrators of crime and violence and those crimes are being committed at an ever earlier age. To give 'life' to these tables and statistics, more anthropological and descriptive studies are required. An illustration of the latter is the book *Writing Rage, Unmasking Violence through Caribbean Discourse* (Morgan and Youssef 2006). However, even these kinds of studies do not touch the heart and soul as incisively as anecdotal and real-life stories, as do those that are presented by the media, or even more directly, told by the children themselves or by their kin. To this end, as mentioned above, the national newspapers have been scrutinized over a period of some six years and accounts of VAC carefully recorded. At a later stage, a third national newspaper was added.

Here follows a selection of these reports:
— No fathers: According to National Security Minister, John Sandy, there are too many fathers who fail to be fathers to their sons, with the result that these children turn to a life of crime (Simon 2011a).
— Schoolgirls taken to hospital after fight: two female pupils of the Tranquillity Government Secondary School had to be treated at the Port of Spain General Hospital. One of the pupils, police said, reportedly stabbed the other with a broken bottle during a scuffle (Simon 2011b).
— Teen pregnancy a big headache: Education Minister Tim Gopeesingh says of the 17,000 births recorded annually in T&T, an estimated 2,500 involved teenagers who become pregnant before the age of 18. He said because pregnancies under the age of 16 would be statutory rape, there might have been an under-reporting of such pregnancies; this in light of primary school girls becoming pregnant (Swamber 2012).
— Accused in midnight slaughter in Dow Village in court today: A 23 year-old man is … charged with the slayings of infant … and his father. The couple's five other children managed to escape unhurt during the ordeal (Ragoonath 2011).
— Baby Ashley is a fighter: Three weeks overdue (and pronounced dead by doctors) and also surviving an attempt by her mother to end her life prematurely, baby Ashley fought against all odds and came into the world. The family lives in abject poverty … in a dilapidated two-bedroom wooden shack infested with rats and cockroaches … Unable to read or write, [the mother] had her first baby at age 14 (Gumbs-Sandiford 2010).
— Two-year-old boy beaten to death: Domestic abuse claimed the life of a two-year-old boy yesterday even as his mother was at the hospital seeking treatment for her own injuries. The child's mother, 21, who suffered 12 months of abuse at the hands of a close relative had previously lived with another man, the father of the dead child. The boy's biological father knew his son was being beaten and made numerous attempts to take the boy but [the mother] always prevented him from doing so (Gonzales 2010).
— 16-year-old shot, killed by police: A 16-year-old boy was shot dead on Monday night in an exchange of gunfire with a police officer … (Clarke 2011).
— Worker slain in front children: A 34-year-old port employee was killed in front of three children …, after three gunmen burst through the front door of a house … opened fire on him. … a father of two and his relatives say … he was not part of any gang (Gonzales 2011).
— Helping others heal: She fled Trinidad and Tobago several years ago after her ex-husband burned down her house and threatened to kill her and her three children (Sheppard 2011).
— Our children aren't racehorses: As is often the case, over-zealous parents drown their children in extra work. They would like to believe that this is to help the child. Sadly

though, some parents do this because they want their children to pass for "prestige" schools! It is now a competition among parents to get their children into such schools. Children have become racehorses to them. (Scott 2011)

— Losing Tecia: The nation reacted in horror to the barbaric murder of ten-year-old Tecia … sent to a mini mart near her John John home … never made it to the shop. Tecia's body was discovered four days later, stuffed in a dirt hole, a stone's throw away from her home. She had been strangled (Kowlessar 2010).

— Mom, four children evicted: A mother and her four children joined the homeless on the streets of San Fernando last night. [The mother] and her children, Dillon 12, Daniel, ten, Dillia, six, and her two-year-old baby, Isaac Crichlow, were evicted from their one-bedroom shack yesterday (John 2011).

— 4 sent home for beating parent, child at school: Four pupils at the X Secondary School have been suspended from classes for beating a parent and his daughter outside the school (Bethel 2011).

— Headless horror: The dismembered bodies of a woman and boy were found — bagged and dumped — at the Forres Park Landfill near Claxton Bay yesterday. (Charan 2010).

— On Monday Dixon, 14, was stabbed to death by a 16-year-old schoolmate at the Waterloo school during an argument over girl (Wilson 2013).

— Missing boy found dead on river bank: Three days of extensive searches for missing eight-year-old Daniel Guerra ended in tragedy yesterday, as the boy's decomposing body was discovered along the Tarouba Link Road, San Fernando (Trinidad and Tobago Guardian 2011).[5]

4.2 Objectives of the Study

This study examines the phenomena of violence in its multiple forms — direct, structural and cultural violence — in the various arenas of societal life and, in so doing, to analyse the dynamic interplay amongst these three components of violence in promoting a culture of violence-tolerance towards child abuse and to detect and promote ways to lower this tolerance. The research proposes to examine the knowledge, attitudes, perceptions and beliefs (KAPB) of members of society on the issues of violence against children, violence tolerance, and child rights; to assess the general measures of implementation of the Convention of the Rights of the Child (CRC) in the Trinidad and Tobago context; to identify the relationship between violence definition and violence -tolerance, and ultimately, to recommend

---

5. The Prime Minister, Kamla Persad-Bissesar, pronounced on March 2, 2011 a 'Daniel Decree': "a social agenda" involving all NGOs, the police, the army and Government and the private sector in a partnership to tackle "issues of crime and child neglect and abuse in the myriad forms" (Lord 2011). However, to date, nothing of this intention has been materialised (Newsday 2013).

pointers for policy, practice and research that will bring about a cultural shift so that all forms of violence against children — direct, cultural and structural — will be acted upon as unacceptable and be met with zero tolerance. This multi-design research employed both *qualitative and quantitative* research techniques. Observation, in-depth interviews and focus group sessions were utilised as techniques to gather information alongside structured survey questionnaires containing, in some instances, open-ended questions and in others, closed questions. Responses to relevant open-ended questions were "condensed into systematically comparable categories" (Berg 2001). Three sets of data were collected: data associated with the violence assessment component of the research, data associated with the views of children in institutions on VAC, and data associated with the CRC implementation. The data collection techniques involved: observation; drawings; informal and formal in-depth interviews; focus group discussions; and surveys with questionnaires.

4.3 Core Assumptions

— Most people tend to define violence along the limited conceptualisation of 'direct' violence, neglecting to include the 'indirect' dimensions of violence (i.e. the structural and the cultural dimensions);
— The broader and more sophisticated the conceptualisations and definitions of violence i.e. the more the definitions move from being 'direct' to 'indirect' (one that includes 'cultural', 'structural' and 'rights' domains), the less likely people are to be tolerant of violence;
— Violence — tolerance in T&T is fed by structural and cultural elements, both past and present;
— Violence — tolerance can be captioned using the variables of 'violence — acceptance', 'violence — tolerance ', and 'violence — intervention';
— Corporal punishment and domestic abuse are viewed as forms of violence;
— The acceptance of corporal punishment, perception of violence — tolerance, and degree of intervention in domestic violence situation(s) all act as measurable indicators of 'violence — tolerance';
— Violence — tolerance as a phenomenon is also highlighted in the literature and the respondents' treatment of varying situations of VAC in the forms of street children, gender violence, and domestic abuse, amongst others;
— Violence — tolerance is evidenced by the degree of commitment by the nation to the implementation of the CRC — reflected in the evaluation;
— Children's rights do not feature prominently in the nation's discourse on violence and, in light of the nation's commitment to the CRC and the Millennium Development Goals (MDGs), the factoring of children's rights into the violence discourse is critical to the

promotion of a less violent society — "zero-tolerance for violence is a matter of basic human rights".
— Change, therefore, is dependent on increased awareness of the broader definition and multidimensional nature of violence coupled with the injection of 'rights' into the violence discourse.

4.4 The Instruments

The majority of research into violence and aggression has focussed on risk factors (Bjørkly 1997; Monahan 1992; Monahan and Steadman 1994) and anger (Novaco 1975; Novaco and Welsh 1989). Some instruments such as Slaby and Guerra's (1988) '18-item belief measure' included five subscales: 'the legitimacy of aggression', 'aggression increases self-esteem', 'aggression helps avoid a negative self-image', 'victims deserve aggression', and 'victims don't suffer'. Other studies have considered offending by assessing criminogenic or criminal factors, e.g. the Psychological Inventory of Criminal Thinking Styles (PICTS) (Walters 2003 and the 'Psychopathy Checklist—Revised'). The PICTS and the PCL-R represent generic measures of offending and are not specific to violence. Many instruments test anger, hostility, paranoia, impulsivity and empathy levels. There are over 40 that relate to violent and aggressive behaviour, but these tend to be personality measures, risk assessments or behavioural measures (Gothelf, Apter, and van Praag 1997; et al. 1996). Those instruments claiming to measure specific thoughts, beliefs and attitudes which may principally relate to violence do not do so in a comprehensive manner (Dahlberg et al. 2005). The Maudsley Violence Questionnaire (MVQ) which was designed according to Walker and Gudjonsson (2006) with the intention to evaluate individuals' thoughts and beliefs about violence, violent acts and beliefs about what is acceptable, justifiable and reasonable in various situations was consulted. The FAVT, another violence-specific measure which has undergone adequate factor analysis and assesses thoughts and feelings from the perspective of an internal 'voice' was referred to. It consisted of "an integrated system of negative thoughts and attitudes, antithetical to self and cynical and hostile thoughts toward others" (Doucette-Gates, Brooks-Gunn, and Chase-Lansdale 1998, 116) e.g., "you're stupid", "you're a failure". The FAVT factor analysed into four robust factors: social mistrust, perceived disrespect/disregard, negative critical thoughts, and expression of overt anger. There are other attitude scales which have been developed for use with children, but one is specific to gun violence (Shapiro et al. 1998) and the 'Attitudes towards Violence Scale' is brief (15 items on two factors) and has not been compared to self-reported violence (Funk et al. 1999).

In T&T, the issue of agenda setting as it relates to national social problems is often dictated by the political will of the prevailing political powers. Furthermore, 'reasons' for, or 'causes' of these societal malaises are often distributed and re-distributed to serve the politico-socio-economic agendas. VAC has too long been on the nation's back burner while debate has raged on 'assigning blame' for conflict and violence to demographic variables of poverty, race, class, religion, and gender. This researcher is in agreement with Blumer (1971, 298) when he says that

> "... social problems are fundamentally products of a process of collective definition instead of existing independently as a set of objective social arrangements with an intrinsic makeup."

Public identification of social problems is often a dangerous game that many governments play without paying due attention to the 'emergence' and 'legitimation' of the real social problems at hand. The developing world has for too long seen its social problems identified by market-oriented, multi-nationalistic neo-liberalism, defining and identifying social ills from poverty or gender inequity in one decade to racism, environmental pollution or terrorism in yet another. Research on violence, as noted earlier, has also suffered the onslaught of race and class underpinnings. To this end, data collection *instrument I,* was designed to glean information from respondents devoid of demographic categorisations. This was done in light of the reality that factors such as race, class, religion, ethnicity, and gender continue to feature prominently in the nation's public discussions on critical social issues; sometimes proving counterproductive to policy reformation because of socio-political and legislative deadlock. It is also becoming more and more an internationally accepted policy of respect for privacy to refrain from enquiring about people's status (such as income level, marital status, age, religious affiliation and racial background). Much valuable international and local research has already been done and can be accessed on the relationships between/among race, class, gender, ethnicity, religion, crime, delinquency and violence and it is not the intent of this research to explore these factors. Taken in aggregate, the researcher accepts that these factors all influence the ideology and cultural beliefs and practices of the respondents and is more interested in accessing the respondents' views (in their multicultural entirety) on violence. It was the intention to *maintain* the focus solely on the opinions, views and attitudes towards violence of people living in T&T, *regardless* of race, class, colour, religion, age, and sexual inclination. *Nationality* then became the critical *identifier.*

Instrument I (Appendix I) is a survey questionnaire comprising twenty questions, most of which were open-ended so as to capture 'emerging' issues in order to determine if notions of 'child rights', 'agency', and 'children's participation' formed a natural part of the dialogue of individuals in Trinidad and Tobago when discussing violence against children. It was designed to gain information regarding people's knowledge, attitudes, beliefs and perceptions about children's rights, violence and violence — tolerance. Likert testing was not used so as to avoid the associated response distortion issues, such as central tendency bias, acquiescence bias, or social desirability bias.

It explored the following: Definitions of violence; Perceptions of violence; Attitudes towards violence; Tolerance to different examples and types of violence; Role of violence in the lives of individuals; Reactions to violence; Tendency to report violence; Tendency of persons to display violent behaviour; Reasons for not reporting violent acts; Experience with violence; Perceived impact of violence; Exposure to violence; and Whether 'rights' factored in the discourse on violence.

Instrument II (Appendix III) is the Survey Questionnaire which was simple in layout with questions designed to get straightforward yes/no responses from children in institutions; to ascertain children's perceptions, attitudes and exposure to violence. Included also, were the additional dimensions: Awareness of rights as children; and the meaning of the CRC to these children.

Instrument III (Appendix IV) is an evaluation tool designed to conduct a situational analysis of VAC in Trinidad and Tobago. Questions regarding the following were asked: Knowledge of violence legislation; Knowledge of children's rights legislation; Opinions on the mechanisms that are present to deal with violence; Perceived impact of violence; Understanding of children's rights; Exposure to children's rights issues; Opinions on children's rights and children's participation.

These interviews served to act as informal evaluations to assess T&T's status with respect to its achieving the general measures of implementation of the UNCRC. This would display the level of the state's commitment to its national and international obligations re: the CRC. Many of the questions asked are tasks that will formulate the performance and evaluation criteria and they are based on the following categories: The process of law reform; Existence of independent national institutions to deal with children's issues; Formulation of comprehensive national agendas or intervention strategies; Networking of various children's agencies; Allocation of resources; Systematic monitoring of the implementation of the CRC; Education, training and awareness-raising exercises; Involvement of civil society.

The Dailies: Since the idea of looking into the high tolerance of violence against children found its genesis seven years ago, the on-line versions of the three leading daily national newspapers — the *Trinidad and Tobago Newsday*, the *Trinidad and Tobago Guardian* and the *Trinidad and Tobago Express* — were alternately scrutinised for pertinent information, often on a day-to-day basis. Also daily, issues of *The New York Times* (USA), the *Toronto Star* (Canada), and a sprinkling of other dailies and weeklies — among which the *Moscow Times* and the *NRC Handelsblad* (Netherlands) were perused. In addition the websites of BBC News, Voice of America and Al-Jazeera were visited.

The Researcher as Investigator: The researcher was born in Trinidad in the true spirit of its multiculturalism; she was part of an Indo-Trinidadian Hindu family in rural central

Trinidad, educated in a Convent school in South Trinidad, was initially married into a mixed Indo-African family of Christian and Islamic faiths, has two children and has worked in the fields of education and teacher training, research and evaluation in the urban sprawl, and human resource development. Her life experience on the island brought her in touch with many boys and girls, including those who suffered from neglect, abuse and ill treatment. In this way, she functions as a potent research tool that helps to attach meaning to research findings and place them in the right kind of context. Her later encounters with comparable situations in African, Asian, European, Latin- and North American, and Middle-Eastern countries have served to broaden the scope of analysis and erase some of the biases that may be inherent to being much a 'product' of any one culture and society. Needless to say being a member of a minority group in Canada, where she now resides with her two children and Dutch, atheist, caucasian spouse lends her additional lens of observation.

4.5 Data Analysis and Limitations of the Study

The data collected were analysed both qualitatively and quantitatively. Data from the interviews and focus group sessions produced a rich body of text on violence. Pertinent questions that were required for hypotheses testing had the summed responses grouped. The summed responses fulfilled relevant assumptions and parametric statistical tests were applied. This was vital to understanding the correlation between violence — definition and violence -tolerance. The quantitative data were analysed using the Statistical Package for Social Sciences (SPSS).[6] Admittedly, while the multi-design approach of the research allows for the marrying of two major techniques to provide a more broad-scope analysis of violence, it is not without some compromise. Quantitative analysis allows for statistical validation but it limits the in-depth probing that would be facilitated by discourse analysis for example, and runs the risk of losing valuable messages as a result of the quantifying of attitudinal and perceptual notions. However, great care was taken when handling the data so as to allow sufficient emergence of issues from the responses garnered. The use of a smaller purposive sample rather than a larger and random selection of respondents naturally meant a compromise in statistical accuracy and representativeness. Thus, the researcher is very modest in her claims, however, when amassed, the sample fulfils the purpose of the study and yields additional insights into this narrative on violence. As they varied from category to category, the replies were transformed into percentages where possible, so as to make mutual comparisons and statistical treatment feasible.

---

6. Many thanks to statistician Julia Tretiak for her assistance with the statistical data analysis.

5.0 The findings

5.1 Analysis of the Data

Eight (8) groups comprising teenagers, parents, teachers, NGO staff, police officers, ECD certificate student teachers, children and policy makers were interviewed.[1] The views of a mixed selection of Bangladeshi, Canadian, Dutch and Nicaraguan nationals comprising NGO staff, parents, police officers, and children were also solicited.

TABLE 5.1 Categories and Number of Respondents

Respondents	Number	Percentage of Total Sample
Children	27	10.1
ECD students	24	9.0
NGO staff	23	8.6
Parents	32	12
Police	32	12
Policy makers	23	8.6
Teachers	28	10.5
Teenagers	78	29.2
Total[2]	267	100

---

1. In looking at 'Who can help to educate for tolerance?', Reardon (1997) identified key players in the process as school authorities, parents, social workers, and community personnel. These categories were identified as the purposive sample frame for this research, and to these were added police officers, early childhood specialists, teenagers and children.
2. To this number, 34 were added (children ages 8 and under, whose opinions were sought via drawings), making the total 301.

5.1.1 Definition of Violence

In the main violence is conceptualised along two main divisions: that of 'direct' violence and 'indirect' violence. Direct violence was defined as any act that caused harm to an individual(s) and included neglect and mental, psychological and emotional damage. Indirect violence embraced the elements of structural, cultural and rights. The raw responses were recorded and then grouped into three conceptual clusters:

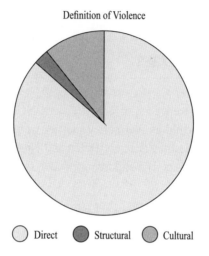

FIGURE 5.1 Response Percentage for Three Conceptual Dimensions of Violence

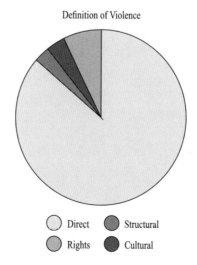

FIGURE 5.2 Response Percentage for Four Categories of Violence

— *Direct Violence*: Physical harm; physical and mental harm; neglect; bullying; hurting vulnerable persons;
— *Structural Violence*: Against the law; systemic; breach of the CRC (legal component);
— *Cultural Violence*: Zero tolerance; rights violation (moral and values component), and God's will.

TABLE 5.2 Definitions of Violence against Children by Interviewees[3]

Interviewees (%)	Physical harm	Physical and mental harm	Against rights	Against God's will	Against the law	Hurting vulnerable persons	Structural violence	Zero tolerance
Parents	78	16	3			3	3	6
Police	53	31		3	9			3
NGOs	68	27	9					
Teachers	72	32					12	
Policy makers	64	32	5					
ECD certificate students	52	48						
Teenagers	47	38	1		9			
Children	52.5				47.5			
All T&T groups combined	61	28	2.3	0.38	8.1	0.38	1.9	1.1

5.1.2 Most Common Forms of Violence

The responses revealed the following:

Direct Violence: Crime, drug abuse, violence against animals, violence against the elderly, robberies and thefts, murders and shootings, gang-related violence, suicide, teenage pregnancy, neglect, kidnapping, violence in schools, violence against children, domestic violence, sexual abuse, mental abuse, verbal abuse, physical violence;

Structural Violence: Abuse of power, exploitation at work, child labour;

---

3. The number of replies (frequencies) per group of interviewees in all tables in this section is presented in percentages to make them mutually comparable.

TABLE 5.3 Most Common Forms of VAC Identified by Interviewees

Observed forms of violence	Teachers	Parents	Police officers	NGOs	Policy makers	ECD students	Teenagers	Children	T&T Average
Percentage of Respondents									
Physical violence	46	35.5	37.5	36	41	52	28		34.5
Verbal violence	25	10	9	14	18	28	9		14
Mental abuse	14		6	5	4	8	51	33	15
Sexual abuse	14	39	16	18	45	8	24		20.5
Domestic violence	54	39	50	27	64	40	37		39
Violence against children	4	16	12.5		27	16	20.5	7	13
Violence in schools	4	6					9		2
Kidnapping	4						2.5	19	3
Child labour			3						4
Neglect									0
Teenage Pregnancy						8			1
Suicide		3							4
Gang-related violence	14	16	6	27	32	8	9		14
Murders and shootings	18	30	22		18		28	78	24
Robberies & thefts		3		4			9		2
Exploitation at work		3	6	4					2
Violence against the elderly					4				0.5
Abuse of power									0
Violence against animals			3	4		4			1
Drug abuse									
Crime								7	1
Structural violence		3	3	9	4				2

The under-twelve category of students saw mental abuse (33%) as a form of violence. Worth noting is that the under-twelve children did not point out corporal punishment as a form of violence and this ties in with the common notion that corporal punishment is accepted by many children as a sanctioned form of discipline (Jualla-Ali 2003). Verbal abuse was especially and not surprisingly picked up by teachers (25%) and ECD certificate student teachers (28%). Mental abuse was highlighted by teenagers (51%) and children (33%); this is also to be expected, as well as applauded, as young people have a stronger developed sense of fairness. Sexual abuse was mentioned most by parents (39%); teenagers (24%). Policy makers (45%) were alert to the phenomenon of sexual abuse and there was mention of violence against the elderly — a group often overlooked. It is understandable that children under twelve years of age see murders, shootings, and kidnappings as main forms of violence as these events appeal most strongly to their imaginations and emotions at this age. In addition to this, the fact is that in recent times kidnappings in T&T have been on the rise and pose a genuine threat to many and may have elicited the necessary parental warnings of safekeeping leading to the responses recorded. Kidnapping has been on the rise throughout the Caribbean and Latin America, but it has soared in Trinidad. In 2001, this country of 1.2 million had fewer than 10 kidnappings. In 2002, the number was 29. In the last couple of years, the figure has been about 150.[4]

4.1.3 Worst Forms of Violence

The worst forms of violence identified were all direct violence: Sexual abuse; physical abuse; psychological abuse; verbal abuse; murder and shootings; domestic violence. It is interesting to note that in T&T, where domestic violence is prominent, it is not singled out by the respondents as being the worst form of violence; but this can be explained also by the fact that they categorise it as physical violence and reported it as such without using the terminology. Important to recognise is that verbal abuse is identified as a worse form of violence; though it does not capture the representation as do physical forms of violence such as rape, beatings and shootings.

Psychological abuse was not mentioned in this category. Local social scientist, St. Bernard (2010), in his study 'Exploring Childhood Victimization in Trinidad and Tobago: A Mixed Method of Analysis of Homicidal Cases' identified the most common deaths among children as being caused by gunshot, stabbing, being beaten, burnt or poisoned, chopped or strangled. There appeared to be a consensus between all the people interviewed: they all abhorred the sexual abuse of children (children: 68%, NGOs: 65%, teenagers: 55%) and their physical mishandling (teachers: 72%, ECD students: 68%, parents: 59%). Even the police saw these two manifestations as most abhorrent (67% and 37% respectively); noteworthy was that murders and shootings did not feature prominently in the responses of the officers. Young children as well feared sexual abuse (68%) and physical harm (16%) but a large contingent of them were also afraid of murder and shootings (47%). Verbal cruelty was also a factor of concern for teenagers (10%), ECD students (28%), teachers (20%) and NGO

---

4. **Kidnappings Send a Chill through Sunny Trinidad *LINK*** cited on 25 June 2013 at: http://www.trinidadandtobagonews.com/forum/webbbs_config.pl/noframes/read/2734.

staff (15%). Among policy makers there were a fair number who were very worried about domestic violence (27%).

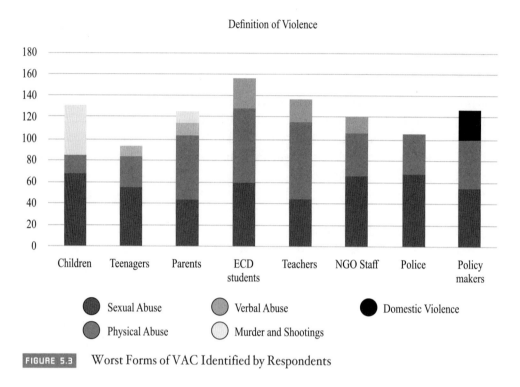

FIGURE 5.3 Worst Forms of VAC Identified by Respondents

5.1.4 The 'Causes' of Violence

The question 'What do you think are the causes of violence?' triggered a variety of responses which when taken together cover a wide range of so-called causal factors as well as show their inter-connectedness. The responses clustered around the following (sub-) themes, which, although listed separately, are indeed overlapping and interlinked:

Direct Violence
— Substance abuse (alcohol and drug abuse, smoking, disagreements and fights);
— Media violence (music, TV/movies, electronic games, print media);
— Domestic violence

Structural Violence
— Poverty[5] (unemployment, financial problems);
— Family structure (family breakdown — single parenting, broken unit, unplanned, unwanted pregnancies, poor parenting, poor upbringing — "no brought-upsy but dragged-up");
— Education (lack of education/knowledge, illiteracy);
— Power/control (abuse of power);
— Environment (bad examples/role models, rough/rundown neighbourhood, growing up on the streets, crime, gangs and gangsters, easy access to guns);
— Political system (lack of formal support systems, under-utilisation of services, no commitment by the government, lack of punishment of violent acts, no law enforcement, political tactics, governmental indifference, no communication with government).

Cultural Violence
— Insecurity/low self-esteem, feelings of hopelessness, depression/post-partum, poor anger management, inability to cope, lack of self-control/impulse control, revenge, jealousy, hatred, [sexual] frustration, need to control, need to feel superior, loss of power, sadism);
— Morals and values (lack of empathy/compassion, disrespect of others, lack of spiritual development, lack of love, care and attention, no proper supervision/guidance, "bad siblings");
— Social factors (poor communication skills, peer pressure, lifestyles, rivalry, arguments, desire and greed, poor social upbringing, the company one keeps);
— Culturally-sanctioned acts;
— Cyclical nature of violence[6] — "violence breeds violence" — (cycle of abuse, cycle of violence, cycle of poor education, cycle of bad childhood, cycle of bullying).

Monahan and Steadman (1994, 188) noted that

> "The complexity of violence — in a violent act — is a result of multiple causal and exacerbating factors, ameliorating or protective factors, individual differences, and the influences of other factors such as the environment and victim behaviour and characteristics".

The responses do not represent scientific causal factors of violence but rather reflect an overview of what people perceive to be plausible reasons why violence occurs. It is clear from the responses given that the 'causes' of violence are multiple. There is often an interplay and interconnectedness of the three dimensions of violence, with one feeding into and

---

5. Galtung's (1990) typology of violence renders poverty as satisfying both the structural and direct dimensions of violence. Hunger, illness, malnutrition are all direct manifestations of poverty. However, poverty as a state of being determined by inequity and injustice is structural in concept (Farmer 2007).
6. The perpetuation of a cycle of violence is as a result of an adherence to cultural norms and values and often of being in a structural and cultural gridlock.

causing the other to manifest itself more prominently. The respondents cited 'causes' of violence as having their roots in the structural and cultural elements of society, thus displaying recognition of structural and cultural violence. However, the *'disconnect'* lies in their failure to identify these two dimensions as playing a decisive role in shaping and defining the violence concept. As it is, they are viewed as 'causes' of violence and have not yet been translated in the mainstream mind-set that by their very existence they represent violence in a different form or manifestation. This shows where inroads have to be made re: sensitizing the populace.

Steinem (2013), one of the pioneers of the feminist movement, said that the "normalization of violence is one of the major causes of violence".[7] St. Bernard (2010) identifies four case studies to highlight critical *components of the culture of the society* that can serve as plausible *risk factors*; these include breakdown in family life, lack of parental supervision, teenage pregnancy, children living in children's institutions, single-mother-headed households, the stepfather syndrome, domestic violence, and use of drugs and alcohol. These factors also are proposed here by some respondents. In the Trinidad and Tobago *Draft National Progress Report 2006* on the follow-up to the United Nations Special Session on Children: *A World Fit for Children*, a host of constraints were identified in addressing the situation of abuse, neglect, exploitation and violence including: Delay in implementing the package of legislation enacted since 2000 to the absence of transitional homes for victims; Lack of skilled human resource; Absence of facilities; Inadequate programming; and *The negative impact of cultural beliefs and practices* (25). Cultural beliefs and practices can themselves easily become forms of cultural violence when they impact so negatively on children. These cultural beliefs, practices, and norms are also used to promote direct or structural violence and have the power to legitimize violence, to make it appear correct, appropriate, acceptable and therefore to be *tolerated*; much like Teeple (2004) who believes that it becomes an entity that perpetuates itself.

5.1.5 Sources of Information

People's understanding of violence against children and what causes it are naturally fed and shaped by diverse sources of information. When the eight groups of interviewees — were asked to respond to the question: 'What are your main sources of information?', They mentioned a range of resources. Television; Internet; Radio; Newspapers;
— Personal observations and experience (there is a blurry line between 'personal observations' and 'personal experience' as the observation of violence, even when not directed to the observer can have a harmful effect, especially on children);

---

7. As of 13 December, 2013; BBC News Interview *HardTalk*.

- On the job/in school (Information collected from directives, colleagues/ students);
- Education, training, research (information obtained via education, training, workshop and lectures);
- Ministries (information and messages and programmatic data issues by key department and governmental agencies, including the police);
- NGOs (information and messages sent out by non-governmental agencies);
- Library, books and pamphlets;
- Community (the information provided by community and spiritual leaders, friends, neighbours and also the grapevine);
- Common sense (the "knowledges" that comes with being part of society).

In the main, television and newspapers were the most common sources of information for most of the groups. Parents (69%), teenagers (64%) and children (87%) accessed their information most often from the television, while the NGOs (81%) and policy makers (77%) seemed to favour newspapers over television. The police and teachers were tied in both categories of television and newspapers (53% and 78% respectively). Radio also featured prominently in homes as a source of information (teachers, 60%; policy makers, 59%; NGOs, 54.5%). The main source of information for the ECD student teachers was the Internet. Television, newspapers and radio are the main providers of information; of the population of some 1.3 million in Trinidad, over 650,000 are users of the Internet,[8] thus it is not surprising that the Internet also forms a major source of information, albeit relatively low among police officers and NGO staff. Personal observations and experience, education and training, and the community at large also contribute to dispensing information and shaping an opinion on what violence against children entails.

5.1.6 Is There a Difference between Violence against Girls and Violence against Boys?

A significant cross-section of the population, with the possible exception of teenagers and children under 12 years of age, was of the opinion that there was no difference between the violence that boys and girls endure. Eighty-three percent (83%) policy makers, seventy-eight percent (78%) NGOs, seventy- four percent (74%) parents, seventy-one percent (71%) teachers, and sixty-six percent (66%) police all thought that there was no difference in violence against girls and violence against boys. Those who saw differences felt that girls are more prone to sexual abuse while boys are more open to physical abuse, like beatings. These groups were children under 12 (59%), teenagers (47%), and ECD teachers/students (36%). There was also a strong opinion that violence against girls was less acceptable than

---

8. As of 12 June, 2012; see: www.bbc.co.uk/news/world-latin-america-20073045, accessed 22 June, 2013.

violence against boys and that girls might appear more vulnerable, for example, to street robbery. For 2011, the police recorded 330 cases of sexual abuse; of these 315 involved girls.[9] Some people wondered whether instances of sexual abuse — especially rape of girls — which was seen as more common, were underreported.

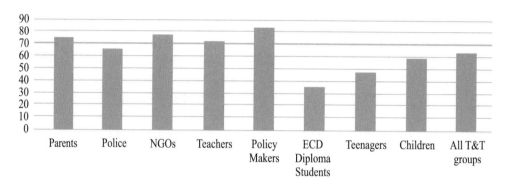

FIGURE 5.4   'No Difference' In Violence against Girls and Violence against Boys

The findings relating to whether there is a difference between violence against girls and violence against boys should be set off against the current growing debate on 'genderizing violence', which is often, but wrongly, interchanged with the notion of 'violence against girls and women'. The latter recognises that women and girls are more open to certain forms of abuse than men. The large number of 'no difference' replies by the interviewees was rather surprising as one would expect that men and boys and women and girls, although entitled to similar rights, given their differences in psychological and biological makeup, would have, for this reason alone, also different vulnerabilities and strengths. As such, males and females could be impacted and violated in different ways.

The responses did not consider rights violation. Interestingly, Criminal violence, of which gender violence is an important component, has been increasing in recent years and has taken its toll on the health system. Data on this however is not easily available but can be discerned by the increase in offences against the person brought to courts in Trinidad and Tobago (UNDP 1999). As Malala addressed the UN[10] and the world on empowering via education of girls, many Trinbagonian girls were unaware of how similar their lives were as that knowledge is shrouded in an illusory veil of tolerance. In 2013 in Trinidad there were still instances of arranged marriages in many Hindu families; female children are still denied

---

9. Children's Authority (2012).
10. 'Pakistani schoolgirl Malala Yousafzai addressed the United Nations as part of her campaign to ensure free compulsory education for every child'. www.bbc.co.uk/news/world-asia-23291897, accessed 13 July, 2013. Malala says, "Poverty, ignorance, injustice, racism, and the deprivation of basic human rights are the main problems faced by both men and women".

secondary school education in favour of the male child — being required to stay home to 'help out with the chores' for example — and incest is still practised and viewed as the right of the male head in some Tobago households.[11]

5.1.7 How Can We Protect Girls from Violence?

The replies though manifold could be meaningfully grouped into eight categories:
— Clubs/cadets/sports (all girls/boys sports clubs; scouts groups);
— Close supervision/monitoring/adult accompaniment;
— Role models;
— Self-defence/street wisdom;
— Educate on VAC;
— CRC/implementation of laws;
— Teach values/respect/open communication;
— Counselling/protection; role of state/social services.

5.1.8 How Can We Protect Boys from Violence?

As can be seen from the data, the majority of the respondents (teachers, 73%; policy makers, 63%; ECD students, 48%; NGO staff, 47%) saw "education on VAC" as the most important way of protecting boys from VAC. "Teaching values" (policy makers, 37%; parents and police, 33%; NGOs and teenagers, 26% and 25% respectively) and "close monitoring" (children under 12, 38%; parents, 33%) followed next as important means of protecting our children. Noteworthy is that children (35%), not completely like others, thought that involvement in clubs and similar organised activities was another way to safeguard them. The responses were similar for the question 'How can we protect girls from violence?'.

5.1.9 Do You Think Physical Punishment is Okay or Not Okay?

The numbers convincingly demonstrate that large segments of the population in T&T still see physical punishment as an appropriate form of discipline. Police, ECD teachers, and parents reported ninety-two (92%), eighty-six (86%) and sixty-eight (68%) percent

---

11. "The de-legitimization of many forms of accepted sexual violence has raised new questions about this practice. For example, meetings in Tobago brought to the fore the view that a high prevalence of incest exists in Tobago and it is also known that a high incidence also exists in certain parts of Trinidad. Yet, the crime statistics produced by the CSO, do not reflect this incidence. Incest involving minors, according to the introduction to the CSO Report on Crime Statistics, is considered to be a minor crime in that it attracts a penalty of under five years imprisonment" (UNDP 1999, 39).

respectively. Teachers, Policy makers, and Teenagers reported sixty-three (63%); fifty-three percent (53%); and fifty-eight (58%) percent in favour of corporal punishment. Only in two categories of respondents — NGOs (67%) and children (56%) — were the numbers above fifty percent against corporal punishment. Interviewees were inclined to physically punish children when they were "disrespectful", "when other measures failed", "to teach them a lesson", "when they committed major crimes", and "as a last resort". They were not in favour of inflicting severe bodily damage; it was frequently argued that, the punishment was "all right" if it was a "tap on the head", "a pinching of the arm", and "not so much as to leave marks on the skin".

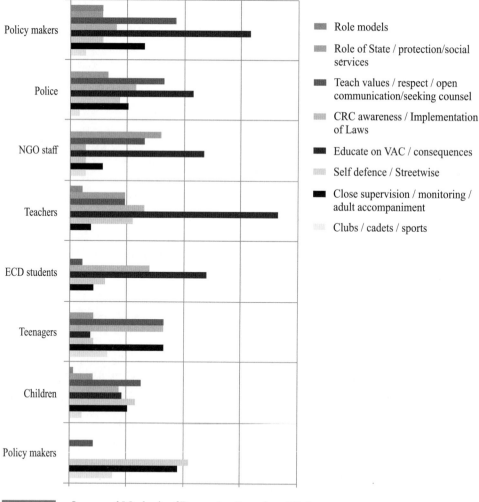

FIGURE 5.5 Suggested Methods of Protecting Boys from Violence

5.1.10 What Would You Do If You Suspected an Incidence of Abuse or Domestic Violence?

There were in many instances, multiple responses noted, for example, 'report to the police and inform the media'. The responses to this question could be grouped into three main categories: First, *'stay out of it'*, followed by *'notify the authorities'* (which included three groups: 'police', 'social services', and 'media', and thirdly *'intervene personally'*. In the category "stay out if it", the teachers reported (13%), followed by the policy makers (10%) and then the teachers (4%). The highest degree of intervention came from the teachers (54%), followed by the children (52%), and the police (42%). The children's high figure again points to their more developed sense of fair play, made mention of earlier. Children, in particular, are keen on seeking advice from their parents or adults they trust, while teachers look to their principals for advice. Importantly, children also see the media, particularly, the popular 'Crime Watch' TV programme, as potentially helpful and as a relevant authority to which to report crimes. The people who prefer 'to stay out of it', mainly do this out of a sense of impotence: "whatever we do, it won't do any good, so why bother?", or out of fear of repercussions. For as one parent said: "Nothing. I afraid of telling the police; I may get killed".

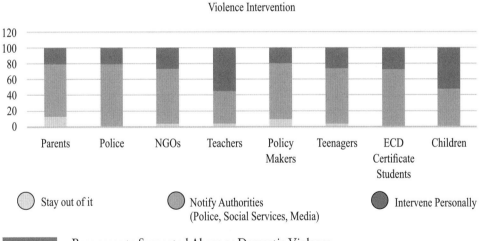

FIGURE 5.6 Responses to Suspected Abuse or Domestic Violence

Intervention in Incidences of Abuse or Domestic Violence

The responses emphatically reflected the fact that most people look heavily to the police as the body to call upon, also when domestic violence is suspected. This fact alone demonstrates a deep trust in the police force and places a deep responsibility on their shoulders, as domestic violence is a complicated and sensitive issue and effective approaches, let alone remedies, are not easily accessed. It is evident then, that specialised expertise is required. From their replies it is also clear that, in addition to following the legal route — filing a report and bringing the case to court — police officers seek to find solutions by reasoning with the people involved and by involving the social services. There are also those who, rather than going to the police or social services, try to intervene personally.

The role of the social services is mentioned, but dwarfs in comparison to that of the police force. Could it be, then, that domestic violence is mainly framed as a criminal act, rather than a social problem? If so, then, a form of punishment will be likely the chosen approach, rather than that of support, both preventative and curative, for the victims and perpetrators. This begs the question as to which strategy is more effective. It is suggested that this issue be discussed in the country's critical forums and that these debates be informed by experience gained, both inside and outside the country.[12] This on top of the need for a country-wide policy as to how witnesses of domestic violence could best be guided. The findings reveal that, as a society we have yet to reach the point where we are willing to intervene personally in the face of violence or take ownership of violence as every person's problem; not only that of the victim. The issue of violence — tolerance and the degree of societal intervention are dependent on these common perceptions, assumptions, beliefs and even knowledge, as they shape behaviour and action or in this instance, inaction.

5.1.11 What Kind of Violence Do You See Street Children Faced With in T&T?

Figure 5.7 presents the kinds of violence experienced most frequently-mentioned by each group. The majority of the respondents — an average of seventy-three percent (73%) — saw sexual abuse as a form of violence confronting street children. Every group recognised this danger. Physical harm (43%) followed as a second threat, then emotional/mental abuse (23%).

However, as can be seen, the variation, even within these three forms of violence was wide. This disparity grows with respect to the other frequently-mentioned forms of violence. The individual understandings of the respondents proved insightful and those responses not visually represented are mentioned here: these include starvation, intervention by the police — so called "haul outs", or "slap downs" — gang-related violence, poverty, sickness,

---

12. The literature on 'helping the perpetrator' is growing; for a brief introduction, see Meicchenbach (2006). Respectponeonline in the UK, offers anonymous and professional help to those concerned about violence and/or abuse towards a partner or ex-partner www.respectphoneline.org.uk. There are similar programmes in a number of other countries.

robbery, and bullying. Problems such as lack of respect and love, discrimination, humiliation, missing education, lack of basic needs and protection were cited.

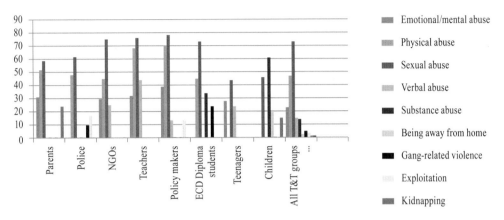

FIGURE 5.7 Kinds of Violence Most Frequently Encountered by Street Children

The following is a typical comment about Trinidad and Tobago's children that one can encounter in the international literature:

> "There is an increasing number of children living in the streets of Trinidad and Tobago. However, no correct figure can be given because of their mobility, in particular between Port of Spain and other cities. These children are often involved in illegal activities such as drug trafficking or prostitution. Qualified organizations have been able to determine that more and more children living in the street have been infected with AIDS."[13]

These findings illustrate that the lives of the nation's street children are for most people only partly accessible and that much more research is required to obtain a more comprehensive picture. George and Van Oudenhoven (2002), writing about foster care from an international perspective, note that in 'high machismo' countries, foster care is not a common course of action. Adoption at a young age and institutionalisation are the usual ways of taking care of children without families. Whatever approach is taken, they do recommend staying in touch with the biological family — if not the parents, then in any event, the other members of the child's family. Some respondents, among whom teenagers, mentioned foster care as a way out. It is something worth pursuing in Trinidad and Tobago. Suriname, for example, where foster care was an unknown phenomenon some 15 years ago, now has a blooming service. It prevents children from being institutionalised and often succeeds in reuniting them, or at least keeping them in touch, with their biological families.[14] In 2004, the Government

---

13. This text is taken from Humanium's website: www.humanium.org/en/trinidad-and-tobago, accessed 17 July, 2013.
14. See: www.pleeggezinnen.com, accessed 3 July, 2013.

initiated a pilot project on foster care that has been regularly renewed. As of 2012, there were 17 active providers and some 40 children in foster care (Children's Authority 2012).

It is also telling that respondents recognized the potential that community engagement had to offer; indeed a wide range of options are open. They were recognised by quite a few police officers, policy makers, teachers and parents as they listed such effective interventions as sport clubs, community groups, and collaboration with social workers, schools and police youth clubs. Apprenticeships with people known and trusted in the community were yet another option. Without a doubt, community organisation, responsibility and engagement seem the most rewarding path to follow. By entering the debate on street children, one encounters a strong sensation of *déjà vu*; the same stories, analyses, complaints and recommendations seem to have been repeated without being heeded by those on whose watch these children live. Some of them are much to the point and should be given the attention they deserve (see, for example, among others: Jones 2007; Julien 2008; Marshall 2003; Mills 2005; Swamber 2007). Any further comments will undoubtedly run the risk of being looked upon in this light and easily dismissed as the umpteenth but futile expression of indignation. Yet, there is no other option than to push and spread the central messages that emerged from these investigations and this paper: "listen carefully to the children, and treat them as experts of their own lives, their views matter", "follow a rights-based approach", "look at street children not as individual failures, but as a failure of the society as a whole" and, most importantly: "there is no reason for the existence of street children in Trinidad and Tobago". For most, whether they were children, teenagers, parents, teachers, NGO staff, police officers or policy makers, the preferred option was for street children to be placed in homes — orphanages, shelters, institutions and the like. Although well-intentioned, the feeling that they ought to disappear or just "get off the streets" resonated loudly on the paper.

With Julien (2008), a plea is made for more action research; this should not only collect data about their numbers, physical condition, nutrition, and grasp of literacy and numeracy, but also about their family background. Indeed, no street child should remain unknown to the caring institutions, particularly those staffed by social workers. From the interviews emerge an understandable demand for better legislation; rules and laws that actually prevent children running away from home and which protect them when out on the streets and guide them back to modes of well-being and an adequate future. Related to this is an equally justifiable wish for stronger and more consistent enforcement of this legislation. The risk here, though, is that this may deteriorate into punitive action, which may make street children only more invisible.

Some children noted that not 'having a home', the risk of being kidnapped, and domestic violence plagued street children, and that living on the streets had a detrimental effect on all domains of a child's life. Striking was the claim of unawareness of the presence of street children in Trinidad and Tobago by certain NGO and Ministry respondents. The role of the media, highlighted by the respondents, should also be given a higher profile, so as to help raise public awareness and indignation and backstop campaigns, and also to bolster and motivate people, foremost the street children themselves and especially report on successful approaches and effective community initiatives that draw on the children's strengths and local assets. Their collective opinion is a veritable source of pertinent intuitions and pointers for actions.

TABLE 5.4 Types of Violence Most Frequently Encountered by Street Children

Respondents (%)	Four Types of violence most frequently encountered by street children (top four cited by each respondent group)									
	Emotional/Mental abuse	Physical abuse	Sexual abuse	Verbal abuse	Substance abuse	Being away from home	Gang-related violence	Exploitation	Kidnapping	Murder
Parents	31	52	59							24
Police		48	62				10	17		
NGOs	30	45	75	25						
Teachers	32	68	76	44						
Policy Makers	39	70	78	13				13		
ECD Students		45	73		34		24			
Teenagers	28	0.5	44	24						
Children			46		61	19			15	
All T&T groups combined	23	47	73	15	14	3	5	4	2	3

5.12 Who are the Main Perpetrators of Violence against Street Children?

The writer is aware that much of the information given by the respondents was not based on research and was more a reflection of their perceptions based on observation and their experiences living in the country. However many of the groups that were included in this research often come into contact with street children and interact with them in their official capacity so the responses were not without merit. In the main, nine groups of perpetrators were identified by the respondents as being responsible for acts of violence against street children (figure 4.12 and table 4.12).

It is interesting that the parents (44%) and children (58%) cite the parents as being the perpetrators of violence against these children or, in their eyes, the ones most responsible for their situation of living out on the streets. The category that came in second for these two groupings was 'unknown adults' — parents (37%); children (27%). Thirdly, for the parents were other street people, while the children identified the drug dealers and addicts in our society. NGOs (38%) identified 'drug dealers and addicts' as being major players, saying that first and foremost it was the 'unknown adults' (52%). The respondents described 'the unknown adults' as being wealthy, old and young; some were businessmen, some were taxi drivers and were in search of pleasure or entertainment or sought to exploit street children for cheap labour.

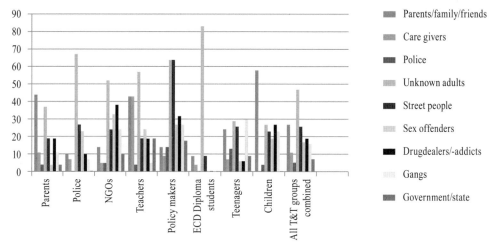

FIGURE 5.8 Main Perpetrators of Violence against Street Children

Child trafficking was also identified as a crime committed against these children by unknown adults. NGOs (10%), policy makers (18%) and teachers (19%) pointed to the state as being a perpetrator of violence against street children by its failure to intervene and get them off the streets, and by its complacency towards the situation. This is expected as these are the people who work at the state level and interact with both the state and street children. The ECD student teachers identified unknown adults as the main offenders (83%) and ignored completely the role of the state. This stands similarly with the police officers who claim unknown adults as sixty-seven percent (67%) and government/state, zero percent (0%). The teenagers were a curious group as they somehow always lent a new and insightful slant to the questions posed. Their responses covered the span of all nine categories with gangs

(30%) followed by unknown adults (29%) and street people (26%) being the main wrongdoers in their eyes. It is a pointed observation that teenagers (24%), like many of the other groups, identified parents as being responsible. Teenagers also saw the role of the state (9%).

5.1.13 What Can Be Done To Lower the Violence against Street Children?

The various replies by the total number of respondents could be readily grouped into seven main clusters:
— Family support: active intervention by governmental agencies, parenting programmes, availability of social workers, financing mentoring programmes (15%);
— Foster care: provision of longer-term care and protection by people other than the biological parents (2%);
— Homes: orphanages, shelters, institutions, safe houses. Places where children can sleep and have a meal and ideally, receive care and support (63.5%);
— Community engagement: walk-in centres, sports clubs, meetings and activity centres, youth clubs, parents' groups, interaction with local schools, police and social workers (9%);
— Education: special training programmes, back-to-school programmes, vocational training, raising awareness about their rights, counselling, and life skills (19%);
— Training of professionals: motivational, material, and technical support for those people who professionally are in touch with street children (5%);
— Legislative reform and law enforcement: policy patrolling, deterrence (36.5%).

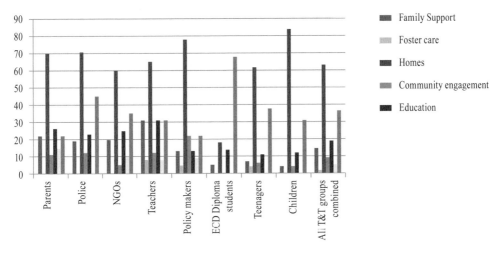

FIGURE 5.9 Ways of Reducing Violence against Street Children

TABLE 5.5 Ways of Reducing Violence against Street Children

Respondents (%)	Family Support	Foster care	Homes	Community engagement	Education	Training of professionals	Legislative reform/law enforcement
Parents	22	0	70	11	26	15	22
Police	19	0	71	12	23	0	45
NGOs	20	0	60	5	25	10	35
Teachers	31	8	65	12	31	8	31
Policy makers	13	4	78	22	13	9	22
ECD Diploma students	5	0	18	0	14	0	68
Teenagers	7	4	62	6	11	0	38
Children	4	0	84	4	12	0	31
All T&T groups combined	15	2	63.5	9	19	5	36.5

5.1.14 What Situations Do You Think Help Lessen Violence?

For practical reasons the response have been grouped into eight clusters:
— Family support: provide counselling and mediation to parents, encourage open communication among family members, show love and care towards each other, income support, employment (37%);
— Education: skills training, information on consequences of violence, anger and stress management, self-defence, information about substance abuse, public education (36%);
— Community-based activities: camps, sports and cultural activities, children's centres, collaboration between people and police, schools, social workers, health facilities, parks, collective responsibility (17%);
— Religious and spiritual strengths: participation in religious activities, faith-bound programmes (11%);
— Social support: access to social workers, social benefits (6%);
— Security: increased police surveillance and patrols, adult supervision in schools, cameras, reporting to police (26%);
— Punitive approaches: fines, jail, capital and corporal punishment (10%);
— Government intervention: law enforcement, more effective child protection laws, funding for community-based pro-child and -youth activities, pro-employment policies, promoting social equity, equality and fairness, political will, public awareness raising (5%).

The findings reflect the importance of consulting and involving *all* stakeholders in matters pertaining to the well-being of our children; *even the children*. Noteworthy is that children, not completely like others, were the only group who identified 'involvement in clubs and similar organised activities' as another way to safeguard them. This begs the question: to whom do we listen when we are formulating our policy decisions and who knows better than the actors in the particular situations (in this case the children) as to what is in their best interest? Much research points to the significance of structured activities and group involvement as deterrents to violence and here it is offered mainly and almost solely as an option by the children. This also goes against common notions that "children do not really know what is good for them and need strict guidance". The responses tell us that foremost, what is needed is for people to "stand up" and "speak out", especially those who are in leadership positions.

5.1.15 What Are Some Things That You Can Do As an Individual To Stop the Cycle of Violence against Children?

For this question, the emphasis was double: as individuals in their own right, but also in their capacity as child, teenager, parent, teacher, ECD certificate student, staff member of an NGO, police officer or policy maker. The following *'Suggestions'* were made:

Children (<12 years): Go to school, join policy youth clubs/other clubs, write letters to the minister, tell teacher and parents, ask parents to send them clothes, protest and speak out, help children in homes, send children to a home, 'take them into our house'.

Teenagers: Report crimes, stay in groups to be safe, write essays, protest, campaign for new legislation, join 'anti-violence gangs', encourage police patrols, talk to parents, influence others, teach younger children proper behaviour, participate actively in sports, look after younger children in school, be a role model, spread the word that violence is not a good thing, follow good education and get a job, write to members of parliament, intervene, ask for funding of community-based activities, talk with teachers, parents. But also, sadly: "*We cyah do nothing because we go get beat up*", "*Alone I cannot make a difference; together we can.*"

Parents: Form parents' groups, speak up and out, respect yourself and your children, intervene when violence is observed, seek education and information about violence, advocate children's rights, look out for and use 'best practices', participate in community-based organizations, report when violence is noticed, prevent discrimination, engage children in group activities, try to get parks, youth clubs, CBOs in the community, organise karate classes, talk to teachers.

ECD diploma students: Know where the children are, raise my children properly, organise family meetings, run radio programmes, get children to see good movies, report, see that they have good friends, set up training centres, introduce school guidance, teach children values, educate youth leaders, speak out, report, "hang them" (the criminals).

Teachers: Speak up and out, educate and inform students, report, teach about moral values, set a good example, become an advocate, report, tell children the 'don'ts and do's', form a committee, refer children to the relevant services, help abused children, talk to the parents.

NGO staff: Re-educate the public, educate parents and children to be less violent in speech and behaviour, promote and engage in groups that have effective programmes, report, offer counselling and rehabilitation, build up trust with children, promote parent outreach programmes, advocate children's rights, speak out on behalf of children, as they don't have power, be aware of the needs of young parents. But also: "*I only do something when somebody is hitting my child*".

Police: Speak out and report, promote sports, support parents, put criminals in jail, set a good example, promote family planning, talk to children in the community and in schools, support NGOs, improve the referral system, promote anger management, lobby with interest groups, promote community police, don't turn a blind eye, set up information centres.

Policy makers: Maintain moral code, set the example — also to other staff, report, speak up, take risks, seek support for affected children, promote different disciplinary methods instead of physical punishment, work with all relevant partners, conduct training exercises for child workers, talk to parents, promote the notion of dialogue between parents and children, introduce 'big brothers' and 'big sisters' and mentorship programmes, initiate awareness-raising/information campaigns.

5.1.16 What Could Be Done To Combat Violence?

The responses were grouped into categories but the division of the replies into these categories did not do justice to the collective wisdom and rich experience of the respondents. Almost without fail, their individual recommendations and suggestions made good sense. (See *Chapter 6*).

Combating Violence

When perusing the wealth of suggestions on how to combat violence, it becomes apparent that few respondents looked at the cultural and structural dimensions. Things such as safe playgrounds, municipally organised festivities, games, and sports, national awareness raising campaigns, and teacher- training were not really touched upon. It is also telling that the role of the media was under lit. Perhaps most importantly is the notion, as said above, that the safety and healthy development of *all* children is the responsibility of *all* Trinbagonians and therefore also of *all* segments of the society, without exception.

In the main, what shines through was the punitive nature of many of the suggestions. Many of the recommendations to arrest the situation nestled in dealing with the so-called bad elements that cause violence — mainly the perpetrators of direct violence — and though some suggestions were offered to address the structural and cultural violence, they did not seem to be sufficient. The most obvious conclusions that these findings permit is that there is wide support for strengthening families and education. This is encouraging, as these are 'instruments' that intuitively make sense and are also backed up by research. The wish for more security is also understandable and proves to be effective especially when police is employed in 'hot spots' (La Rose 2013). Similarly, the recommendation for community-based activities should be taken seriously as it is there where children and youth grow up and form their personalities and learn to relate to each other and the society at large.

What ought to be the role of the government in all of this violence discourse? This was mentioned, and deemed necessary by the respondents as they are in the best place to lead the way, display the right kind of attitude and emotions and to use its influence to get partners on board so as to effect change. It is worrisome that the children and teenagers did not even look at the government as a serious actor. A few responses across the various groups mentioned that the death of a loved one seemed to be the only effective recipe to move people away from violence, while others saw capital punishment as a panacea to rid the society from this bane. As can be seen, both approaches have so far not really delivered. More promising were the suggestions by a few others of showing a good example, and this dictates the availability of role models and of trusted adults. This, in itself, deserves a special investigation and canvassing of society's human resources.

Poverty, unemployment, and exposure to inequality[15] — especially between men and women — and unfairness were also seen to be at the root of violence. There were also voices that pleaded for the elimination of vile and violent language in the media. Above all, people were encouraged to "not turn a blind eye to violence against children".

---

15. It is now increasingly recognised that exposure to inequality and inequity has a adverse effect on all people in society, rich and poor, young and old, and both physically and psychologically. See for an extensive discussion on this topic: Gini Growing Inequality Impacts: www.gini-research.org, accessed 15 July, 2013.

5.1.17 How Do People in T&T Look at Violence from an Historical and International Perspective?

Three questions were put to the eight groups:

In comparison with the outside world would you say that in T&T we are?
(a) More violent   (b) Less violent   (c) Same as

Which do you do as a citizen of T&T?
(a) Tolerate violence   (b) Stand up against violence

Which do you think makes for a less violent T&T?
(a) T&T 20 years ago   (b) T&T now   (c) T&T 20 years from now

In comparison with the outside world would you say that in T&T we are more violent, less violent, or equally as violent?

In the main, the data supports the literature that exposure to situations of continuous violence alters one's perception of violence. Often people in violent situations become more tolerant and acceptant of the phenomena and are more likely to view the situation as 'normal', 'same as' or even 'less violent' than external situations. The opinions vary as to how Trinidad and Tobago compares with the international world.

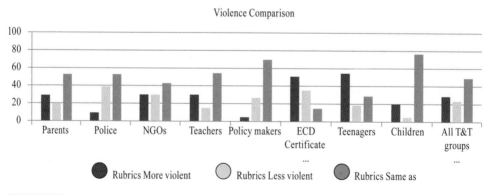

FIGURE 5.10 T&T's Violence Ranking Compared with the Rest of the World.

There is some consensus that we are thought of as being 'as violent' and 'less violent' rather than 'more violent'. This reinforces the disparity in the findings of the subscales of the Global Peace Indicator (GPI) for T&T between the levels of 'violent crime — 5' and 'perceived criminality — 3' (see table 2.4). In fact, Trinidad ranks higher in 'violent crime' than their Caribbean neighbours, Cuba, Grenada, Guyana, Haiti, Jamaica, and Venezuela, which is contrary to the perception, but supportive of the research on violence — tolerance and perception.

Two groups, the police (39% vs. 8%) and policy makers (26% vs. 4%) said that the nation is 'less violent' rather than 'more violent' when compared to the outside world. The majority of the respondents within all the groups, with the exception of the teenagers (28% and 18% vs 54%) and ECD student teachers (14% and 35% vs. 51%), felt that T&T is 'as violent as' and 'less violent' than the outside world as compared to 'more violent'.

TABLE 5.6 T&T's Violence Ranking Compared with the Rest of the World

Respondents (%)	More violent	Less violent	Same as
Parents	28	19	53
Police	8	39	53
NGOs	29	29	42
Teachers	30	15	55
Policy makers	4	26	70
ECD certificate students	51	35	14
Teenagers	54	18	28
Children	19	4	77
All T&T groups combined	28	23	49

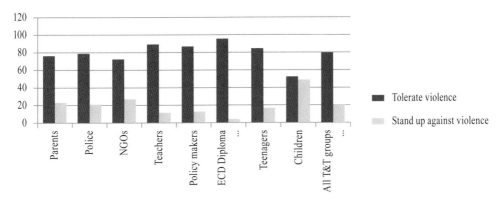

FIGURE 5.11 Respondents' Tolerance of Violence

Tolerate Violence or Stand up Against Violence

With respect to the country's tolerance of violence and whether we in T&T (a) Tolerate violence, or (b) Stand up against violence, the responses confirm one of the main underlying hypotheses of this paper, that there exists a 'culture of violence — tolerance' in Trinidad and Tobago and that people are aware of it. The responses point heavily to a people who are very much tolerant and acceptant of a situation of violence of which they are aware but somehow feel disinclined or powerless to change. Fairclough (2001, 2-3) suggests that "ideology is the prime means of manufacturing consent and the means by which 'social relations' and power differences are legitimized". Postcolonial theory then indeed offers, as Morgan and Youssef (2006, 7) claim, "lenses for understanding colonialism as a system based on terrorism and perpetuated by means of denigrating ideologies" and its concomitant epistemological and ontological violence. It is evident that a consideration of one sphere of violence — in this case the structural — leads inevitably and ultimately to an analysis of the others, as all three dimensions feed into each other. A glance at the statistics shows the high degree of tolerance vs. taking a stance against violence as testified to by all of the groups interviewed: ECD student teachers (96% vs. 4%); teachers (89% vs. 11%); policy makers (87% vs. 13%); teenagers (84% vs. 16%); police (79% vs. 21%); parents (77% vs. 23%); NGOs (73% vs. 27%); and children (52% vs. 48%).

TABLE 5.7 Respondents' Tolerance of Violence

Respondents (%)	Tolerate violence	Stand up against violence
Parents	77	23
Police	79	21
NGOs	73	27
Teachers	89	11
Policy makers	87	13
ECD certificate students	96	4
Teenagers	84	16
Children	52	48
All T&T groups combined	85	15

When one examines the violence and plundering of this region that occurred at the time, one can see that it is with good reason that the Caribbean psychiatrist Frederick Hickling contends that its peoples have been exposed to the centuries-long 'collective psychosis' of Europeans (Hickling and Sorel 2005). This is not to imply that Caribbean people are a violent people but rather that the contact with violence has been so much a part of their existence, as history shows, that society has developed in a way, an immunity to violence; a degree of tolerance that allows violence to perpetuate and exist and co-exist without causing much disturbance to the psyche and it is within this context that the *cultural dimension* of violence is being examined. In this light, one can comprehend the high tolerance towards violence against children in the form of abuse and neglect and further accept that the tolerance constitutes one major cause of its persistence, if not of its increase in intensity and spread. In some societies, many people, including parents and children, look at forms of violence as "normal", "part of growing up", "belonging to life". Thus, when queried, parents in Trinidad and Tobago argued that teachers were allowed to hit their children when they saw fit, otherwise they "would not learn"; even children, or at least some of them, agreed with their parents' view (Jualla-Ali 2003). Small wonder then, that the country features negatively on international crime rates.[16]

Which do you think makes for a less violent T&T: T&T 20 years ago, T&T now or T&T 20 years from now?

The replies to the third question indicate that most people (69%) were of the opinion that things were better in the past than now (9%) and only a few (21%) saw a brighter future ahead (the majority of them were teenagers and children). The most nostalgic of the groups were the ECD group of student teachers (96%), the NGOs (86%), and the policy makers (76%). Interestingly the parents were the most forward-looking (28% vs. 53%). The figures display a grim image of the present, with children advocating zero percent (0%), teenagers (4%), and NGOs (5%). The police also present a similar dismal view of the present (21%) and an even more hopeless take on the future of T&T (14%).

Violence Then, Now, and in the Future

The World Health Organisation, looking at the rampant violence in Africa during the late 1990s, notes that people learn 'to cope' rather than 'to manage', which is a healthier and more realistic way of addressing violence. Coping mechanisms are culturally defined and also depend on the individual situation of the person under stress, but a common feature is to deny the situation for what it is.[17] It is an intriguing hypothesis to explore given our colonial legacy: could it be that large sections of T&T society 'get used to' and 'just learn to cope' with violence, rather than know how to 'manage' it?

---

16. According to the website numbeo.com, Trinidad and Tobago ranks third on the world ranking list, right after Venezuela and Guatemala. www.numbeo.com/crime/rankings_by_country.jsp, accessed 25 February 2013.
17. See: WHO/EHA (1990). 'Emergency Health Training Programme for Africa,' www.who.int /disasters/ repo/5517.pdf., accessed 25 September, 2008.

Vertigans (2011) claims that colonialism continues to cast a shadow over contemporary "freed nations with experiences under British governance, in particular", that it informs present day perceptions is unsurprising. He notes that the past continues to live on, as:

> "There is a legacy of political violence that has been communicated and reinterpreted across generations and frequently through narrative, behaviour, memory agents, symbols and songs." (43)

In an attempt to understand which "residues of violence remain embedded within social and individual personality structures", we examine the concept of 'habitus'. Elias (1996):

> "Social memory is narrated by legitimised agents of memory and reflective, symbolic practices. Representations of the past are entwined within individual and social habitus and the fortunes of a nation over centuries become sedimented into the habitus of its individuals. As such historical narrative helps to shape contemporary meaning and behaviour." (Quoted in Vertigans 2011, 45)

TABLE 5.8 T&T 20 years ago, T&T now, T&T 20 years from now?

Respondents	T&T 20 years ago	T&T now	T&T 20 years from now
Parents	28	19	53
Police	66	21	14
NGOs	86	5	9
Teachers	73	15	12
Policy makers	76	10	14
ECD certificate students	96	4	0
Teenagers	76	4	20
Children	52	0	48
All T&T groups combined	69	9	21

Through the contributions of Bourdieu and Elias, 'habitus' has become an influential concept in understanding conformity, change, and tolerance. Bourdieu (1977, 189-90) considered habitus to be

> "... the product of the work of inculcation and appropriation necessary in order for these products of collective history (e.g. language, economy) to succeed in reproducing themselves more or less completely, in the form of durable dispositions". It is thus "both structured and structuring, product and producer of social worlds." (Quoted in Crossley 2003)

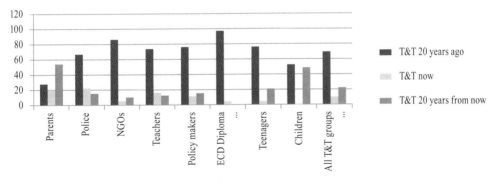

FIGURE 5.12 T&T 20 years ago, T&T now, T&T 20 years from now?

5.1.18 What Role Should the Government Play in Fighting VAC?

With the exception of the odd remark that the "government couldn't do anything", most respondents felt that the government could and should play a big, if not the biggest, role in the fight against violence against children. This segment also forms a sound body of recommendations (See *Chapter 6*).

5.2 Testing the Hypotheses

Research Statement 1: The most common dimension in the definition of violence is direct violence.

Definition 1 of Violence

		Frequency	Percent	Valid Percent	Cumulative Percent
Valid	Direct	228	85.4	87.0	87.0
	Structural	7	2.6	2.7	89.7
	Cultural	9	3.4	3.4	93.1
	Rights	18	6.7	6.9	100.0
	Total	262	98.1	100.0	
Missing	No Response	5	1.9		
Total		267	100.0		

Definition 2 of Violence

		Frequency	Percent	Valid Percent	Cumulative Percent
Valid	Direct	228	85.4	87.0	87.0
	Indirect	34	12.7	13.0	100.0
	Total	262	98.1	100.0	
Missing	No Response	5	1.9		
Total		267	100.0		

The results show that the most common definition of violence by the respondents was that of direct violence (85.4%), thus we can unequivocally accept that the most common definition of violence is 'direct' violence. The dimensions of violence were further categorised into 'direct' vs. 'indirect'.[18]

Research Statement II: In T&T we are acceptant of violence as a form of punishment.

Acceptance of Violence

		Frequency	Percent	Valid Percent	Cumulative Percent
Valid	Not Okay	97	36.3	37.6	37.6
	Okay	161	60.3	62.4	100.0
	Total	258	96.6	100.0	
Missing	No Response	9	3.4		
Total		267	100.0		

Research Statement III: In T&T we are tolerant of violence.

Violence-Tolerance

		Frequency	Percent	Valid Percent	Cumulative Percent
Valid	Tolerate violence	193	72.3	75.1	75.1
	Stand up against violence	64	24.0	24.9	100.0
	Total	257	96.3	100.0	
Missing	No Response	10	3.7		
Total		267	100.0		

---

18. This was due in large part to: (i) the relatively small cell sizes of the 'structural, 'cultural' and 'rights' domains; (ii) 'direct' vs. 'indirect' are clearly two distinct typologies identified by Galtung (1969) to allow for greater statistical accuracy.

We can unequivocally endorse the perception of violence — tolerance, which stands at: 'tolerate violence' vs 'stand up against' — 72.3% versus 24%.

Hypothesis I

Ho: There is no relationship between definition of violence and acceptance of violence.
HI: There is a strong positive relationship between definition of violence and acceptance of violence.

Definition of Violence * Acceptance of Violence Cross Tabulation

Count			Acceptance of Violence		
			Not Okay	Okay	Total
Definition of Violence	Direct		70	150	220
	Indirect		25	9	34
Total			95	159	254

		Acceptance of Violence	Definition of Violence
Acceptance of Violence	Pearson Correlation	1	.297**
	Sig. (2-tailed)		.000
	N	258	254
Definition of Violence	Pearson Correlation	.297**	1
	Sig. (2-tailed)	.000	
	N	254	262

**. Correlation is significant at the 0.01 level (2-tailed).

The results of the Kendall's tau b and the Spearman's rho were statistically significant at the 0.01 level of significance showing a fairly moderate correlation ($0.1 < |r| < 0.3$) between 'definition of violence' and 'violence acceptance'. We therefore, reject the null hypothesis and accept the alternative hypothesis. The Pearson's Chi-Square rendered a value of $x^2(1) = 21.884$, $p<0.001$, statistically significant at the 0.01 level of significance.

Nonparametric Correlations

Correlations

			Acceptance of Violence	Definition of Violence
Kendall's tau_b	Acceptance of Violence	Correlation Coefficient	1.000	.297**
		Sig. (2-tailed)	.	.000
		N	258	254
	Definition of Violence	Correlation Coefficient	.297**	1.000
		Sig. (2-tailed)	.000	.
		N	254	262
Spearman's rho	Acceptance of Violence	Correlation Coefficient	1.000	.297**
		Sig. (2-tailed)	.	.000
		N	258	254
	Definition of Violence	Correlation Coefficient	.297**	1.000
		Sig. (2-tailed)	.000	.
		N	254	262

**. Correlation is significant at the 0.01 level (2-tailed)

Chi-Square Tests

	Value	df	Asymp. Sig. (2-sided)	Exact Sig. (2-sided)	Exact Sig. (1-sided)
Pearson Chi-Square	21.884a	1	.000		
Continuity Correctionb	20.138	1	.000		
Likelihood Ratio	21.303	1	.000		
Fisher's Exact Test				.000	.000
Linear-by-Linear Association	21.798	1	.000		
N of Valid Cases	254				

a. 0 cells (.0%) have expected count less than 5. The minimum expected count is 12.72.
b. Computed only for a 2x2 table

The results are depicted graphically below, showing the tendency of the respondents who define violence along 'direct' lines being more apt to be in favour of physical punishment whereas, of those who defined violence as 'indirect', there was a higher percentage of respondents against physical punishment.

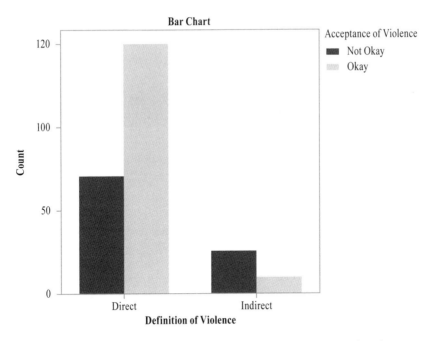

FIGURE 5.13 Relationship between Definition and Acceptance of Violence

Hypothesis II

Ho: There is no relationship between definition of violence and violence tolerance.
HI: There is a strong relationship between definition of violence and violence tolerance.

Case Processing Summary

	Cases					
	Valid		Missing		Total	
	N	Percent	N	Percent	N	Percent
Definition of Violence * Violence Tolerance	252	94.4%	15	5.6%	267	100.0%

Definition of Violence * Violence Tolerance Cross Tabulation

Count		Violence Tolerance		Total
		Tolerant of Violence	Stand Up Against Violence	
Definition of Violence	Direct	176	42	218
	Indirect	14	20	34
Total		190	62	252

Chi-Square Tests

	Value	df	Asymp. Sig. (2-sided)	Exact Sig. (2-sided)	Exact Sig. (1-sided)
Pearson Chi-Square	24.811[a]	1	.000		
Continuity Correction[b]	22.725	1	.000		
Likelihood Ratio	21.464	1	.000		
Fisher's Exact Test				.000	.000
Linear-by-Linear Association	24.713	1	.000		
N of Valid Cases	252				

a. 0 cells (.0%) have expected count less than 5. The minimum expected count is 8.37.
b. Computed only for a 2x2 table.

Symmetric Measures

		Value	Asymp. Std. Error[a]	Approx. T[b]	Approx. Sig.
Ordinal by Ordinal	Kendall's tau-b	.314	.072	3.829	.000
	Spearman Correlation	.314	.072	5.225	.000[c]
Interval by Interval	Pearson's R	.314	.072	5.225	.000[c]
N of Valid Cases		252			

a. Not assuming the null hypothesis.
b. Based on normal approximation
c. Using the asymptotic standard error assuming the null hypothesis.

A Kendall's correlation coefficient indicated a fairly moderate relationship. The result of the chi square is statistically significant at the 0.01 level of significance. We therefore reject the null hypothesis and accept the alternative. The results of cross tabulations show that there is a higher tendency for those who define violence with the 'indirect' component tend to be less tolerant of violence.

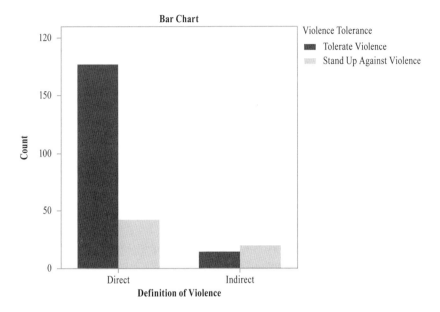

FIGURE 5.14   Relationship between Definition and Tolerance of Violence

Hypothesis III

Ho: Violence intervention is not affected by definition of violence.
HI: Violence intervention is affected by definition of violence.

Violence Intervention

	N	Mean	Std. Deviation	Std. Error	95% Confidence Interval for Mean		Min	Max
					Lower Bound	Upper Bound		
Direct	212	1.98	.291	.020	1.94	2.02	1	3
Structural	7	2.14	.378	.143	1.79	2.49	2	3
Cultural	27	2.33	.480	.092	2.14	2.52	2	3
Total	246	2.02	.337	.021	1.98	2.07	1	3

Violence intervention was scaled along three levels of intervention ranging from *least intervention* ("stay out of it") to *medium intervention* ("inform authorities") to *high intervention* ("intervene personally") representing the degree of tolerance to violence. The statistical analysis shows that the means are increasing based on the definition of violence. As the responses of the definition of violence tend towards a broader, more sophisticated definition of violence (one that includes the structural and cultural dimensions), the more likely people are to "intervene personally". For the most basic definition (direct) the mean is 1.98, meaning that people are more likely to "stay out of it", while for the broadest definition of violence the mean is 2.33, meaning that people are more likely to "intervene personally"

Test of Homogeneity of Variances

Violence Intervention 2			
Levene Statistic	df1	df2	Sig.
20.831	2	243	.000

The Levene statistic is significant at the 0.01 level meaning that we reject the hypothesis that the variances are equal. The assumption of equal variances is not satisfied allowing for the use of Welch and Forsythe.

ANOVA

Violence Intervention 2					
	Sum of Squares	df	Mean Square	F	Sig.
Between Groups	3.072	2	1.536	15.061	.000
Within Groups	24.782	243	.102		
Total	27.854	245			

Robust Tests of Equality of Means

Violence Intervention 2				
	Statistic[a]	df1	df2	Sig.
Welch	7.097	2	13.622	.008
Brown-Forsythe	8.630	2	26.211	.001

a. Asymptotically F distributed.

Welch and Brown-Forsythe tests that are robust to inequality of variances are both significant at 0.05 level indicating that there are differences in degree of intervention between the groups with direct, structural and cultural definitions of violence. Post-hoc analysis shows that although the nearby definitions of violence (i.e., direct/structural and structural/cultural) are not significantly different from each other, the more extreme definition difference (direct vs. cultural) is statistically significant at 0.05 level. Further analysis, which treats the violence definition data as two broader groups of direct vs. indirect violence, shows a significant difference between the groups.

Descriptives

Violence Intervention 2

	N	Mean	Std. Deviation	Std Error	95% Confidence Interval for Mean		Min.	Max.
					Lower Bound	Upper Bound		
Direct	212	1.98	.291	.020	1.94	2.02	1	3
Indirect	34	2.29	.462	.079	2.13	2.46	2	3
Total	246	2.02	.337	.021	1.98	2.07	1	3

Test of Homogeneity of Variances

Violence Intervention 2			
Levene Statistic	df1	df2	Sig.
41.495	1	244	.000

ANOVA

Violence Intervention 2					
	Sum of Squares	df	Mean Square	F	Sig.
Between Groups	2.870	1	2.870	28.033	.000
Within Groups	24.983	244	.102		
Total	27.854	245			

Robust Tests of Equality of Means

Violence Intervention 2				
	Statistic[a]	df1	df2	Sig.
Welch	14.638	1	37.314	.000
Brown-Forsythe	14.638	1	37.314	.000

a. Asymptotically F distributed.

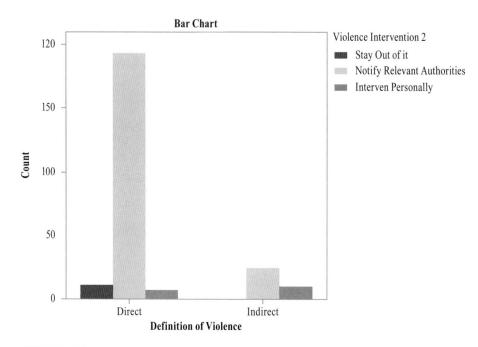

FIGURE 5.15 Relationship between Definition of Violence and Violence Intervention

We can see that the distinction between the two groups is statistically significant confirming our hypothesis. $F(1, 244) = 28.003$; $P<0.01$. We therefore reject the null hypothesis and accept that violence intervention is affected by violence definition.

5.3 Children Living in Institutions

The views of children living in institutions were solicited and several children's homes in T&T were accessed with the aim of acquiring some information from them. The charts depict the responses very aptly, making words almost redundant. It appears that when violence is justified, it is less likely to be perceived as violence; there exists a gender bias in children's perception of violence; and when violence is 'legitimised' as per marriage/relationship, there is less likelihood of violence being called violence. Of the 40 children, 75% thought that physical punishment was okay for children. The findings showed that the scope of children's conceptualisation of violence was direct (100%). However, when questioned about whether they thought that a child not being able to get help in the hospital was violence, 62.5% deemed it so, while 55% said that a child not being allowed to go to school was violence, showing that these dimensions, though not in the forefront of the definition of violence, can and do factor in when they are added to the discourse. The responses to the question "Which of the following do you think is an example of violence?" are indicated via tables and charts below.

TABLE 5.9   Example of Violence: A Parent Hitting a Child for No 'Good' Reason

	Frequency	Percent
No	3	7.5
Yes	37	92.5
Total	40	100.0

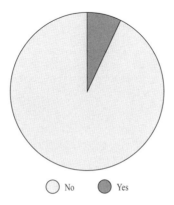

FIGURE 5.16   Example of Violence: A Parent Hitting a Child for No Good Reason

TABLE 5.10 Example of Violence: A Parent Hitting a Child for Misbehaving

	Frequency	Percent
No	30	75.0
Yes	10	25.0
Total	40	100.0

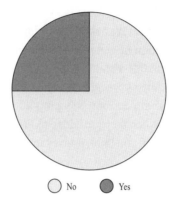

FIGURE 5.17 Example of Violence: A Parent Hitting a Child for Misbehaving

TABLE 5.11 Example of Violence: A Boy Hits a Girl

	Frequency	Percent
No	5	12.5
Yes	35	87.5
Total	40	100.0

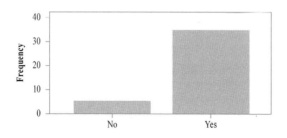

FIGURE 5.18 Example of Violence: A Boy Hits a Girl

| TABLE 5.12 | Example of Violence: A Girl Hits Boy |

	Frequency	Percent
No	16	40.0
Yes	24	60.0
Total	40	100.0

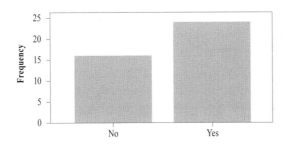

FIGURE 5.19 Example of Violence: A Girl Hits Boy

| TABLE 5.13 | Example of Violence: A Husband/Boyfriend Hitting His Wife/ Girlfriend |

	Frequency	Percent
No	3	7.5
Yes	37	92.5
Total	40	100.0

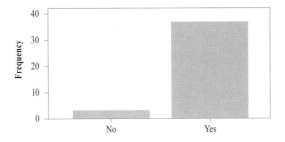

FIGURE 5.20 Example of Violence: A Husband/Boyfriend Hitting His Wife/ Girlfriend

TABLE 5.14 Example of Violence: A Wife/Girlfriend Hitting Her Husband or Boyfriend

	Frequency	Percent
No	13	32.5
Yes	27	67.5
Total	40	100.0

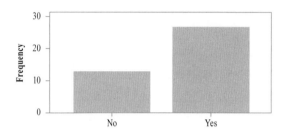

FIGURE 5.21 Example of Violence: A Wife/Girlfriend Hitting Her Husband or Boyfriend

TABLE 5.15 Example of Violence: A Child Not Being Allowed To Go to School and Have an Education

	Frequency	Percent
No	18	45.0
Yes	22	55.0
Total	40	100.0

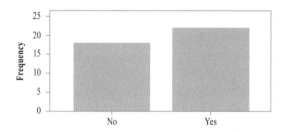

FIGURE 5.22 Example of Violence: A Child Not Being Allowed To Go to School and Have an Education

5.0 THE FINDINGS

TABLE 5.16 Example of Violence: A Child Not Getting Help in the Hospital

	Frequency	Percent
No	15	37.5
Yes	25	62.5
Total	40	100.0

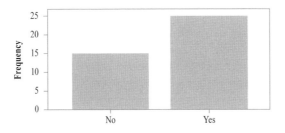

FIGURE 5.23 Example of Violence: A Child Not Getting Help in the Hospital

TABLE 5.17 Example of Violence: Someone Shouting Bad and Hurtful Words at another Person

	Frequency	Percent
No	7	17.5
Yes	33	82.5
Total	40	100.0

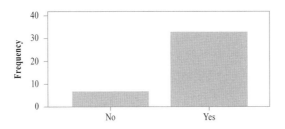

FIGURE 5.24 Example of Violence: Someone Shouting Bad and Hurtful Words at another Person

TABLE 5.18 Example of Violence: Do You Think Physical Punishment Is Okay When a Child Does Wrong?

	Frequency	Percent
No	10	25.0
Yes	30	75.0
Total	40	100.0

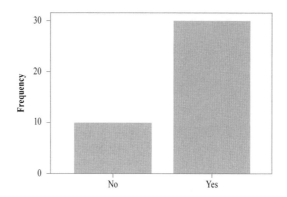

FIGURE 5.25 Example of Violence: Do You Think Physical Punishment Is Okay When a Child Does Wrong?

TABLE 5.19 Example of Violence: Do You Think Physical Punishment Is Okay When An Adult Does Wrong?

	Frequency	Percent
No	15	37.5
Yes	25	62.5
Total	40	100.0

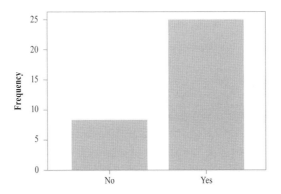

FIGURE 5.26 Example of Violence: Do You Think Physical Punishment Is Okay When An Adult Does Wrong?

Do you see any of the following as bad forms of punishment for children? Yes/No

TABLE 5.20 Bad Forms of Punishment: Hitting With the Hands

	Frequency	Percent
No	19	47.5
Yes	21	52.5
Total	40	100.0

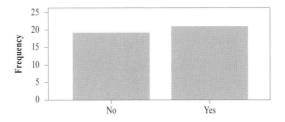

FIGURE 5.27 Bad Forms of Punishment: Hitting With the Hands

TABLE 5.21 Bad Forms of Punishment: Beating With a Stick or Strap

	Frequency	Percent
No	3	7.5
Yes	37	92.5
Total	40	100.0

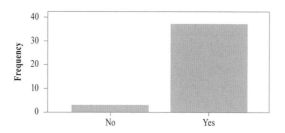

FIGURE 5.28 Bad Forms of Punishment: Beating With a Stick or Strap

TABLE 5.22 Bad Forms of Punishment: Locking Child in a Closet

	Frequency	Percent
No	5	12.5
Yes	35	87.5
Total	40	100.0

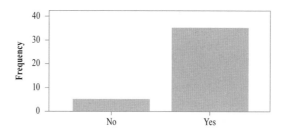

FIGURE 5.29 Bad Forms of Punishment: Locking Child in a Closet

5.0 THE FINDINGS

TABLE 5.23 Bad Forms of Punishment: Locking Child in a Room

	Frequency	Percent
No	10	25.0
Yes	30	75.0
Total	40	100.0

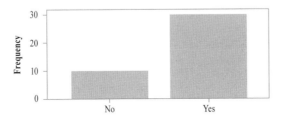

FIGURE 5.30 Bad Forms of Punishment: Locking Child in a Room

TABLE 5.24 Bad Forms of Punishment: Taking Away Food from the Child (No Lunch or Dinner)

	Frequency	Percent
No	3	7.5
Yes	37	92.5
Total	40	100.0

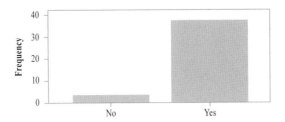

FIGURE 5.31 Bad Forms of Punishment: Taking Away Food from the Child (No Lunch or Dinner)

TABLE 5.25 Bad Forms of Punishment: Cursing the Child (Using Bad Words)

	Frequency	Percent
No	3	7.5
Yes	37	92.5
Total	40	100.0

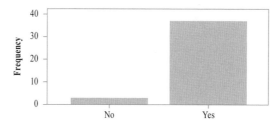

FIGURE 5.32 Bad Forms of Punishment: Cursing the Child (Using Bad Words)

TABLE 5.26 Bad Forms of Punishment: Tying Up the Child

	Frequency	Percent
No	2	5
Yes	38	95
Total	40	100.0

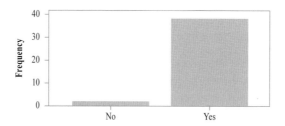

FIGURE 5.33 Bad Forms of Punishment: Tying Up the Child

With regard to what children consider to be 'bad' forms of punishment, there was almost a tie (47.5%: 52.5%) for no/yes response to 'hitting with the hands' as compared to the (7.5%: 92%) response for 'beating with a stick or strap'. There was less tolerance for being beaten with a stick or strap than with the hands. 'Locking away' the child, whether in a closet or room did not meet the approval of the children either: 87.5% and 75% respectively saw these acts as bad forms of punishment. 'Taking away food', 'tying up the child', and 'cursing the child', were also cited as bad forms of punishment (92.5%; 95%; 92.5%). It seems children just do not enjoy being punished.

TABLE 5.27 Have You Ever Heard About the Rights of the Child?

	Frequency	Percent
No	5	12.5
Yes	35	87.5
Total	40	100.0

TABLE 5.28 Do You Think That Children in T&T Have Rights?

	Frequency	Percent
No	7	17.5
Yes	33	82.5
Total	40	100.0

TABLE 5.29 Rights of the Child Identified by the Children

	Frequency	Percent
1	1	2.5
2	1	2.5
3	22	55.0
4	3	7.5
5	1	2.5
6	2	5.0
7	3	7.5
8	4	10.0
9	3	7.5
Total	40	100.0

When asked about the CRC, 87.5% of them had heard about the CRC and 82.5% thought that children in T&T have rights. It was painful, but not surprising, to hear that 82.5% of them had experienced violence in their short lifetimes and "no" they did not think it was 'normal' (92.5%), as they were quite aware that some children do not experience violence in their life (72.5%). When asked to name one (1) right of the child, the responses given were as follows:[19] 1- right to protection and not be hurt (7.5%); 2-right to play (10%); 3- right to education (55%); 4-right to a name (7.5%); 5-right to parents (7.5%); 6-right to be able to read (5%); 7-right to be unable (2.5%); 8-right to be heard (2.5%); 9-right to speech (2.5%). Interestingly the two main answers given by the children, the 'right to education' and the 'right to play' are two of the most significant and critical components of the CRC and two essential ingredients for development.

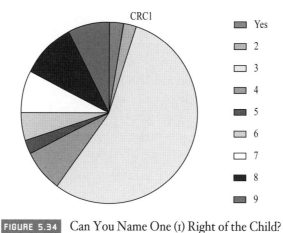

FIGURE 5.34   Can You Name One (1) Right of the Child?

TABLE 5.30   Have You Ever Experienced Any Violence in Your Life?

		Frequency
Valid	No	7
	Yes	33
	Total	40

---

19. Categories 1-9 are in keeping with the legend of the pie-chart showing the identification of one 'right'.

TABLE 5.31 Do You Think It Is Normal?

	Frequency	Percent
No	37	92.5
Yes	3	7.5
Total	40	100.0

TABLE 5.32 Do You Think Some Children Never Experience Violence in Their Life?

	Frequency	Percent
No	11	27.5
Yes	29	72.5
Total	40	100.0

12. How Do You Feel About Violence?

TABLE 5.33 How Do You Feel About Violence?

Categories of feelings and the scores per category					
Badly	Sadly	Angrily	Helpless	Normal	Wrong
38	39	34	30	9	28
95%	97.5%	87.5%	75%	22.5%	70%

The researcher wanted to capture a response as to whether children perceived violence as 'normal' or 'part of life,' in addition to their emotions and feelings about this phenomenon that engulfs them. The majority of the children living in institutions had been exposed to some form of violence or another (82.5%). In the main, almost all of the respondents (97.5%) felt sadly, badly (95%), and helpless (75%) about the violence in their lives. There was a high expression of anger (87.5%) and many thought that it was wrong (70%) and not normal (22.5%).

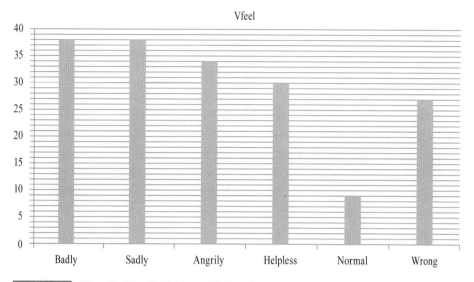

FIGURE 5.35 How Do You Feel About Violence?

Children's Feelings about Violence

The indicator of 'normalcy' was important for the researcher as prolonged exposure to violence often renders the perception of the phenomenon as 'normal'. The reliability measure was corroborated with (Q10) rendering a response of 92.5% against violence normalcy. These children have been taken out of their violent situations and as such are in a position to differentiate between life situations; this provides pointers for comparative research. The article 'Child Abuse/Children Exposed to Family Violence' noted that children understand:

> "Abuse is not normal. At some point, the children are exposed to a healthy environment and healthy relationships between people. They realize that not everybody lives the way they do. They become aware that what is happening in their home is violent. They learn that violence and abuse are not normal or acceptable, and that it does not have to be that way."[20]

13. 'Who do you think can help stop violence?'

Most children were not fazed by the questions 'who do you think can help stop violence?' and 'any ideas how?' Nonetheless, these are difficult questions, Their replies, *taken together*, show that children, even of this age, have sensible opinions about these issues, but, above

---

20. http://www.child.alberta.ca/home/documents/familyviolence/doc_opfvb_booklet_child_abuse _colour.pdf, accessed January 12, 2010.

all, that they trust the people around them: their parents, adults, teachers, the police, social services, the government, and, almost by extension, Jesus. In expressing these views they are also right: it is indeed the unity of these groups 'enveloped' in a meaningful 'belief system' that is the prerequisite for harmony and mutual tolerance, if not acceptance.

TABLE 5.34 Answers by Children <12 to the Question: 'Who Can Help Stop Violence?

Rubrics	Frequency	Percentage
Government	3	7.5
Police	15	37.5
Social services	11	27.5
Trusted adults	5	12.5
Awareness campaign	2	5
Teacher	2	5
Parents	4	10
Everybody	2	5
Children themselves	2	5
Jesus	3	7.5
No reply	5	12.5

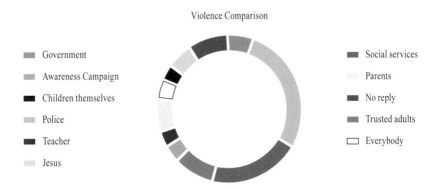

FIGURE 5.36 Who Can Help Stop Violence?

TABLE 5.35 Answers by Children <12: 'Any Idea On How To Stop Violence Against Children?

Rubrics	Frequency	Percentage
Teacher	2	5
Laws protecting children	5	12.5
Education (workshops in school)	2	5
Talking about it	3	7.5
Ask adults for help	6	15
Inform community on CRC	2	5
Arrest/discipline perpetrators	4	10
Strengthen police	1	2.5
Strengthen social services	2	5
Promote collaboration among services	2	5
Awareness raising	2	5
Stop bullying	2	5
Improve social values	2	5
Pray	1	2.5

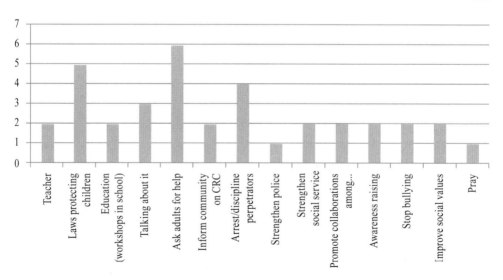

FIGURE 5.37 Answers by Children <12 to the Question: 'Any Idea On How To Stop Violence Against Children?'

Children's Demographics

TABLE 5.36 Religion of Children

		Frequency	Percent	Valid Percent	Cumulative Percent
Valid	Hindu	16	40.0	40.0	40.0
	Muslim	5	12.5	12.5	52.5
	Christian	19	47.5	47.5	100.0
	Total	40	100.0	100.0	

TABLE 5.37 Ages of Children

	Frequency	Percent	Valid Percent	Cumulative Percent
5.00	1	2.5	2.5	2.5
7.00	2	5.0	5.0	7.5
8.00	2	5.0	5.0	12.5
9.00	4	10.0	10.0	22.5
10.00	4	10.0	10.0	32.5
11.00	6	15.0	15.0	47.5
12.00	6	15.0	15.0	62.5
13.00	4	10.0	10.0	72.5
14.00	4	10.0	10.0	82.5
15.00	2	5.0	5.0	87.5
16.00	2	5.0	5.0	92.5
17.00	3	7.5	7.5	100.0
Total	40	100.0	100.0	

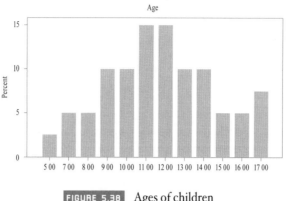

FIGURE 5.38 Ages of children

TABLE 5.38 Sex of Children

		Frequency	Percent	Valid Percent	Cumulative Percent
Valid	Male	17	42.5	42.5	42.5
	Female	23	57.5	57.5	100.0
	Total	40	100.0	100.0	

5.4 Children: Violence, Fears and Happiness

The views of teenagers and boys and girls in the 9 to 12 age bracket contributed to a substantial degree to the present discourse; an effort was also made to hear the views of younger children. Because of a number of constraints it was decided to limit this approach to asking two groups of children totalling 34 children, all second grade and standard 1 pupils, to make a drawing on two subjects: 'what scares you' and 'what makes you happy'.[21] Asking to draw images of 'violence against children' was considered, again given various constraints, not feasible and a bit invasive.

Looking at their 'scary' drawings there are familiar pictures such as snakes, monsters, creepy animals, getting drowned in the sea, bulldogs, but also those of knives, killings and, ominously of 'Uncle Dillon'. The happy scenes talk about such things as playing on the beach,

---

21. There is sufficient evidence that children's drawings can be used for getting an impression of how they think and feel about certain things; see, for example, Malchiodi (1998).

swimming and boating, reading at twilight, working, computer games, seeing 'friendly' animals, flowers, butterflies, dollars (!) and, foremost play. And not to forget: 'Mummy'.

They give massive support to the notion of 'antidotes to violence' that will be discussed later in this text. Indeed, by making children happy in the manner they see fit — and most of it does not require a great deal of exertion — the incidence of violence can possibly be stemmed.

FIGURE 5.39 Child's Depiction of Happiness

FIGURE 5.40 Drawing by a Child Showing Happy Feeling

FIGURE 5.41 Child's Concept of Violence

FIGURE 5.42 Drawing Done by a Child to Show Violence

FIGURE 5.43 Violence Depicted On a Wall Painting[22]

---

22. Photo taken by researcher during a field visit in Shu'fat camp in East Jerusalem, November 2014.

6.0 Recommendations

The recommendations that emerged from the research are as follows:
  i. Examine the multidimensionality of violence through a multi-angular lens;
  ii. Adopt a rights-based approach to dealing with the situation of VAC;
  iii. Include all stakeholders in the violence discourse;
  iv. Engage antidotes to violence;
  v. Explore positive deviance and its relevance for combating VAC;
  vi. Create a VAC epistemic community;
  vii. Conduct research on violence; and
  viii. Be visionary in approach.

In summary, it is recommended that the UN Convention on the Rights of the Child be implemented fully and generously. Unlike the reports by the Committee on the Rights of the Child and the Human Rights Committee, with their recommendations taken together, these eight recommendations seem rather modest. This seeming diffidence is rooted in two arguments, the first being that this document is already littered throughout its pages with sound recommendations from the responses gleaned in the field and the extensive literature review. At best this chapter will attempt to capture in broad spectrums the majority of these recommendations. The other, more tactical argument is that too many recommendations are futile as the persons or agencies for which they are intended[23] may easily feel overwhelmed and paralysed.

---

23. In this case, for a broad audience that recognises policy makers, practitioners — teachers and parents included — researchers, students and, actually, all people who feel they have a stake in the well-being and healthy development of the nation's children and young people.

6.1 Multi-angular Lens

On a global level, any dialogue on violence inevitably lends the discourse to the inherent implications for conflict analysis and resolution and ultimately the fostering of a peace culture and a culture of tolerance. Much of Galtung's work focuses on peace discourse in a global perspective. Youssef (2010a, 2-3) argued:

> "Our focus on a 'culture of violence' needs to be distinguished from the use of the same term by the United Nations ... aiming not just to build peace after conflict had occurred but to promote a culture of peace which would actively prevent violent conflict from arising. Its ongoing programmes to promote a Culture of Peace are wide-ranging and include the eradication of poverty; the preservation of the environment; the empowerment of all oppressed groups including, especially, women; the equipping of peoples with dialogue and mediation skills; information-sharing and transparency among governments. It must be clear then that its agenda is somewhat different from our own more contained approach."

She goes on to propose that the situation in Trinidad and Tobago,

> "... is not a world agenda but a local one, and it focuses not on nations and national wars, global environmental and socio-economic issues, important as these unquestionably are. It is concerned with the comprehension and eradication of a societal malaise, which, like a cancer, eats away at the mind and body of a people, until it consumes them. It looks deep within the society, puts the society under a microscope if you will, in order to determine the cause of the disease, the environment which enables it to flourish, and to find means, include by a collaboration of minds, to suppress the virus which is feeding and undermining the body politic." (p. 2-3)

The text and sentiments espoused in Youssef's writings[24] echoed much of what is said here on violence in the Caribbean and it forms a sustainable mould for continued work; hence the lengthy quotations. However, it is at this juncture that we differ slightly in our focus, for although this research examines the phenomenon of violence in the Trinidad and Tobago context, it does so on a broader plateau and in conjunction with a very regional and global perspective. It is all embracing in its philosophy, in its analytical approach and in its discourse. It is global, universal and yet contextually specific. It examines the local psyche while at the same time looking at gender inequity and poverty as all reflections of violence. The researcher acknowledges that it is only by looking from all angles can solutions be found to target the phenomenon in its entirety. Recommendations will therefore penetrate

---

24. See also Youssef (2010b).

every level of society from all angles. They may be direct or indirect; they may target systemic and structural change and they will certainly involve cultural reformation.

Solutions must be embraced against the backdrop of basic democratic ideals and human rights. This calls for, first and foremost, a local and global 'ownership of the problem'. Quainton (1983) proposes "intentional opposition" which demands development of a

> "... comprehensive strategy that looks on the issue of violence as a long-term fundamental challenge to democratic values ... that can be grappled with comprehensively and concretely using moral suasion, humane and effective law enforcement, and media restraint." (p. 58)

As Ahmad (1993) reasons, humanity's survival depends on the adoption of nonviolent methods to solving its problems, whether these pertain to individuals, communities or nations.

The Cultural Domain

Pinheiro's (2006) recommendation of promoting non-violent values and awareness-raising addresses ways of stemming the culture of violence and can be taken as critical but, if not allowed to filter and soak into the very cracks of society, becomes a lost voice in the wind. In the Trinidadian and Tobagonian context it is evident that one cannot simply plant the seeds of non-violent values without first clearing the land of the weeds of violence doctrine that continue to prevail. When the land is stripped bare and the preparatory work is done, only then will one see results. This requires adjusting skewed perceptions to be able to call a phenomenon by its real name; to see an action for what it is: to call violence, violence. No more ought corporal punishment be a euphemism for harsh discipline; it is an act of violence against a minor and a cruel and humiliating form of punishment and it is not discipline. Incest ought no longer to be viewed as a slightly embarrassing family matter that is quickly and quietly chucked under the mattress but should be acknowledged as an act of violence against a child by someone whom he or she trusts. Gang rape of a teenage girl by her male peers should not be allowed to be dismissed as a flippant and slightly frowned upon "rite of passage". AIDS discrimination has to be seen as an infringement on the rights of the infected child and as an act of VAC. Child pornography and child trafficking are acts of VAC.[25]

---

25. This paragraph draws on the researcher's initial research proposal, *A Culture of Violence: A Rights-Based Analysis of Child Abuse in Trinidad and Tobago*. Rona Jualla-Ali, 2007. Institute of Social Studies, The Hague, Netherlands. Acknowledgement is made to Rekha Wazir for her guidance in this effort at the time.

When violence is strongly deep-rooted in the cultural sphere, then cultural perceptions and sanctions are less easily done away with. For example, genital mutilation, though seen by many as a violation of the girl-child, is still considered an accepted ritual, as are child marriages in many cultures, which are less physical in their dimension but which in many instances go against the will and wishes of the child and often involves depriving the child of an education; so too is the contentious issue of child labour. Is it okay to deprive a family of an income that may mean the difference between survival and collapse, if a child is underage and employed? What if depriving that child from working part-time, for example, translates into the family not being able to afford sending that child to school? The situations can be complex indeed, which is why adopting a straight and strict definition along the clear line of rights issue — in this instance, children's rights — goes a long way in making the path ahead more visible. The role of the state is critical at this point in promoting and protecting the rights of children, allowing for a decent family life and access to education instead of being sent off to work in the coffee fields of Sierra Leone, for example, at the age of eight, regardless of how much society sanctions it.

The Structural Domain

Addressing structural violence requires approaches of a different nature and, as Farmer (2006) notes,

> "Structural violence is the result of policy and social structures, and change can only be a product of altering the processes that encourage structural violence in the first place ... 'Structural interventions' are one possible solution. Countries such as Haiti and Rwanda have implemented these interventions with positive outcomes. Examples include prohibiting the commodification of the citizen's needs, such as health care, ensuring equitable access to effective therapies, and the development of social safety nets. These examples increase citizen's social and economic rights, thus decreasing structural violence."[26]

Farmer (2006) acknowledges that, although some of the structural interventions can make a situation better, such as by decreasing premature morbidity and mortality, the social and historical determinants of the structural violence cannot be omitted, for more interventions are needed for improvement. This is usually the case; change has to be consistent and it has to be promoted at the local and regional level in a manner that is sustainable in conjunction with a global perspective. Guaranteeing the rights of children and adolescents does not only imply a legal and moral responsibility, it also has implications for the economic and social policies adopted by the government and, consequently, for the allocation of a country's financial resources (UNICEF 2005). Unless the measures for implementation of the rights

---

26. Farmer (2006) quoted at http://en.wikipedia.org/wiki/ Structural violence, accessed 2 September, 2013.

in the Convention are put in place, child rights advocacy will continue to be mere dialogue without action.

Recommendation I

It is, therefore, recommended that the problematic of violence against children, particularly as it relates to children's rights and tolerance of violence, be approached from the widest possible range of perspectives ('applying a multi-angular lens'), recognising its multi-dimensionality.

6.2 Adopt a Rights-Based Approach to dealing with the situation of VAC

The 'Pinheiro Report' builds on and incorporates numerous in-depth country studies from all over the globe, including the Caribbean region with data on Trinidad and Tobago (UNICEF 2005), and is the foundation *par excellence* for any serious attempt to contribute to the debate on policy, training, intervention, advocacy, and research.

The Pinheiro report lists a dozen overarching recommendations:
— Strengthen national commitment and action;
— Prohibit all violence against children;
— Prioritize prevention;
— Promote non-violent values and awareness raising;
— Enhance the capacity of all who work with children;
— Provide recovery and social reintegration services;
— Ensure participation of children;
— Create accessible and child-friendly reporting systems and services;
— Ensure accountability and impunity;
— Address the gender dimension;
— Develop and implement systematic data collection and research;
— Strengthen international commitment.

These recommendations form a thematic guide to the UN study and provides a useful tool for non-governmental organisations reporting on violence against children to the UN Committee on the Rights of the Child (NGO Group for the Convention on the Rights of the Child 2008). A set of concrete and measurable indicators developed by UNICEF (2007) and partners should facilitate the implementation of these recommendations as they offer guidelines on how to monitor progress, raise awareness, play an advocacy role and enable local and international comparisons. These indicators are, briefly:

Violation Indicators

— Self-reported violence against children;
— Child homicide rate;
— Hospital discharge rate due to assaults in children;
— Children who skipped school due to violence.

Protective Environment Indicators

— Children's life skills;
— Adults' attitudes towards violence against children;
— Official reports of violence against children;
— Substantiated cases of violence against children;
— Child victims referred to services;
— School violence policy.

It should be appreciated that the existence of these widely-endorsed recommendations and accompanying indicators do not necessarily result in immediate action or in rapid reductions of violence against children. They are only one set of tools in a human development process that has many other instruments, dynamics, components and actors which are governed by a diversity of courses of action and it would be delusionary to assume that major changes would occur overnight. And yet, in contradicting this last statement, transformations are occurring: interviews with educators in Nicaragua in 2008, for example, showed that they were much more aware of their rights compared to those of less than a generation before. It was striking to hear that they felt that media had played an important role in turning around this consciousness. "They raised awareness about children's rights, both in the teachers, as in the children themselves."[27]

This is a hopeful given as it demonstrates that such processes as awareness raising, motivational and attitudinal change, education, training and capacity building can result in far-reaching impacts, even in situations where financial means are in short supply. In Trinidad and Tobago, it was demonstrated that child-focused teacher training courses led teachers

---

27. School teachers in Matagalpa, in discussion with the author, Spring 2008.

to hit their children less or not at all (Jualla 2007), while in Nicaragua, the *Policía Nacional*, changed its policies from a reactive to a preventive approach to VAC, also with notable beneficial effects (Cordero Ardila, Gurdián Alfaro, and López Hurtado 2006).

In considering the use of the objectives and indicators, it should be appreciated that they were written for a universal audience and therefore have to be contextualized for each country or region to become truly relevant and functional. At best they form a conceptual and programmatic framework. The underlying causes of violence are, of course, multiple, wholly complex and interlinked; many of them are engendered or related to poverty such as unemployment, poor living conditions, alcohol and drug abuse, child trafficking, lack of (access to) basic services such as education, judicial support and health, ill-functioning public administrations, to mention a few. These causal factors were endorsed by the findings of this research. That social factors, relatively unrelated to poverty issues, play a major role in the fight against VAC is also borne out by worldwide human development data. Rosling (2006) notes that many countries, including a number of Latin American and Caribbean countries, are attaining comparatively far better socially beneficial results, such as child survival, longevity and literacy, with far less economic resources — this compared with the United States — and are moving ahead at a faster pace.

Recommendation II

It is, therefore, recommended that the views presented in the United Nations World Report on Violence against Children become mandatory reading for all formal child rights duty bearers with the additional assignment that the Report's recommendations be implemented. It is further recommended that the Report be promoted as recommended reading for individuals professionally involved in children's and youth's issues and that policies, projects and programmes adopt a rights-based approach.

6.3 Including All Stakeholders in the Violence Discourse

The question '*What could be done to combat violence against children?*' was posed to all the respondents in the survey so as to formulate a list of coherent recommendations for change that came from the ground:

— Prepare laws that are more focused on the protection of children and give due credit to the UN Convention on the Rights of the Child;
— Revise outdated laws;
— Close loopholes in the law;
— Pass a VAC law;
— Enforce the existing laws "without exception";
— Employ 'specialised' police officers;
— Strengthen community policing;
— Train teachers, community leaders, and police officers in conflict resolution;
— Introduce better monitoring and reporting practices;
— Collect and document statistics on VAC;
— Put more severe penalties and punishments in place; even "hang a few paedophiles to set an example";
— Offer parenting courses at community level;
— Teach parents anger management;
— Teach teachers/parents alternative forms of discipline;
— Teach educators/parents/public at large to recognise symptoms of VAC;
— Engage media in informing public on VAC;
— Create more jobs for parents;
— Stop using violent and abusive language;
— Allow parents to spend more time with their children by limiting their working hours;
— Offer financial planning to parents;
— Improve family planning services;
— Strengthen value education in schools;
— Make secondary schools compulsory;
— Offer counselling/therapy to victims;
— Offer counselling/therapy to perpetrators;
— Offer special programmes to abused children;
— Communicate with children on a daily basis;
— Encourage children to watch less violent movies, play less violent games;
— Engage boys and girls in creative activities, sports, drama;
— Celebrate annual 'Combating VAC' days;
— Organise youth clubs;
— Keep children off the streets;
— Teach and help children to speak up;
— Teach and help abused children on what to do;
— Teach children self-defence;
— Teach boys and girls life skills;
— Teach children anger management;
— Teach children about their rights;

6.0 Recommendations

— Teach boys and girls about their bodies;
— Create a help/hotline for children;
— Stop bullying in school and in the community;
— Teach children to respect each other;
— Remove children from violent situations;
— Organise public awareness campaigns;
— Develop a range of abuse prevention programmes;
— Try to intervene at an early age/early stage;
— Set up special communities, at national, regional and community levels;
— Create better and more safe-houses, shelters, half-way homes;
— Provide more health centres;
— Introduce neighbourhood watches;
— Encourage community-based collaboration among police, teachers, religious and other community leaders;
— Create safe environments for children;
— Create caring communities;
— Make NGOs more proactive;
— Establish specialised NGOs;
— Establish a body of volunteers;
— Strengthen social work departments;
— Deploy more and better trained social workers, both in schools and the community;
— Introduce community counsellors;
— Talk to the abusers;
— Prevent teenage pregnancy;
— Employ more police in 'troublesome' areas;
— Make visible the consequences of violence;
— Gather more information on VAC; conduct research;
— Study the environment of the child;
— Collect data on perpetrators;
— Introduce visible solutions; and finally
— Create stronger political will; and
— Protest! Break the silence!

The list is long but not too long and, upon reflection, most of their suggestions, barring only a few, seem doable and within the reach of the political, social and economic resources of the country. Each of them deserves further discussion and scrutiny as they all hold potential for the good of the nation's girls and boys. It is also evident, as one respondent made clear, that VAC is not a task for one person or department, but is incumbent on everybody, as each and every citizen is a major stakeholder. Their joint opinion also points to the importance of government-supported and sustained community action. Striking is the fact that the joint recommendations also touch on the three dimensions or forms of VAC: the direct, structural and cultural. By so doing, inadvertently, the recognition of the causes of violence as recorded earlier and the solutions of VAC clearly lie in addressing all three dimensions as is admitted in these responses. The solutions are in making sound structural changes to the systems that currently exist such as "revise outdated laws", "collect data on perpetrators", and "employ specialised police officers". It also involves attending to cultural reformation such as "create stronger political will", "teach and help children to speak up", "create caring communities", and "break the silence".

Respondents were also questioned as to the '*Role of Government in fighting VAC*' and the following recommendations were made by the different groups:

Children: Government should: have meetings about violence, introduce programmes for abused children, pay for school supplies, provide homes and shelter, put police on the alert, supply food, offer counselling, put up signs, stop bullying, and protect children.

Teenagers: "*I don't care what the government does to fight violence, because nothing can stop violent people we have in T&T ... *"
"*I want to leave this country because I like myself.*"
"*Try and hire more good police and less corrupt police.*"
"*Listen to the cries of children.*"
Implement and enforce laws, stiffer penalties, death penalty for abusers, ban on drugs, public awareness raising, organise groups for children, create places for counselling, give children good education so they can get a good job, more police, financial help to poor families, launch children's programmes and youth camps, "put more interest in kids".

Parents: Implement and enforce the law, harsher penalties, set up programmes to keep children off the streets, have more counsellors for children, inform parents about laws, organise public lectures, provide training for parents, have sex education in schools, provide homes and shelters, have supervised after-school activities, set up community programmes, support families at the community level, improve the police force, create a special body to deal with violence against children, introduce monitoring and evaluation systems, teach society the values of respect and honesty, strengthen child protection services, "give voice to the children".

ECD Certificate Students: Enforce the law, enact the Children's Act, promote the rights of the child, train professionals, be an example.

Teachers: Implement and enforce the law, stiffer penalties, more accountability by the police and parents, better education programmes, introduce programmes to educate the people, promote hotlines, more social workers and guidance officers, see that schools and homes are safe, form support groups, adjust the school curriculum, set up intervention centres, monitor street families, better infra-structure.

NGO Staff: Implement and enforce the law, stiffer penalties, become more involved, design and introduce new programmes, create more safe homes, rehabilitation centres, shelters, take children off the streets, work with and support NGOs, provide information and educational programmes, have consultations, spend more money on intervention strategies, create infrastructure, promote foster care, see to it that people in authority (e.g. the police) should abide by the law, show more political will and take responsibility for the nation's children, become more involved.

Police: "*If we save one child, we would have saved society.*"
Introduce stiffer penalties, develop better policies, introduce developmental programmes, organise workshops, seminars, lectures at schools, provide shelter, half-way houses, and safe homes, train more social workers, raise public awareness and conduct information campaigns, set up sports activities at the community level, reinforce community police. Strengthen youth police groups, support community groups, pass more and better laws, provide financial aid to disadvantaged families, train more people, assist NGOs, support poor families, see that every child is regularly seen by the school doctor for medical and mental check-ups, bolster 'big brother' and 'big sister' programmes, deal with the social ills of society.

Policy Makers: Implement and enforce the laws pertaining to violence against children, introduce social programmes, provide education and rehabilitation, build up public awareness, run sensitisation workshops in communities, stricter laws for criminals, strengthen social work, offer counselling services, provide safe havens, reduce availability of drugs and alcohol, adapt school curricula, train professionals — police, media workers, counsellors and teachers — to deal with violence against children, establish hotlines, follow up on victims, promote code of conduct also for use of the Internet, make list available of sexual offenders, provide rehabilitation programmes, engage the media.
"*Don't think the government cares much*".

Recommendation III

It is, therefore, recommended that all activities related to combating violence against children and to implementing the UN Convention on the Rights of the Child, fully and generously involve all stakeholders and validate their contributions to the debate, practice, and research on violence against children. It is also recommended that all stakeholders — in addition to professional workers and policy makers, in particular — recognise the quintessential status of children, young people and parents. It is further recommended that a National Children's Council be established.

6.4 Engage Antidotes to Violence

This section explores approaches that deviate from the norm and focus on a cure for the malady and provide impetus for change. It is a speculative piece as not all the ideas that are developed are as yet deeply rooted in hard-core research but are rather based on anecdotal evidence and a vision of how things pertaining to children, their families, and communities ought to be. These ideas can be captured by two concepts: 'antidote against violence' and 'positive deviance'. Looking at international politics and policies on violence and terrorism, Selvam (2013) sees the promotion of community cohesion and a foreign policy that conveys a commitment to peace as 'antidotes' to violence.

Play as an Example of a Natural Antidote to Violence[28]

> *Managua, Nicaragua, 18 January 2008, afternoon*[29]
> First there were about eight or so children — boys and girls — of ages ranging from about six to fourteen years old who roam the streets near Lake Managua. We talk with them about their lives, their homes, parents, things they like and don't like, and inevitably about violence. We walk in the direction of their homes, a section of town where broken down and derelict houses dominate. "You should stop here", they tell us, "it's dangerous for outsiders". After a while, the girls have somehow vanished; the boys take us around and we drink cola with them. Then they show us some interesting points in the neighbourhood. We are startled that they can read so well and know their country's history. When we part, a boy receives a nod from the leader and approaches us: "nos podriás comprar una pelota de fútbol", they'd love to play football and so far they only have used a ball they made of rags and rubber bands. The ball they have in mind costs about one Euro.

---

28. This discussion draws on Jualla and Van Oudenhoven (2009).
29. This insert represents fieldwork on violence conducted by the researcher, accompanied by colleagues, in Nicaragua, 2008.

Even the naïve observer may see that the children in this scene, in addition to acquiring physical skills, learn to cooperate, divide roles, share responsibilities, abide by rules, and cope with competition, loss and victory, satisfaction and disappointment — all elements, that come into play in curtailing violence. Children at play are usually also less the butt of aggression by others; at least, they arouse less suspicion and wariness than when they loiter and hang about, ostentatiously bored and looking for something to do.

What is meant by Antidotes?

Simply put, an antidote, as defined by dictionary.com,[30] is "a medicine or other remedy[31] for counteracting the effects of poison, disease, etc.," and, pertinent to this discussion, "something that prevents or counteracts injurious or unwanted effects; good jobs are the best antidote to teenage crime". Here, the label is used to describe those activities or events that are incompatible with violence, that diminish the situations that promote violence, in this way preventing it from emerging. It is, in fact, a matter of mutual exclusivity.

> *Pochimil, Nicaragua, 22 February 2008, evening*
> It is getting dark in the small low-income coastal town of Pochimil, one hour's drive by bus west from the capital Managua. On a small field, flanked on three sides by houses and wooden structures, some 20 people play baseball. The teams are mixed; boys and girls as young as seven or eight as well as mature women and men play the game. A muscular woman is pitching. When young children are on, she throws them a low-speed ball; older children receive faster balls; adults face her full force. Onlookers cheer on, comment and, at times, jeer in a friendly fashion. In the back of the field refreshments are taken. Once in a while, one of the grown-up spectators joins the game to show off special skills.

In scene two, this simple, uncomplicated pastime in Pochimil, which can be seen all over the country, has all the ingredients that bring children, young people and adults together in reasonable harmony. Violence is far from their minds, and constructive, pleasurable behaviours are being developed and sustained. When hints of violence begin to emerge, they are quickly dealt with and diffused by laughter or soothing remarks by the adults, who themselves refrain from quarrelling or fighting as they have to keep cool in front of the young

---

30. www.dictionary.com; accessed 8 March 2013.
31. The people behind 'Cure Violence', take this medical definition literally and argue that to 'cure' violence one has to apply methods and strategies borrowed from disease control; thus such activities as detection and interruption, identifying 'carriers' of violence. In practice, they seem to endorse the same kind of 'healing' and 'antidotal' approaches as described here. See: http://cureviolence.org.

children. The all-inclusive approach is not unlike that which was successfully introduced in the UK to combat a special form of violence — football hooliganism (Lowrey 2002). In 2008, while meeting with street children in Matagalpa and Managua, Nicaragua, and in the streets of Port of Spain in Trinidad, it was realized that much was needed in the form of sport, play, music and art as means of intervention in the lives of these children and it was evident that these could act as 'something that prevents or counteracts the injurious effects' of exposure to life on the streets to violence. Rather than focusing exclusively on expressions of violence and all that these entail, the 'antidote' approach looks at the plus points and builds on positive features, skills and qualities that are incompatible with VAC.

The importance of *play* and, with its more organized expression, *sport*, among children and between children and adults cannot be overemphasized; most people would accept this intuitively, but this statement is also backed by a vast amount of experience and research.[32] In short play and sport promote wholesome lifestyles, foster empathy, cooperation, attachments and identity, increase the ability to delay gratification, make the players more socially acceptable to their peers and strengthen their ties to their families and community, and strengthen their social knowledge and willingness to act in teams; this among other multiple gains (Bonne 2000). For example, the mission statement of the international NGO, Right to Play, reads as follows:

> "The UN recognizes play as the right of every child. Play is not a luxury; it is a tool for education and health. It can bring entire communities together and inspire every individual. A game of football can teach children about tolerance and peace, and a game of tag can teach about malaria. Play helps teach important life lessons and develop skills like cooperation, leadership, and teamwork."[33]

Gaming and play are indeed natural antidotes to violence, especially when teams are involved — never mind the occasional eruptions of poor losers. When the children in the institutions were asked to identify a single right of the child, the right to play featured as the second highest response after the right to education.

Other Antidotes to Violence

The example of play as an antidote to VAC has been given generous attention as it is certainly a potent asset, but also as it is an activity that is wholly child friendly. Other such

---

32. The literature on the importance of play and sport on development is too vast to mention here, and interesting overviews are presented by Kenneth Ginsburg and the Committee on Communications and Committee on Psychosocial Aspects of Child and Family Health. *The Importance of Play in Promoting Healthy Child Development and Maintaining Strong Parent-Child Bonds*, American Academy of Pediatrics, 9 October 2006.
33. See: www.righttoplay.com/International/about-us/Pages/mission.aspx; accessed 22 Dec. 2012. It is also an excellent site for pertinent information on play and efforts to promote play by children.

countervailing tools are certainly present anywhere in the world. Rosling (2006) suggests that *culture* is perhaps the most powerful of them all and this stands to reason. *Music, song, dance*, and *drama* come immediately to mind as activities that appeal to both young and old people, and this is significant as it may be assumed that activities in which both children and adults participate have greater beneficial effects (Dunkin and Hanna 2001). Other possibilities or antidotes include *voluntarism* or other *forms of social engagement*, such as employment of young adults especially in the more creative and child-oriented forms of education. It is telling that Early Head Start, an intervention programme in the USA, directed to the youngest children and their parents, sees as one of its main outcomes that parents spank their children less than those who did not participate (Love et al. 2002). Fujioka et al. (2006), using magneto encephalography found positive behavioural as well as morphological changes in young children's brains after they had been exposed to violin tones as compared to noise bursts. These changes included enhanced memory and cognitive skills as well as neural networks. They also noted that these effects were greatest when started at an early age. Their findings are in agreement with those of a spate of other studies on the impact of playing/listening to music with credible claims of boosting self-confidence and group work.

Music, Sport, Culture of Respect and the Happiness Factor

A visit again to Nicaragua, this time to the mountainous village of Rancho Grande in 2013, reinforced the impression that music, play and sport act as antidotes to violence and that reforms directed solely at 'stamping out violence' do not work and seem only to create more hostility. Antidotes to violence serve to reinforce the preventative versus the remedial approach to developmental scourges. It is common for policies and practices to be geared towards 'righting' the 'wrongs' and Central, South America and the Caribbean are no exception. The 'antidote' approach looks at combating violence before it surfaces; it entails creating spaces that are incompatible with violence, thus preventing it from rearing its head and diffusing it before it can come to life.

> Rene Oliver, member of staff of the NGO *Asociación Amistad* in Matagalpa, Nicaragua, sits under a tree and strums his guitar. This guitar is his work tool, and it allows him to not only create music but to reflect the voices of the young children around him in his lyrics and music. They flock to him like moths to the light. We all sit in the dark sharing stories of life and the night and our countries and he tells us what the children say to him about the violence they encounter in their daily lives and he tells of how he takes their stories and together with them creates songs for them to sing so that they have an outlet and in the meantime learn how to cope with 'violencia'.[34]

---

34. This insert represents fieldwork on violence conducted by the researcher, accompanied by colleagues, in Nicaragua, 2013.

The more one looks, the more antidotes will be identified. Winterman (2005), reports that families which regularly sit down and eat together show fewer pastimes associated with drugs, smoking or drinking and seem to contribute to a *'culture of respect'*. Caring for and relating to animals provides yet another antidote as children become less aggressive, more cooperative, and tend to gain a better understanding of other people's needs (Katcher 2002). The counter-violence power of antidotes such as dancing, making music together, and performing plays is also increasingly recognized. The mission, for example, of the Brazilian NGO *Grupo Cultural Afro Reggae* has a clear mission: to reduce the use of drugs, disease, and crime in the favelas through artistic education. In addition to soul, reggae, rap and hiphop, it organizes free workshops on dance, recycling, football, percussion, and more. It succeeds in offering people alternatives to a life of violence.[35]

Violence against children in institutions is extremely difficult to get a grip on and no wonder, as onlookers are not allowed in and children will think twice before they complain, as the retaliation by the staff might be serious. They do speak out, however, when asked about previous experiences in other 'homes' and many of them have indeed moved from institution to institution. There seems ample support for the findings that homes without or with low degrees of violence have clean and functioning bathrooms and kitchens; clean and comfortable bedrooms and living rooms; there is no broken furniture, dirty linen or holes in the carpet. The walls are not besmirched and are well painted. This kind of entourage apparently also serves as an antidote. When these conditions were not met, then, indeed the children and young people reported high incidences of violence (Van Oudenhoven 2007). José Antonio Abreu is the founder of *El Sistema*, a Venezuelan NGO that has absorbed hundreds of thousands of people, including very young children, into orchestras and musical ensembles. He sees this as creating an antidote to violence and other ills of poverty! And, *inter alia*, sees the right to art as 'the most holy of human rights' (Wakin 2012). *El Sistema* calls it also a 'social right'.[36] We would like to add that it is already an internationally recognized children's right as laid down in the UN Convention on the Rights of the Child.

> It is in the middle Issigeac, this old town in the Dordogne in France. It is a warm summer evening and the square is covered with long tables. At the side, gigantic pots with simple dishes are simmering on a fire. The villagers — grandparents, teenagers, mothers and fathers with their babies — are there, as well as a fair scattering of tourists. They are seated at the *table longue* and partake of the food and drinks that can be obtained for a few Euros. The mood is good, there is laughter and some people move around quietly. Yet another antidote.

---

35. See: www.Afroreggae.org; accessed 19 March, 2013.
36. The Simón Bolívar Music Foundation (FundaMusical Bolívar) is the governing body of the National System of Youth and Children's Orchestras and Choirs of Venezuela, commonly known as *El Sistema*. See: http://www.fesnojiv.gob.ve/en/el-sistema.html.

Another way of looking at these antidotes is that perhaps they make the participants 'feel good about themselves' or go through moments of 'happiness'. In this light, it is interesting to see that the emerging 'happiness' studies, in addition to such factors as health, income, relationships, expectations, and social status, see 'agency' increasingly as crucial to feeling happy (Graham 2012). Many therapists, for example, are aware of the stress-relieving power of play, music, art, theatre and sport, each with its distinctive healing attributes. It is not risky to assume that for most people, happiness works as an antidote to violence. In a roundabout way, the crucial place of 'agency' in feelings of happiness and antidotes to violence leads the discussion back to education and to the manner in which children and young people are being raised: are they given agency, do they meaningfully participate and are they allowed to decide about events concerning their own lives? The discussion on agency, of course, is a discussion on rights.

Mini Democracies as Antidotes

Winston Churchill was not very fond of democracies, but did not see an alternative either, hence his famous observation that "Democracy is the worst form of government except all those other forms that have been tried from time to time."[37] Here, democracy goes perhaps further than Churchill envisaged and moves beyond the power of a majority vote. Here, democracy is about allowing space to all members to contribute and participate in action and decision making. It is a matter of maximizing the rights and the position of the weak, the vulnerable and the minority. These principles should not only apply to nations, but could easily be realised in small groups, such as in schools or classes, neighbourhood associations, the workplace, the soccer club, the family. There are no hard data as to whether these 'mini democracies' also work as antidotes to violence, but it seems likely. In any event, described in this manner, 'mini democracies' seem to fit nicely in the explanatory framework of Pinker's *The Better Angels of our Nature* as discussed earlier. All forms of antidotes to violence seem to have a number of features in common: they occur repeatedly and the activities are best carried out by hybrid groups — ethnically mixed, young and old, male and female, high and low social status. They are largely voluntary, non-competitive but collaborative, rewarding to all. All members play an active role and in this way each and everybody experiences a sense of 'agency'. Important to note is that meeting these criteria is certainly not easy, but also not impossible.

---

37. "Many forms of Government have been tried and will be tried in this world of sin and woe. No one pretends that democracy is perfect or all wise. Indeed, it has been said that democracy is the worst form of government except all those other forms that have been tried from time to time."The Official Report, House of Commons (5th Series), vol. 444, 11 November 1947.

A Debate on the Power of Art as an Antidote to Violence

> Art as Antidote to Violence
>
> Many view art — especially modern art forms — as expressions and promoters of violence among the youth. To that end, what follows is a debate on the power of art as an antidote to violence. Can art transform a culture of violence into a culture of peace? Can it serve as an antidote to violence? The following lines contain insights into the nefarious concept of violence as it is linked to art and art's designated transformative power when it comes to violence. Expressions of violence are everywhere: embedded deep in the cultural habits and mind-sets of a people; wielding their power from the structural power towers that exist and at times expressing themselves directly — which we encounter and attempt most of the times to come to terms with. This is so partly because we do not really feel empowered to touch the 'structural', we are overwhelmed by the 'cultural', or for the most part still exist in a state of "false consciousness".
>
> The lesson from the great thinkers such as George Hegel, Friedrich Engels, Karl Marx and Frantz Fanon is that violence is a structure. Engels argues that the economic is a fundamental force for subjugation, that capital has a logic of its own that justifies the use of whatever means are available to achieve economic prosperity. So politics and world order and capital dictate to a large degree the extent of violence: whether it is the ongoing massive violence that one is seeing now in Syria and most of the Middle East or the transnational ethnic violence that persists in South Asia, or the legacy of violence in the form of colonialism, or the war on terror after 9/11 as the US attempts "to make the world safe for democracy."[38]
>
> Postmodernist Abel (2008) claims, that violence is all-pervasive by ontological necessity. It may well be that violence is intrinsic to the human condition, an inescapable fact of life that can be channelled and reckoned with but never completely suppressed. So, then, are people inherently violent? Can the teachings of philosophers, the likes of Hobbes, Locke and Rousseau help us to come to grips with the duality of man: peaceful man versus violent man? What are the implications if indeed violence is intrinsic? By interfering and altering and transforming the violent into the non-violent, is one disturbing nature's essence — the very essence of man — and by extension his expression, his art?

---

38. On April 2, 1917, President Woodrow Wilson went before a joint session of Congress to seek a declaration of war against Germany in order that the world "be made safe for democracy," www.whitehouse.gov/about/presidents/woodrowwilson.Cached — Similar; accessed 14 March, 2013.

Does all art promote peace? Can art promote violence? Is there violence in art? What about films and their violent images? Can one defend the right of art galleries to display, for example, Tapanila's graphic photographs or paintings of bloodied representations of battered and murdered women? Is 'Shaved Heads and Marked Bodies' a therapeutic, artistic representation of a culture of trauma? What about the expressions of some music icons: Movado and Fifty Cents? Rihanna and her "I found love in a hopeless place"? Are these violent lyrics the natural expression of these artists? Can they express themselves in this fashion because it is what they live? It is their life, their art. Indeed then art can be violent and have violent expressions, one can argue. The derogatory language, the use of expletives, the constant reference to warfare and bloodshed has become commonplace and is not necessarily seen as violence. It is seen as contemporary culture; contemporary art, even? Is it not then that art is more shaped by violence than violence affected by art? Or is it a relationship of reciprocity? Do these natural expressions promote peace and allow for the healthy venting of stored negative emotions that dissipate once they have been vented or do they serve to in turn create and promote a culture of violence? Or even a culture of peace? Is art therapeutic for the artist in this instance at the expense of the ill-health of all the avid young followers? Or old as the case may be?

At which point does violence become an accepted part of the psyche? When did certain societies start accepting violence as natural and normal? Why is the citizenry so tolerant of the violence around it? One is not talking about the wars or the bloodshed where one feels powerless but the small instances where one is exposed to systemic violence; for example, when a child dies because of negligence in a hospital, or when a young girl is sexually abused, or when a woman is beaten. When are the seeds of violence actually sown? Surely it is not at that moment when a teenage boy hits his girlfriend in a jealous rage, but before, long before.

So can art transform a culture of violence into a culture of peace? Is art mere outlet, mere expression; a form of catharsis? Is it, as Marx says of religion, an opiate of the masses; a feel-good form of relief to alleviate the scourge of violence? Like the chant of Bob Marley's 'One love'? When can it and when does it become transformative? Does art target all aspects of violence or does it act as a temporary plaster on a festering sore? Can art change the world? Can it stop the next suicide bomber from going through with his violent act of destruction? Can it stop the next mother from throwing acid on her teenage daughter simply for looking unconsciously at a boy? Can it stop a blotched teenage abortion that results in the death of both mother and child?

Maybe or maybe not, but can it reach one person and affect her/him in a most profound way that causes her/him to be an agent of change? In other words, can it empower? Can it shape the life skills that are gleaned by our young ones? If the answer is yes, then there is a chance and art may well be an antidote to violence. Change must begin somewhere, however miniscule.

Drawing by Chloe R, 8, from Mayaro, submitted to the 'International Art Contest for Young People, Art for Peace 2012', Trinidad and Tobago.

Recommendation IV

It is, therefore, recommended that, in efforts to combat violence against children, the notion of 'antidotes' is further researched as an effective and practical tool to create and sustain situations in which violence against children cannot occur. It is further recommended that effective antidotes be introduced and sustained when and wherever feasible.

6.5 Explore Positive Deviance and its Relevance for Combating Violence against Children

The Positive Deviance approach

Positive deviance[39] is the given that, in almost all settings of widespread despair, misery or malfeasance, a few at-risk individuals follow uncommon, beneficial practices and consequently experience better outcomes than their neighbours who share similar risks. The positive deviance approach then seeks to identify these individuals or 'positive deviants' whose behaviours go 'against the grain' and yield wholesome results. A next step then is to bring this phenomenon to scale, to empower their peers or community members to follow the practices of these successful 'positive deviants'. A further characteristic of these 'positive deviants' is that they share the same conditions and live in similar circumstances as the others; critical also is that their positively deviant behaviours are affordable, acceptable, and sustainable and do not conflict with local culture.

This approach to behavioural and social change benefits therefore, from the community's readily available assets and strengths, and builds on them. It follows the strategies adopted by the people themselves. This community-based approach stands in sharp contrast to many customary initiatives, which are alien to the community and often not sustainable or require constant external support. The solutions offered by the 'positive deviance' approach are, by virtue of their very existence, always culturally acceptable, within the conceptual and emotional reach of the pertinent people, and affordable. These solutions can also be implemented immediately. The positive deviance approach has proven to be effective both in high- and low-income countries and with an ever expanding inventory of issues, ranging from child malnutrition, use of condoms in brothels, to cleanliness in hospitals. Experience has shown that, even in the most desperate situations, there are always a few 'positive deviants' whose exemplary behaviour could be followed. Maybe the positive deviance approach can be helpful in finding 'antidotal' activities or events in Trinidad and Tobago? Training, research and dissemination capacity may be built up that promotes the use of the positive deviance approach in policy, practice and training.

---

39. The notion of positive deviance as a tool for research, policy and practice is rapidly gaining traction in human development policy and practice and any Internet search will attest to this; using the words 'positive deviance', even with 'specifiers' such as country (e.g., Trinidad and Tobago) or subject (e.g., 'children', 'youth' — however, PD applied to VAC is pretty rare!) will yield a rich harvest of interesting and helpful information. The place to visit is the Positive Deviance Initiative (PDI): www.positivedeviance.org. See also Marsh et al. (2004), Pascale, Sternin and Sternin (2010), Richard et al. (2010), Spreitzer and Sonenshein (2004) and Jualla and Van Oudenhoven (2011).

TABLE 6.1 Issues Deemed Suitable for the Positive Deviance Approach

During two workshops on 'The Positive Deviance Approach and Violence against Children and Youth' in Kenya,[40] the fifty participants were asked to identify issues suitable for the 'positive deviance' approach. They produced a very long list indeed; some of the issues are mentioned below.

– Development of the 'whole' child	– Sexual abuse
– Alcoholism	– Climate change
– Negligence	– Insecurity
– Discipline without the cane	– Harmful cultural practices
– Safe places to play	– Media and child protection
– Education and the girl child	– Parents in conflict with the law
– Domestic violence	– Children in conflict with the law
– Life Skills	– Non-custodial sentences
– Substance and drug abuse	– Child malnutrition
– Harm reduction	– Gender inequality
– Child trafficking	– Divorce
– Poor hygiene and sanitation	– Peer pressure

Both the antidote and the positive deviance approaches must, of course, be case specific, contextually couched and generated from a bottoms-up approach versus a top-down imposition if it is to have any effect whatsoever. Trinidad and Tobago is unique, in more than one way, but the issues faced are not so different from those experienced by others who successfully embraced the positive deviance approach. A first move would be to locate areas where violence against children and youth is rife. These could be certain geographical areas, such as some areas in Port of Spain or Laventille, specific institutions, such as schools, ways of reporting in the media, such as portraying young women as sexual objects, lack of developmental opportunities for disadvantaged children, such as lack of playgrounds or employability schemes, or lacunae in the law, such as a prohibition on corporal punishment both in school and at home. Then, the challenge is to find people who buck the trend, or the situations that cause the change and show, in ways acceptable and affordable for everybody, how things could be changed for the better. The next step is the application of these findings or the bringing to scale of these 'best practices'.

Recommendation V

It is, therefore, recommended that, in efforts to combat violence against children, the notion of 'positive deviance' is further explored as a potential tool to create and sustain situations in which violence against children do not exist. It is further recommended that practices of

---

40. See: Van Oudenhoven and Van Oudenhoven (2011).

positive deviance are carefully evaluated for their relevance for situations where violence against children is common and introduced when feasible.

6.6 Creating a VAC Epistemic Community

Violence against children has become a growing issue of concern to many people in Trinidad and Tobago, whether in their capacities as parent, teacher, researcher, policy maker, religious leader, media specialist or those who work outside the sphere of children's matters, such as lawyers, bankers, business people or taxi drivers. Indeed, many good initiatives are already in place or are being envisaged. The past years have seen the adoption of universal preschool and secondary education, government GATE intervention for those pursuing tertiary education and the establishment of the University of Trinidad and Tobago in response to the growing demand for access to tertiary education by the Trinidad and Tobago citizenry. This speaks volumes for the nation. The establishment of a Family Services Ministry is a critical factor in addressing many of the violence issues facing our families, and the honouring and establishment of the Children's Authority shines a light on the efforts of those engaged in the fight against VAC. There is still a need to set up A Children in Need of Special Protection (CNSP) national database, and to do so much more. However, much work is being done by the Ministry of National Security to follow the trend of violence by documenting data and conducting in-depth research and evaluation. Acknowledgment is made of the work done by the Ministry of the People and Social Development for the establishment of children's centres and mobile career guidance offices, and the Ministry of Education for the injection of an increasing number of school counsellors and the universalising and enabling of free preschool education. There is evidence all around that things are happening in Trinidad and Tobago; that our children's interests are being considered and that this is not happening in a haphazard manner but as a result of some planning and dialogue. It is with this in mind that the following is proposed.

Here it is proposed to move a significant step further and, drawing on the expertise and experience of all people, including children involved in the programmes and activities, by strongly recommending the creation of a 'Violence against Children Epistemic Community'.

Epistemic[41] Community: A New Approach

The word *episteme* in the Platonian sense means knowledge or justified true belief, and in its analytic tradition invited formal and informal approaches. Epistemic means relating to knowledge or its degree of validation. The definition of epistemic community used here has its roots in the one proposed by Haas (1992). In his view, an epistemic community consists of diverse people who have:
— A shared set of normative and principled beliefs, which provide a value-based rationale for the social action of community members;
— Shared causal beliefs, which are derived from their analysis of practices leading or contributing to a central set of problems in their domain and which then serve as the basis for elucidating the multiple linkages between possible policy actions and desired outcomes;
— Shared notions of validity — that is, inter-subjective, internally defined criteria for weighing and validating knowledge in the domain of their expertise; and
— A common policy enterprise — that is, a set of common practices associated with a set of problems to which their professional competence is directed, presumably out of the conviction that human welfare will be enhanced as a consequence.

Thus, an epistemic community may be seen as a group of people who do not have any specific history together and could comprise a network of professionals from a variety of disciplines and backgrounds. The approach advocated here is different from that of Haas' in that it emphasizes the motivational and emotional commitment of the members of the community and — this is critical — the amount of formally validated experience or expertise they possess. This adaptation also differs from Gramsci's (1971) 'intellectuals' to whom solely was entrusted the role of political consciousness and the charge for change as a result of their elite position in society and their struggle for progressive self-consciousness. In this new understanding of an epistemic community, everybody who genuinely cares about the well-being and healthy development of children and young people would be welcome to join. Following from this, less prominence is placed on 'certified' professionalism and everybody with a credible track record of involvement in VAC-based work is seen as *bona fide*. It is further important to stress the importance of the presence of diversity, in disciplines, backgrounds, and social status or power, and at the same time the need to accept each other as complete equals.

The main functions of a VAC epistemic community are five-fold:
— Generate new understanding about VAC;
— Create a supportive platform for policy, research, training, and implementation;
— Access and establish new networks;

---

41. Epistemic: 'of or relating to knowledge or knowing', Merriam-Webster Dictionary.

— Provide encouragement, resources and validation to those actively fighting against VAC; and ultimately
— Create and sustain a movement against VAC.

Forming a VAC Epistemic Community

Epistemic communities do not come off the ground by their own accord and external intervention seems almost always a requirement. This external intervention should most likely come from a governmental or non-governmental agency with the right mandate and track record, as well as with the necessary human and financial resources. These resources need not be extravagant, but are indispensable, nonetheless. The main function of this agency would be to marshal, under one roof so to speak, a critical mass of like-minded people, and further to act as an administrative and coordination structure that brings people together, sets and oversees the agenda, monitors follow up, records development and informs and motivates its members. Once an epistemic community starts to perform well and starts to self-generate initiatives, its involvement can be reduced. An epistemic community is not to be confused with a committee that is comprised of selected members and set up to address a particular issue or issues and whose members are called upon once or twice a month to sit on a panel and discuss these issues and propose recommendations; nor is it to be mistaken with a supervisory board, for example. An epistemic community is made up of a large body of people who are empowered by each other to act on issues that they deem important and beneficial. The members are not limited to a role of reporting and recommending but are all actual implementers. This makes a significant difference.

An especially tough point to deal with in the T&T context may be the essential requirement for a well-functioning epistemic community, which is seriously looking at each other as equals and validating each other's experiences as equally relevant. In the best of circumstances this skill does not come to most people naturally. Academic degrees and social status do matter a great deal and are difficult to do away with; the PhD holder may find it uncomfortable not to cling to his/her doctoral title, while the young teenage mother may quickly feel that her experience is not really relevant. Guidance and training would be needed to actually get there and this, too, could be an important additional role of the initiators. The ideal is to promote the emergence of numerous VAC epistemic communities that are organically interlinked.

One or More VAC Epistemic Communities?

The answer to this question is 'both'! As a nationwide epistemic community could easily have its roots as well as engender a large number of local epistemic communities. Thus there is no reason why Couva, Mayaro, Plymouth, San Fernando, or Scarborough should not have their own VAC epistemic communities while being connected to the national one and being 'fed' and informed both locally and nationally.

Recommendation VI

It is therefore recommended that the government of Trinidad and Tobago take the initiative in creating a sustainable structure that leads to the establishment of an enduring, dynamic, and all-inclusive, nationwide VAC epistemic community as well as inter-connected epistemic communities at county and local levels. In doing this, it is particularly recommended that the government encourage all stakeholders to participate in these epistemic communities.

6.7 Conduct Research: What Can You Do to Stop the Cycle of Violence?

When the responses to the question '*What can you do to stop the cycle of violence*' were analysed it was felt that there was an element of 'what's there' and 'what's missing' in those responses. The data was analysed therefore along those lines and the latter category incorporated here as recommendations. The suggestions as to 'what's missing' from the interviewed groups are discussed in the paragraphs.

The suggestions of *the children* are both endearing and helpful and show considerable 'agency'. The boys and girls could also be 'nudged' to think about doing projects on violence and bullying in school. *The teenagers* are quite aware of the options open to them, but what is needed is for them to be heard and listened to in a systemic way and what is even more important is that somehow they need to recognize the fact that they should actually demand this. Not much is missing from *the parents'* suggestions. One could think of parents pushing harder for services benefitting their children. As for *the ECD student teachers,* the following are areas that can also be considered: in-service and pre-service training, collaboration with other stake-holding organizations, better understanding of community work, and networking; and the promotion of a higher awareness of the UN Convention on the Rights of the Child. *Teachers* could be the initiators of a range of community activities and lobby for school premises to be utilized for after-school activities; liaise with social workers, the police and the research community; promote pre-service and in-service training on violence against children; suggest changes in the curriculum to promote a heightened awareness of the UN Convention on the Rights of the Child. *NGOs* can engage in national campaigning, networking with other NGOs, development of training modules, knowledge generation, engaging a research community, and collaboration with police, health workers, social workers, and governmental agencies. They can develop new approaches to the problem and adopt a watchdog function. Greater awareness of the UN Convention on the Rights of the Child is also needed.

Perhaps training (both in-service and pre-service) for the *police* as to what violence against children entails as they do not always have a 'good name' in the public's eye; pointers for policy and action research should be formulated, and they should collaborate with other welfare organizations at the community level. There is also need for a better understanding, awareness and internalization of the UN Convention on the Rights of the Child. While *policy makers* can aim to promote child-friendly policies, forge partnerships with the NGO community, support and promote new community-based initiatives, identify and disseminate affective practices, organise focus groups, contribute to action research agendas, collaborate with the research community, and promote greater awareness of the UN Convention on the Rights of the Child.

The main lesson that presents itself is that people, in whatever position, are not powerless and in the main possess a fair amount of knowledge as to how to act and there is internal consistency across the groups which show a fair degree of validity of the responses. However, none of the respondents mentioned (action-) research as something the government should support, and the researcher believes it is an indispensable element in generating new and essential knowledge on violence against children and that, as a corollary, the research community should assume a more aggressive and pro-active role that is driven by a rights-based approach which universalises violence and allows for a method of political engagement to promote the creation of strategic goals. There needs to be a 'marriage' between academia and practice in the field.

A recent call for proposals from the international NGO Council on Violence against Children, 'Creating Non-violent Juvenile Justice Systems'[42] included the following as possible areas of research:
— Examples of positive models of a non-violent system;
— Studies and data on outcomes of both positive and negative existing systems, in terms of costs, recidivism, future violence, risks to public safety, psychological impact, etc.;

---

42. Cited 21 March 2013 at http://www.crin.org/violence/NGOs/.

— Relevant jurisprudence including on legal frameworks and successful litigation against violence; and data on
— Forms and incidence of violence in the existing system;

Each of these topic areas listed above provide strong directives as to the structural and cultural reformations that can be adopted in T&T. Two important reports issued by the Consortium for Street Children, a group that combines the thinking and experience of over 60 member agencies working in over 130 countries, provide state-of-the art overviews on current views on, and approaches to, street children. The first, *The State of the World's Street Children: Violence* is of particular relevance to the topic of this study. In summary, the Report's key findings are:
— Street children are exposed to many experiences of violence from an early age and in many situations. Their plight is generally overlooked by policy makers and official 'helpers';
— The experiences of street children from all over the world are very similar, even of those in poor and rich countries;
— A better appreciation and understanding of the lives of street children is essential for effective policy and intervention;
— Governments continue to deal with street children in a violent manner, often contravening their rights;
— New and effective approaches are inclusive and support families and their communities.

Not surprisingly, it makes the following recommendations:
— Put children at the centre of policy making and community action;
— Support families;
— Develop and connect community-based organisations;
— The state should promote and actively enforce a child protection policy;
— Create an 'inclusive' society with an emphasis on poverty reduction;
— Strengthen research (Thomas de Benítez 2007).

The second, *The State of the World's Street Children: Research*, focuses on results of intensive and extensive study and reflection. The outcomes seem also pertinent for the situation in Trinidad and Tobago. The major findings, very briefly, are listed hereunder.

As to the top four research findings:
— Street children are young people who experience a combination of multiple deprivations and 'street connectedness';
— Street children's experiences and relationships are essential to understand their lives and for undertaking any form of action;
— Street children should participate, as standard practice, as informants and co-researchers;

— Longitudinal, repeat and comparative studies are vital in developing an understanding of street children's present and future role in society.

As to the top four gaps in current research:
— Academic and developmental studies are carried out in isolation of each other and fail to inform policy and practice and *vice versa;*
— Research on street children is fragmented;
— Research on children is not systematic;
— No 'motor' exists to promote a 'body' of research on street children.

As to the top four findings related to advocacy:
— Street children must be distinguished but not isolated from other children;
— Transparency about budget allocations, child protection systems, and evaluation of their impact on children is needed;
— Local level policies and involvement by NGOs must be backed up by laws and budget allocations;
— Investment in research is needed.

As the two most important 'next steps' to be taken, the Report recommends the creation of 'space' on national and local policy agendas and investment in more knowledge gathering (Thomas de Benez 2011). So far the issue of stating exactly what is meant by 'street children' has been avoided as a precise definition takes us away from our central claim which is that the spectacle of street children is an expression of violence which should not be tolerated, neither by the government nor by people on the streets of the nation. In all of this it is being recognized that many street children possess extraordinary survival and other skills and are extremely resourceful. At the same time there are no easy solutions to build on their capabilities, to protect them from harm and to help them on the path to healthy development.

Posner and Roth (2014), in their debate on whether human rights law is too ambitious and ambiguous; the latter, argued that human rights, including those pertaining to women and children', are ineffective, too costly to be implemented and useless in the hands of corrupt and bureaucratic governments, and for those reasons should be abandoned. However, the former claims that to a certain extent, the collective of human and children's rights campaigners are succeeding in codifying the views of the public as to how governments should act.

Recommendation VII

It is recommended that the Government as well as knowledge-generating institutions enhance and expand their research on violence against children and related issues. It is further recommended that the notions of 'practitioners as researchers' and 'children as researchers' be fully appreciated. To this end, it is also recommended that people working in social service organisations be encouraged to, and supported in, creating new insights and understanding, and that schools be stimulated and assisted in running 'children as researchers' activities. It is moreover recommended that the new knowledge thus engendered be optimally validated and mutually shared.

6.8 Being Visionary in Approach

Listverse.com (2009) mentions the top 10 terrible issues facing children; they are in ascending order: violence through indoctrination, poverty, life as a refugee, lack of access to education, child neglect, child labour, child prostitution, Internet child pornography, trafficking and slavery, and military use of children.[43] Although Trinidad and Tobago does not score on all of these ten threats to the well-being of children, there's no reason for complacency as things that look 'strange', 'incidental' and 'far away' at first sight, may well become reality, as Van Oudenhoven and Wazir (2006) note in their study, *Newly Emerging Needs of Children*. Could it have been predicted a few decades ago that Trinidad and Tobago would become a source and transit point for adults and children subjected to sex trafficking and forced labour (Charan 2013)? The recommendation to set up rapid assessment, policy and intervention mechanisms (RAPIMs) that register, attempt to understand, attach meaning to and formulate pointers for policy and practice on these newly emerging issues is a proactive step in the right direction by authorities. Those RAPIMs would comprise a hybrid range of stakeholders in children's issues, such as policy makers, parents, social workers, professionals, media specialists and also children (Charan 2013).

Violence against children, even vaguely defined as it is, knows many expressions and the list of the ways in which boys and girls are and can be debased, corrupted, degraded, disrespected or otherwise violated is very long indeed and has no end. There is also a long list without an end of the studies, reports, statements, analyses or research, training modules, examples of good practice, websites, resource centres, and policy documents on violence against children and its many forms. There is currently a veritable 'tsunami of tsunamis'

---

43. See: http://listverse.com/2009/07/06/top-10-terrible-issues-facing-children-worldwide/, accessed 12 May 2012.

of information production taking place and it is easy to get drowned in these high floods of material. Each self-respecting government and here there are few exceptions, has a policy in place on how to combat VAC or intends to do so. Thus the CARICOM Heads of Government concluded at their 33rd regular three-day conference in Saint Lucia, 2012, to emphasise the need for "concerted action, at ALL levels, to address the increasing challenge of child abuse — particularly sexual abuse." They also agreed that an integrated response was needed:

> "[a] holistic approach that includes parenting education, public awareness and education, and legislative reforms to protect our Region's children and to deal appropriately, not only with perpetrators, but also with those who support abuse through ... non- reporting of incidents ... [and] ... and hopefully arrive at a consensus on legal and other measures to stamp out corporal punishment." (Government of Trinidad and Tobago 2012)

Recommendation VIII

It is therefore recommended that the Government and stake-holding entities appoint in decision- and opinion-making positions people who demonstrate solid track records in the fight against violence against children and who are capable of and have the motivation and sense of both mission and vision to advance the cause of all children and young people in Trinidad and Tobago. It is further recommended that they be given all the needed resources to carry out this task fully and generously.

7.0 Conclusion

Galtung's theory of structural and cultural violence has promoted an increasingly rights based approach to international development issues; and current thinkers inspired by Galtung (Barash and Webel 2008 and Morvardi 2008, among others) increasingly point in the same direction as, they too, see egalitarian ideas as particularly relevant to the understanding of conflicts, extremism and the 'clash of cultures' and, noteworthy frame their arguments, like Galtung does, in terms of human rights and social justice. The basic premise that violence might be understood and addressed through an understanding of structural inequity and the cultural acceptance of violence paved the way for this empirical research and will most likely continue to do so by the research community.

This research, which adopts a rights-based approach in its analysis of violence, is premised on several core assumptions; the main one being that the broader and more sophisticated the conceptualisations and definitions of violence, that is, the more the definitions included cultural, structural and rights domains, the less likely people are to be tolerant of violence. The proven hypotheses displayed a significant relationship between the manner in which violence is understood and defined and the degree of tolerance that is accorded to the phenomenon. In instances where rights played a role in people's understanding of violence and where violence was perceived along systemic and cultural lines, there was a tendency for those individuals to be less likely to 'tolerate' or 'accept' violence and more likely to 'stand up against' violence and 'intervene' to make a change. The evaluation of the country status with regards to the implementation of the CRC served to corroborate the research findings in the field, supporting the claim that the discussion on rights issues does not yet form as critical a component on the nation's agenda as it ought to especially as it relates to the implementation of the CRC.

Gramsci (1971) noted that political consciousness is the first step towards a further progressive self-consciousness. The researcher suggests that the opposite is also true and accepts the view that:

> "The unity of theory and practice is not just a matter of mechanical fact but part of the historical process ... to the level of real possession of a single and coherent conception of the world." (Cited in Lemert 2013, 203)

The research, then, is driven by the philosophy that sociological ideologies and practical actions are inextricably linked and is fashioned by the researcher's international experience in the field and guided by the adoption and practical manipulation of a combination of theoretical approaches. The study focuses on one of the most vulnerable members of society, its children, and establishes that the true measure of a nation's progress is the manner in which it treats with its most vulnerable; and this is further dictated by the extent to which it realises its citizens' potential to access their inalienable rights. It acknowledges the link between political consciousness and progressive self-consciousness and the implications for the manner in which violence is defined, expressed and endured, as this determines the degree of acquiescence to any phenomenon. A critical aim of the research is to highlight that a cultural shift is essential to bring to scale these attitudes of low violence — tolerance; a shift that will allow for rights ideology to become the mainstream ideology which will ultimately lead to a decrease in acts of VAC. The research calls for structural and cultural changes that can come about only with a rights-based awareness and approach.

The rights-based approach adopted calls essentially for the integration of the standards and principles of children's rights into any undertaking. In the case of development programming, this means it must form part of the plans, strategies and policies so as to promote greater awareness among governments and other relevant institutions of their obligations to fulfil, respect, and protect these rights and to support and empower individuals and communities to claim their rights. The discourse on rights as they relate to violence is woven into the study from conception to completion. It is embodied in the literature review, the methodological approach, the instruments, the data analysis and interpretation and most importantly it fashions the recommendations. This document is the embodiment of a rights-based approach, calling emphatically for the generous and consistent implementation of the CRC by all members and groups in society. It calls for the violation of children's rights to be viewed as violence. It acknowledges such phenomena as child labour, child marriages, child sexual abuse, neglect, incest, corporal punishment, domestic abuse and infanticide, as violence that is fed by cultural beliefs, norms and practices, and maintained by structural elements. The research contained herein establishes the link between structural, cultural and direct violence and highlights forms of structural violence in the form of child poverty, poor health care, inadequate educational opportunities, and the presence of street children, racism, ageism, classism, ethnocentrism, and sexism among others. It establishes clearly the interconnectedness of the three dimensions of violence showing how one promotes the other.

The anchoring of the study in a rights-based approach renders significance to the study. However, the research is important for several other reasons, those being that it offers a comprehensive narrative on violence both internationally and locally, provides a structural and post-structural analysis of Caribbean society, and applies a unique conceptual framework of analysis of violence in the region. It applies a macro theory of international development and social change to micro national and individual scope of consideration. This allows for the phenomenon of VAC to be observed in a manner that brings to the fore elements of violence that were previously hidden. Quantitative and qualitative data serve to enhance the research and lend testimony to the researcher's claims. The execution of a multi-design methodological approach that provides stark quantifiable data combined with rich and insightful global field narratives and informative qualitative data that project current and emerging issues, hopefully serves to solidify this body of work as innovative and contributory to the ongoing effort to stem the tide of VAC.

This book highlights the scope for further research, in particular as it relates to *antidotes to violence*, *epistemic communities* and *positive deviance*. It suggests the establishment of *children's councils* to promote children's agency and participation and reiterates the need for a country's commitment to the implementation and adherence to the CRC, in both spirit and action.

References

Adamson, Alan H. 1972. *Sugar without Slaves: The Political Economy of British Guiana 1838-1904*. New Haven, CT: Yale University Press.

Ahmad, Razi. 1993. Islam, Nonviolence, and Global Transformation. In *Islam and Nonviolence,* edited by Glenn D. Paige, Chaiwat Satha-Anand, and Sarah Gilliatt, 27-52. Honolulu: University of Hawai'i, Matsunaga Institute for Peace.

Althusser, Louis. 1971. *Lenin and Philosophy, and Other Essays*, translated from the French by Ben Brewster. London: Monthly Review Press.

Amin, Samir. 1974. *Accumulation on a World Scale: A Critique of the Theory of Underdevelopment*. New York, NY: Monthly Review Press.

Anthony, David, ed. 2011. *The State of the World's Children 2011: Adolescence; An Age of Opportunity*. New York: UNICEF.

Arriaga, Ximena B., and Stuart Oskamp, eds. 1999. *Violence in Intimate Relationships*. Thousand Oaks, CA: Sage Publications.

AS. 2011. "Schoolgirls Taken to Hospital after Fight". *Trinidad and Tobago Express,* January 10.

Aslam, Abid, ed. 2013. *The State of the World's Children 2013: Children with Disabilities*. New York: UNICEF.

Bakhtin, Mikhail. 1984. *Rabelais and His World*. Bloomington: Indiana University Press.

"Bangladesh and Development, The path through the Fields." 2012. *The Economist* November 3rd.

Barash, David and Charles Webel. 2008. *Peace and Conflict Studies*. London: SAGE.

Barker, Robert L. 2003. *The Social Work Dictionary*. 5th ed. Washington, DC: NASW Press.

Barnett, Laura. 2008. *The "Spanking" Law: Section 43 of the Criminal Code*. [Parliamentary Information and Research Service of the Library of Parliament].

Baron, Stephen W., and Timothy F. Hartnagel. 1998. "Street Youth and Criminal Violence." *Journal of Research in Crime & Delinquency* 35 (2): 166-92.

Barrow, Christine. 2002. *Children's Rights, Caribbean Realities*. Kingston: Ian Randle Publishers.

Beckford, George L. 1972. *Persistent Poverty: Underdevelopment in Plantation Economies of the Third World*. London: Oxford University Press.

Berg, Bruce L. 2001. *Qualitative Research Methods for the Social Sciences*. 4th ed. Needham Heights, MA: Allyn and Bacon.

Berggren, Niclas, and Therese Nilsson. 2013. "Does Economic Freedom Foster Tolerance?" *Kyklos* 66 (2): 177-207.

Berkeley, Bennie. 2012. The Relevance of Postmodern Epistemologies in Multicultural Studies in the Caribbean. *Journal of the Department of Behavioural Sciences* 1 (2): 118-23.

Best, Lloyd. 1968. "Outlines of a Model of Pure Plantation Economy." *Social and Economic Studies* 17 (3): 283-326.

———. 1971. "Independent Thought and Caribbean Freedom." In *Readings in the Political Economy of the Caribbean,* edited by Norman Girvan, and Owen Jefferson, 7-28. Kingston: New World Group, Ltd.

Best, Lloyd, and Kari Polanyi Levitt. 2009. *Essays on the Theory of Plantation Economy: A Historical and Institutional Approach to Caribbean Economic Development*. Kingston: University of the West Indies Press.

Bethel, Camille. 2011. "4 Sent Home for Beating Parent, Child at School". *Trinidad and Tobago Express,* February 4.

Biebricher, Thomas, and Eric Vance Johnson. 2012. "What's Wrong with Neoliberalism?" *New Political Science.* 34 (2): 202–216.

Bissessar, Ann Marie. 2011. "Slaughter of the Innocents". *Trinidad and Tobago Guardian,* February 28.

Bjørkly, Stål. 1997. "Clinical Assessment of Dangerousness in Psychotic Patients: Some Risk Indicators and Pitfalls." *Aggression and Violent Behavior* 2 (2): 167-78.

Blumer, Herbert. 1971. "Social Problems as Collective Behavior." *Social Problems* 18 (3): 298-306.

———. 1979. *Critiques of Research in the Social Sciences: An Appraisal of Thomas and Znaniecki's "The Polish Peasant in Europe and America"*. New Brunswick, NJ: Transaction Books.

Bolioli, Oscar L., ed. 1993. *The Caribbean: Culture of Resistance, Spirit of Hope*. New York: Friendship Press.

Bonne, Jennifer Cowie. 2000. *Healthy Child Development through Sport and Recreation: Discussion Paper*. [Ontario]: Ontario Physical and Health Education Association.

Bose, Sugata, and Ayesha Jalal. 1997. *Nationalism, Democracy, and Development: State and Politics in India*. Delhi: Oxford University Press.

Bourdieu, Pierre. 1977. *Outline of a Theory of Practice*. Cambridge: Cambridge University Press.

———. 1990. *The Logic of Practice*. Stanford, CA: Stanford University Press.

Boyden, Jo, and Judith Ennew. 1997. *Children in Focus: A Manual for Participatory Research with Children*. Stockholm: Rädda Barnen.

Brathwaite, Kamau. 1974. *Contradictory Omens: Cultural Diversity and Integration in the Caribbean*. Kingston: Savacou Publications.

Brereton, Bridget. 1996. *An Introduction to the History of Trinidad and Tobago*. Oxford: Heinemann Educational Publishers.

Brikci, Nouria, and Judith Green. 2007. *A Guide to Using Qualitative Research Methodology*. Médecins sans Frontieres. Available from http://evaluation.msf.at/fileadmin/evaluation/files/documents/resources_MSF/MSF_Qualitative_Methods.pdf

Brock, Deborah, Amanda Glasbeek, and Carmela Murdocca, eds. 2014. *Criminalization, Representation, Regulation: Thinking Differently About Crime*. North York, Ontario: University of Toronto Press Inc.

Bronner, Stephen E. 1999. *Ideas in Action: Political Thought in the Twentieth Century*. Lanham, MD: Rowman & Littlefield Publishers.

Brown, Catrina. 2003. "Narrative Therapy: Reifying or Challenging Dominant Discourse." In *Emerging Perspectives on Anti-Oppressive Practice,* edited by Wes Shera, 223-46. Toronto: Canadian Scholars' Press Inc.

Bushman, Brad J. 1998. "Effects of Television Violence on Memory for Commercial Messages." *Journal of Experimental Psychology: Applied* 4 (4): 291-307.

Buttell, Frederick P., and Michelle Mohr Carney, eds. 2005. *Women Who Perpetrate Relationship Violence: Moving Beyond Political Correctness*. Journal of Offender Rehabilitation, 41 (4). New York: Haworth Press.

CARICOM Secretariat. 2012. "Sexual Violence against Children: The Elephant in the Room" [press release]. July 9.

Chadee, Derek, and Jason Ditton. 2005. "Fear of crime and the Media: Assessing the Lack of Relationship." *Crime Media Culture* 1 (3): 322-32.

Chambliss, J. J. 1996. *Philosophy of Education: An encyclopedia*. New York: Garland Pub.

Chan, Margaret. 2013. "Linking Child Survival and Child Development For Health, Equity, and Sustainable Development." *The Lancet* 381 (9877): 1514-15.

Charan, Richard. 2010. "Headless Horror." *Trinidad and Tobago Express,* July 22.

———. 2013. "People Trafficking 'a Problem in T&T' ... US Laments Lack of Prosecutions." *Trinidad and Tobago Express,* June 20.

Child Protection Monitoring and Evaluation Reference Group (CPMERG). 2012. *Ethical Principles, Dilemmas and Risks in Collecting Data on Violence against Children: A Review of Available Literature*. New York: Statistics and Monitoring Section/Division of Policy and Strategy, UNICEF.

Children's Authority of Trinidad and Tobago. 2013. *Information Brief*. Port of Spain: Children's Authority of Trinidad and Tobago.

Cicchetti, Dante, and Vicki Carlson, eds. 1989. *Child Maltreatment: Theory and Research on the Causes and Consequences of Child Abuse and Neglect*. Cambridge: Cambridge University Press.

Cicchetti, Dante, and Sheree L. Toth. 1995. "A Developmental Psychopathology Perspective on Child Abuse and Neglect." *Journal of the American Academy of Child & Adolescent Psychiatry* 34 (5): 541-65.

Cimpric, Aleksandra. 2010. *Children Accused of Witchcraft: An Anthropological Study of Contemporary Practices in Africa*. Dakar: UNICEF WCARO.

Clarke, Camille. 2011. "16-Year-Old Shot, Killed By Police." *Trinidad and Tobago Guardian,* January 28.

Coady, Cecil A.J. 2008. *Morality and Political Violence*, Cambridge: Cambridge University Press.

Cohen, William B. 1980. *European Empire Building: Nineteenth-Century Imperialism*. St Louis, MO: Forum Press.

"Confronting Horror in Paradise." n.d. *AVAAZ.Org*. Available from http://www.avaaz.org/en/highlights.php.

Cordero Ardila, Edwin, Hamyn Gurdia/n Alfaro, and Carlos Emilio López Hurtado. 2006. *Alcanzando un Sueño: Modelo de Prevención Social de la Polici/a [CD]*. Managua: Ediciones CRIPTO.

"Corporal Punishment" [Editorial]. 2013. *Express Tribune,* March 4.

Council of Europe. 2007. *Abolishing Corporal Punishment of Children: Questions and Answers*. Strasbourg: Council of Europe Pub.

Craig, Susan. 1982. "Sociological Theorising in the English-Speaking Caribbean: A Review." In *Contemporary Caribbean: A Sociological Reader,* edited by Susan Craig, 143-80. St Joseph: College Press.

Crenshaw, Martha, ed. 1983. *Terrorism, Legitimacy, and Power: The Consequences of Political Violence.* Middletown, CT: Wesleyan University Press.

Crichlow, Wesley. 2002. "Western Colonization as Disease: Native Adoption and Cultural Genocide." *Critical Social Work* 2 (2): 104-26.

Crossley, Nick. 2003. "From Reproduction to Transformation: Social Movement Fields and the Radical Habitus." *Theory, Culture & Society* 20 (6): 43-68.

Crowley, Daniel J. 1957. "Plural and Differential Acculturation in Trinidad." *American Anthropologist* 59 (5): 817-24.

Curet, L. Antonio. 2005. *Caribbean Paleodemography: Population, Culture History, and Sociopolitical Processes in Ancient Puerto Rico.* Tuscaloosa, AL: The University of Alabama Press.

Currie, Cheryl L. 2006. "Animal Cruelty by Children Exposed to Domestic Violence." *Child Abuse & Neglect* 30 (4): 425-35.

Dahlberg, Linda L., Susan B. Toal, Monica H. Swahn, and Christopher B. Behrens. 2005. *Measuring Violence-Related Attitudes, Behaviors, and Influences among Youths: A Compendium of Assessment Tools.* 2nd ed. Atlanta, GA: Centers for Disease Control and Prevention, National Center for Injury Prevention and Control.

"Daniel Decree Falls by the Wayside." 2013. *Trinidad and Tobago Newsday,* September 22.

de Benítez, Sarah Thomas. [2007]. *State of the World's Street Children: Violence.* London: The Consortium for Street Children (UK).

———. 2011. *State of the World's Street Children: Research.* London: The Consortium for Street Children.

Debiasi, Laura B., Annette Reynolds, and Ellen B. Buckner. 2013. "Assessing Emotional Well-being of Children in a Honduran Orphanage: Feasibility of Two Screening Tools." *Pediatric Nursing* 38 (3): 169-76.

Dei, George J. Sefa, and Alireza Asgharzadeh. 2001. "The Power of Social Theory: The Anti-Colonial Discursive Framework." *The Journal of Educational Thought* 35 (3): 297-323.

Denzin, Norman K. 1978. *The Research Act: A Theoretical Introduction to Sociological Methods.* 2nd ed. New York: McGraw-Hill.

Deosaran, Ramesh. 2007. *Crime, Delinquency and Justice: A Caribbean Reader.* Kingston: Ian Randle Publishers.

———.2013. "Equality of Educational Opportunity: The Race, Class and Crime Connection". *FFS Public Lecture.* University of the West Indies. November 27.

Detrick, Sharon, Gilles Abel, Maartje Berger, Aurore Delon, and Rosie Meek. 2008. *Violence against Children in Conflict with the Law: A Study on Indicators and Data Collection in Belgium, England and Wales, France and the Netherlands.* Amsterdam: Defence for Children International.

"Do You Know This Child?" 2011. *Trinidad and Tobago Express,* February 6.

Dobash, R. Emerson, Russell P. Dobash, Kate Cavanagh, and Ruth Lewis. 2000. *Changing Violent Men.* New Delhi: Sage Publications, Inc.

Dobash, Russell P., R. Emerson Dobash, Margo Wilson, and Martin Daly. 1992. "The Myth of Sexual Symmetry in Marital Violence." *Social Problems* 39 (1): 71-91.

Dodson, Michael. 1996. "Power and Cultural Difference in Native Title Mediation." *Aboriginal Law Bulletin* 3 (84): 8-11.

Dos Santos, Theotonio. 1973. "The Structure of Dependence." *The American Economic Review* 60 (2): 231-36.

Doucette-Gates, Ann, Jeanne Brooks-Gunn, and P. Lindsay Chase-Lansdale. 1998. "The Role of Bias and Equivalence in the Study of Race, Class, and Ethnicity." In *Studying Minority Adolescents*, edited by Vonnie C. McLoyd, and Laurence Steinberg, 211-36. Mahwah, NJ: Lawrence Erlbaum Associates, Inc.

Dugassa, Begna Fufa. 2008. "Indigenous Knowledge, Colonialism and Epistemological Violence: The Experience of the Oromo People under Abyssinian Colonial Rule." Thesis (Ph.D), University of Toronto.

Dunkin, Diane, and Pamela Hanna. 2001. "Thinking Together: Quality Adult: Child Interactions." New Zealand Council for Educational Research.

Dunkle, Kristin L., Rachel K. Jewkes, Heather C. Brown, Glenda E. Gray, James A. McIntyre, and Siobán D. Harlow. 2004. "Gender-Based Violence, Relationship Power, and Risk of HIV Infection in Women Attending Antenatal Clinics in South Africa." *The Lancet* 363 (9419): 1415-21.

Duranti, Alessandro, and Charles Goodwin, eds. 1992. *Rethinking Context: Language as an Interactive Phenomenon*. Cambridge: Cambridge University Press.

Dutton, Donald G., Tonia L. Nicholls, and Alicia Spidel. 2005. Female Perpetrators of Intimate Abuse. In *Women Who Perpetrate Relationship Violence: Moving Beyond Political Correctness*, edited by Frederick P. Buttell, and Michelle Mohr Carney, 1-32. Journal of Offender Rehabilitation, 41 (4). New York: Haworth Press.

Ellison, Christopher G. 1991. "An Eye for an Eye? A Note on the Southern Subculture of Violence Thesis." *Social Forces* 69 (4): 1223-39.

Erikson, Erik H. 1950. *Childhood and Society*. New York: Norton.

Escobar, Arturo. 1995. *Encountering Development: The Making and Unmaking of the Third World*. Princeton, NJ: Princeton University Press.

Fairclough, Norman. 1998. *Discourse and Social Change*. Cambridge: Polity Press.

———. 2001. *Language and Power*. 2nd ed. London: Pearson Education Limited.

Fairclough, Norman, and Ruth Wodak. 2007. Critical Discourse Analysis. in *Discourse as Social Interaction*, edited by Teun A. Van Dijk, 258-84. London: Sage Publications Ltd.

Fanon, Frantz. 1965. *A Dying Colonialism*. New York: Grove Press.

Farmer, Ben. 2012. "Afghan Boy Suicide Bombers Tell How They Are Brainwashed into Believing They Will Survive." *The Telegraph,* January 13.

Farmer, Paul. 2006. *AIDS and Accusation: Haiti and the Geography of Blame*. Updated ed. Berkeley, CA: University of California Press.

Faulk, M. 1974. "Men Who Assault Their Wives." *Medicine, Science, and the Law* 14 (3): 180-183.

Felson, Richard B., Allen E. Liska, Scott J. South, and Thomas L. McNulty. 1994. "The Subculture of Violence and Delinquency: Individual vs. School Context Effects." *Social Forces* 73 (1): 155-73.

Fiebert, Martin S. 2007. *References Examining Assaults by Women on Their Spouses or Male Partners: An Annotated Bibliography*. Long Beach: California State University.

Fokkema, Douwe, and Frans Grijzenhout, eds. 2004. *Dutch Culture in a European Perspective 5: Accounting for the past, 1650-2000*. Assen: Royal Van Gorcum.

Foucault, Michel. 1980. *Power/Knowledge: Selected Interviews and Other Writings, 1972-1977*. Edited by Colin Gordon. New York: Vintage.

Fowler, R. 1991. Critical Linguistics. In *The Linguistics Encyclopedia,* edited by Kirsten Malmkjaer, 89-93. London: Routledge.

Frank, Andre Gunder. 1967. *Capitalism and Underdevelopment in Latin America: Historical Studies of Chile and Brazil*. New York, NY: Monthly Review Press.

Frye, Alex. 2011. 'Formerly Enslaved People End Apprenticeship Practices in Trinidad, 1832-1838". *Global Nonviolent Action Database*. Accessed August 28, 2012, http://nvdatabase.swarthmore.edu/content/formerly-enslaved-people-end-apprenticeship-practices-trinidad-1832-1838.

Funk, Jeanne B., Robert Elliott, Michelle L. Urman, Geysa T. Flores, and Rose M. Mock. 1999. "The Attitudes towards Violence Scale: A Measure for Adolescents." *Journal of Interpersonal Violence* 14 (11): 1123-36.

Fuse, Kana, and Edward M. Crenshaw. 2006. "Gender Imbalance in Infant Mortality: A Cross-National Study of Social Structure and Female Infanticide." *Social Science & Medicine* 62 (2): 360-374.

Gaedtke, Felix, and Gayatri Parameswaran. 2013. "Nat Purwa: Where Prostitution is a Tradition." *Al Jazeera,* January 19.

Gaestel, Allyn. 2013. "Nepal: Chaupadi Culture and Violence against Women." *Pulitzer Center on Crisis Reporting*. Published February 5, 2013. Available from http://pulitzercenter.org/projects/nepal-cultural-practice-women-rights-sexual-violence-chaupadi-migration-WHO.

Galtung, Johan. 1969. "Violence, Peace, and Peace Research." *Journal of Peace Research* 6 (3): 167-91.

———. 1990. "Cultural Violence." *Journal of Peace Research* 27 (3): 291-305.

———. 1993. "Kulturelle Gewalt." *Der Burger Im Staat* 43: 106.

———. 1996. *Peace by Peaceful Means: Peace and Conflict, Development and Civilization*. London: Sage Publications Ltd.

Geertz, Clifford. 1973. *The interpretation of Cultures: Selected Essays*. New York, NY: Basic Books.

Gelles, Richard J., and Murray A. Straus. 1979. Determinants of Violence in the Family: Towards a Theoretical Integration. In *Contemporary Theories About the Family: Research-Based Theories,* edited by Wesley R. Burr, Reuben Hill, F. Ivan Nye, and Ira L. Reiss, 549-81. New York: Free Press.

George, Shanti, and Nico van Oudenhoven. 2002. *Stake Holders in Foster Care: An International Comparative Study*. Antwerp/Apeldoorn: Garant.

Gershoff, Elizabeth Thompson. 2002. "Corporal Punishment by Parents and Associated Child Behaviors and Experiences: A Meta-Analytic and Theoretical Review." *Psychological Bulletin* 128 (4): 539-79.

Girvan, Norman. 1971. *Foreign Capital and Economic Underdevelopment in Jamaica*. Kingston: Institute of Social and Economic Research, University of the West Indies.

Glaser, Barney G., and Anselm L. Strauss. 1967. *The Discovery of Grounded Theory: Strategies of Qualitative Research*. Chicago: Aldine Pub. Co.

Global AIDS Alliance. 2006. *Zero Tolerance: Stop the Violence against Women and Children, Stop HIV/AIDS*. Washington, DC: Global AIDS Alliance.

Goldberg, David Theo. 1993. *Racist Culture: Philosophy and the Politics of Meaning*. Oxford: Blackwell.

Gonzales, Gyasi. 2010. "Two-Year-Old Boy Beaten to Death." *Trinidad and Tobago Express,* October 21.

———. 2011. "Port Worker Slain in Front Children." *Trinidad and Tobago Express,* January 29.

Goodwin, Charles, and Alessandro Duranti. 1992. "Rethinking Content: An Introduction." In *Rethinking Context: Language as an Interactive Phenomenon,* edited by Alessandro Duranti, and Charles Goodwin, 1-42. Cambridge: Cambridge University Press.

Gothelf, Doron, Alan Apter, and Herman M. van Praag. 1997. "Measurement of Aggression in Psychiatric Patients." *Psychiatry Research* 71 (2): 83-95.

Graham, Carol. 2012. *The Pursuit of Happiness: An Economy of Well-Being*. Washington, DC: Brookings Institution Press.

Gramsci, Antonio. 1971. *Selections from the Prison Notebooks*. Edited and translated by Quintin Hoare, and Geoffrey Nowell-Smith. New York, NY: International Publishers.

Gumbs-Sandiford, Anika. 2010. "Baby Ashley is a Fighter." *Trinidad and Tobago Guardian,* December 27.

Gunter, Barrie, Caroline Oates, and Mark Blades. 2005. *Advertising to Children on TV: Content, Impact, and Regulation*. Mahwah, NJ: Lawrence Erlbaum.

Haas, Peter M. 1992. "Introduction: Epistemic Communities and International Policy Coordination." *International Organization* 46 (1): 1-35.

Habermas, Jürgen. 1972. *Knowledge and Human Interests*. London: Heinemann Educational Books.

———. 2003. *The Future of Human Nature*. Cambridge: Polity Press.

Hammersley, Martyn, and Paul Atkinson. 1983. *Ethnography: Principles in Practice*. London: Tavistock.

Harris, Marvin. 2001. *Cultural Materialism: The Struggle for a Science of Culture*. Updated ed. Walnut Creek, CA: Alta Mira Press.

Henry, Paget, and Carl Stone. 1983. *The Newer Caribbean: Decolonization, Democracy, and Development*. Philadelphia: Institute for the Study of Human Issues.

Herskovits, Melville. 1948. *Man and His Works: The Science of Cultural Anthropology*. New York, NY: A. A. Knopf.

Heuler, Hilary. 2013. "Uganda's Soaring HIV Infection Rate Linked to Infidelity." *Voice of America,* April 19. Available from http://www.voanews.com/content/infidelity-root-cause-of-ugandas-chaning-aids-epidemic/1644720.html.

Hickling, Frederick, and Elliot Sorel, eds. 2005. *Images of Psychiatry: The Caribbean*. Kingston: World Psychiatric Association.

Holsti. Ole R. 1968. "Content Analysis." *The Handbook of Social Psychology.* Ed. Gardner Lindzey and Elliott Aronson. 2nd ed., Vol. II, Reading: Addison-Wesley.

Hopf, Werner H., Günter L. Huber, and Rudolf H. Wei. 2008. "Media Violence and Youth Violence: A 2-Year Longitudinal Study." *Journal of Media Psychology* 20 (3): 79-96.

Hussain, Murtaza. 2012. "Pakistani Taliban's Indoctrinated Child Bombers." *Al Jazeera,* October 17.

International Labour Organization. 1999. Worst Forms of Child Labour Convention, 1999. ILO Convention, 182. Geneva: International Labour Office.

———. 2010. *Facts on Child Labour 2010*. Geneva: International Labour Office.

Jackson, Richard, ed. 2004. *(Re)Constructing Cultures of Violence and Peace*. New York: Editions Rodopi B. V.

James, C. L. R. 1947. *Dialectical Materialism and the Fate of Humanity*. Accessed April 13, 2010, https://www.marxists.org/archive/james-clr/works/diamat/diamat47.html.

———. 1963. *The Black Jacobins*. 2nd rev. ed. New York, NY: Random House.

Jayaram, Narayana. 2008. "India." In *Toward a global PhD? Forces and Forms in Doctoral Education Worldwide*, edited by Maresi Nerad and Mimi Heggelund Seattle: Washington University Press.

Jilani, Hina. 1992. Whose Laws? Human Rights and Violence against Women in Pakistan. In *"Freedom from Violence: Women's Strategies from Around the World"*, edited by Margaret Schuler. New York: United Nations Development Fund for Women.

John, Yolandra. 2011. "Mom, Four Children Evicted." *Trinidad and Tobago Express,* February 6.

Johnson, Bridget. n.d. "Top Murder Rates in the World." *About.Com World News,* Accessed 4 March 2013, http://worldnews.about.com/od/crime/tp/Top-Murder-Rates-In-The-World.htm.

Jualla-Ali, Rona. 2003. "Corporal Punishment in Trinidad and Tobago: An Insight into Teacher-Training and Teacher Type." MSc thesis, University of the West Indies.

Jualla, Rona. 2007. Corporal Punishment in Trinidad and Tobago: An Insight into Teacher-Training and Teacher Type. Paper presented at *Caribbean Child Research Conference, Kingston, Jamaica, October 23-24.*

Jualla, Rona, and Nico van Oudenhoven. 2010. Lowering the Tolerance towards Violence against Children: Lessons from Nicaragua and Trinidad and Tobago. In *Promoting Child Rights through Research: Selected Papers from the Caribbean Child Research Conference 2007-2008. Volume 2,* edited by Aldrie Henry-Lee, and Julie Meeks Gardner. Kingston: Sir Arthur Lewis Institute of Social and Economic Studies (SALISES).

———. 2011. *The Positive Deviance Approach to Worrisome Children and Youth Issues: Pointers for Policy Action in Kenya*. Leiden: ICDI.

Julien, Gabriel. 2008. "Street Children in Trinidad and Tobago: Understanding Their Lives and Experiences." *Community, Work & Family* 11 (4): 475-88.

———. 2009. "Advocacy among Street Children in Trinidad and Tobago." *The International Journal of Learning* 16 (3): 69-77.

———. 2010. "The Street Child's View of Education in Trinidad and Tobago: The Social and Academic Merits." *The International Journal of Learning* 17 (1): 109-18.

Katcher, Aaron. 2002. Animals in Therapeutic Education: Guides into the Liminal State. In *Children and Nature: Psychological, Sociocultural, and Evolutionary Investigations,* edited by Peter H. Kahn Jr., and Stephen R. Kellert, 179-98. Cambridge, MA: Massachusetts Institute of Technology.

Keating, Daniel P., and Clyde Hertzman, eds. 1999. *Developmental Health and the Wealth of Nations: Social, Biological, and Educational Dynamics*. New York: The Guilford Press.

Kennedy, Leslie W., and Stephen W. Baron. 1993. "Routine Activities and a Subculture of Violence: A Study of Violence on the Street." *Journal of Research in Crime and Delinquency* 30 (1): 88-112.

Kerrigan, Dylan. 2012. "Culture Contact: Trinidad "Pre-History ", Historical Representation and Multiculturalism." *Journal of the Department of Behavioural Sciences* 1 (1): 15-33.

Kiel, L. Douglas, and Euel W. Elliott, eds. 1997. *Chaos Theory in the Social Sciences: Foundations and Applications*. Ann Arbor, MI: University of Michigan Press.

Kong Soo, Charles. 2013. "No Gov't Database on Street Children in T&T." *Trinidad and Tobago Guardian,* January 2.

Kowlessar, Geisha. 2010. "Losing Tecia." *Trinidad and Tobago Guardian,* December 12.

Krug, Etienne G., Linda L. Dahlberg, James A. Mercy, Anthony B. Zwi, and Rafael Lozano, eds. 2002. *World Report on Violence and Health*. Geneva: World Health Organization.

La Rose, Miranda. 2013. "188 Crime Hotspots." *Trinidad and Tobago Newsday,* May 11.

Lahlah, Esmah. 2013. *Invisible Victims? Ethnic Differences in the Risk of Juvenile Violent Delinquency of Dutch and Moroccan-Dutch Adolescent Boys*. Doctoral Thesis, Tilburg University.

Laing, Aislinn. 2010. "Albino Girl, 11, Killed and Beheaded in Swaziland 'for Witchcraft'." *The Telegraph,* August 20.

Lampinen, James Michael, and Kathy Sexton-Radek, eds. 2010. *Protecting Children from Violence: Evidence-Based Interventions*. New York: Psychology Press.

Lang, Olivia. 2013. "Maldives Girl to Get 100 Lashes for Premarital Sex." *BBC News,* 26 February.

Lazaro, Christine. 2013. "Yemeni Child Bride Update: More Real Life Stories Emerge as Young Girls Discover the Value of Education." *International Business Times,* October 15.

LeBaron, Michelle. 1997. Mediation, Conflict Resolution and Multicultural Reality: Culturally Competence Practice. In *Mediation and Conflict Resolution in Social Work and the Human Services,* edited by Edward Kruk, 315-35. Chicago: Nelson-Hall Publishers.

LeBaron, Michelle, and Nike Carstarphen. 1997. "Negotiating Intractable Conflict: The Common Ground Dialogue Process and Abortion." *Negotiation Journal* 13 (4): 341-61.

Levitt, Kari, and Lloyd Best. 1969. *Externally-Propelled Growth and Industrialization in the Caribbean*. Montreal: McGill University, Centre for Developing Area Studies.

———. 1975. "Character of Caribbean Economy." In *Caribbean Economy: Dependence and Backwardness,* edited by George L. Beckford, 34-60. Kingston: Institute of Social and Economic Research, University of the West Indies.

Lewis, Gordon K. 1983. *Main Currents in Caribbean Thought: The Historical Evolution of Caribbean Society in its Ideological Aspects, 1492-1900*. Boonsboro: Sequitur Books.

Londoño, Ernesto. 2013. "Afghanistan Sees Rise in 'Dancing Boys' Exploitation." *The Washington Post,* April 4.

Lord, Richard. 2011. "PM Sets Up Daniel Decree to Protect T&T"s Children." *Trinidad and Tobago Guardian,* March 2.

Loubon, Michelle. 2013. "Gender-Based Violence Figures Alarming, Says De Coteau." *Trinidad and Tobago Express,* October 23.

Love, John M., Ellen Eliason Kisker, Christine M. Ross, Peter Z. Schochet, Jeanne Brooks-Gunn, Diane Paulsell, Kimberly Boller, Jill Constantine, Cheri Vogel, Allison Sidle Fuligni, and Christy Brady-Smith. 2002. *Making a Difference in the Lives of Infants and Toddlers and Their Families: *The Impacts of Early Head Start. Vol. 1: Final Technical Report*. Washington, DC: Dept. of Health and Human Services.

Lowrey, James. 2002. *Football and Families*. Fact Sheet, 14. Sir Norman Chester Centre for Football Research.

Maguire, Edward R., Julie A. Willis, Jeffrey Snipes, and Megan Gantley. 2008. "Spatial Concentrations of Violence in Trinidad and Tobago." *Caribbean Journal of Criminology and Public Safety* 13 (1 & 2): 48-92.

Malchiodi, Cathy A. 1998. *Understanding Children's Drawings*. New York: The Guilford Press.

Malinowski, Bronisław Kasper. 1931. "Culture." In *Encyclopedia of the Social Sciences*, edited by Edwin Robert Anderson Seligman, 621-46. New York: Macmillan.

Manual for the Measurement of Indicators of Violence against Children. [n.d.]. http://www.unicef.org/violencestudy/pdf/Manual%20Indicators%20 unicef.pdf: [UNICEF].

Marsh, David R., Dirk G. Schroeder, Kirk A. Dearden, Jerry Sternin, and Monique Sternin. 2004. "The Power of Positive Deviance." *BMJ* 329: 1177-79.

Marshall, Ronald. 2003. *Return to Innocence: A Study of Street Children in the Caribbean; Theory, Research, and Analysis*. St. Augustine: University of the West Indies, School of Continuing Studies.

Martin, Cedriann. 2012. "The New Fight against Domestic Violence." *Trinidad and Tobago Express*, September 14.

Marx, Karl. 1977. *A Contribution to the Critique of Political Economy*. Moscow: Progress Publishers.

———. 1994. "Critical Notes on the Article "The King of Prussia and Social Reform. By a Prussian"." In *Marx: Early Political Writings*, edited by Joseph J. O'Malley, 97-114. Cambridge: Cambridge University Press.

Marx, Karl, and Friedrich Engels. 1998. *The Communist Manifesto*. New York: Penguin Group.

McFadden, David. 2013. "Jamaica's 'unrelenting violence' against children condemned by UNICEF." *Toronto Star*, June 5.

McGreal, Chris. 2008. "Rape Victim, 13, Stoned to Death in Somalia." *Guardian*, November 2.

McMichael, Philip. 2010a. Changing the Subject of Development. In *Contesting Development: Critical Struggles for Social Change*, edited by Philip McMichael, 1-14. New York: Routledge.

———, ed. 2010b. *Contesting Development: Critical Struggles for Social Change*. New York: Routledge.

Mead, Margaret. 1953. "The Study of Culture at a Distance." In *The Study of Culture at a Distance*, edited by Margaret Mead, and Rhoda Métraux, 3-59. Chicago: University of Chicago Press.

Meichenbaum, Donald. [2006]. *Family Violence: Treatment of Perpetrators and Victims*. http://www.melissainstitute.org/documents/treating_perpetrators.pdf: [Melissa Institute for Violence Prevention and Teatment].

Merton, Robert K. 1957. *Social Theory and Social Structure*. New York: The Free Press.

Mintz, Sidney W., and Richard Price. 1992. *The Birth of African-American Culture: An Anthropological Perspective*. Boston: Beacon Press.

"Missing Boy Found Dead on River Bank". 2011. *Trinidad and Tobago Guardian*, February 21.

Monahan, John. 1992. "Mental Disorder and Violent Behavior: Perceptions and Evidence." *American Psychologist* 47 (4): 511-21.

Monahan, John, and Henry J. Steadman, eds. 1994. *Violence and Mental Disorder: Developments in Risk Assessment*. Chicago: University of Chicago Press.

Moore, Mark H. 1990. "Drugs: Getting a Fix on the Problem and the Solution." *Yale Law and Policy Review* 8 (1): 8-35.

Moore, Richard D., David Stanton, Ramana Gopalan, and Richard E. Chaisson. 1994. "Racial Differences in the Use of Drug Therapy for HIV Disease in an Urban Community." *The New England Journal of Medicine* 330: 763-68.

Mora, Anna Maria. 2013. "More Social Workers too, Please." [Letter to the Editor]. *Trinidad and Tobago Express,* March 17.

Morera, Esteve. 1990. "Gramsci and Democracy." *Canadian Journal of Political Science* 23 (1): 23-37.

Morgan, Paula, and Valerie Youssef. 2006. *Writing Rage: Unmasking Violence through Caribbean Discourse*. Kingston: University of the West Indies Press.

Morvaridi, Behrooz. 2008. *Social Justice and Development*. London: Palgrave Macmillan.

Müller, Ragnar. n.d. *Violence Typology by Johan Galtung (Direct, Structural and Cultural Violence)*. http://www.friedenspaedagogik.de/content/pdf/2754.

Mustapha, Nasser. 2002. "Issues in Education in Trinidad and Tobago." In *Issues in Education in Trinidad and Tobago,* edited by Nasser Mustapha, and Ronald A. Brunton. St. Augustine: School of Continuing Studies, University of the West Indies.

Mustapha, Nasser, and Ronald Brunton. 2002. *Issues in Education in Trinidad and Tobago*. St Augustine: University of the West Indies, School of Continuing Studies.

National Scientific Council on the Developing Child. 2012. *The Science of Neglect: The Persistent Absence of Responsive Care Disrupts the Developing Brain*. Working Paper, 12. http://www.developingchild.harvard.edu: National Scientific Council on the Developing Child, Center on the Developing Child at Harvard University.

Nazroo, James. 1995. "Uncovering Gender Differences in the Use of Marital Violence: The Effect of Methodology." *Sociology* 29 (3): 475-94.

Nettleford, Rex. 1973. *Rose Hall, Jamaica; Story of a People ... A Legend ... And a Legacy*, illustrated by Slim Aarons, and Arnold Newman. Rose Hall Limited.

Novaco, Raymond W. 1975. *Anger Control: The Development and Evaluation of an Experimental Treatment*. Lexington, MA: Lexington Books.

Novaco, Raymond W., and Wayne N. Welsh. 1989. "Anger Disturbances: Cognitive Mediation and Clinical Prescriptions." In *Clinical Approaches to Violence,* edited by Kevin Howells, and Clive R. Hollin, 39-60. Chichester: Wiley.

O'Connor, Anahad. 2013. "When the Bully is a Sibling," Well (blog). *New York Times,* June 17, http://well.blogs.nytimes.com/2013/06/17/when-the-bully-is-a-sibling/?_php=true&_type=-blogs&_r=0.

O'Neill, Michael Foley, and Noirin Hayes. 2011. Journalism Education and Child Rights: Exploring a New Model of Collaboration in Rights-Based Journalism Education. Paper presented at *Cities, Creativity, Connectivity, IAMCR Journalism Research and Education Section, Istanbul, July 13-17.*

Office of the High Commissioner on Human Rights. Committee on the Rights of the Child. 2006. *Consideration of Reports Submitted by States Parties under Article 44 of the Convention, Con-*

cluding Observations: Trinidad and Tobago. Geneva: Office of the High Commissioner on Human Rights.

Ortiz, Fernando. 1995. *Cuban Counterpoint: Tobacco and Sugar*. Durham, NC: Duke University Press.

Pagliaro, Jennifer. 2013. "Celebrated U of T Prof Arrested on Child Porn Charges." *Toronto Star,* July 8.

Pahl, Jan, ed. 1985. *Private Violence and Public Policy: The Needs of Battered Women and the Responses of the Public Services*. London: Routledge and Kegan Paul.

Paige, Glenn D., Chaiwat Satha-Anand, and Sarah Gilliatt, eds. 1993. *Islam and Nonviolence*. Honolulu: University of Hawai'i, Matsunaga Institute for Peace.

Pantin, Gerard. 1979. *A Mole Cricket Called Servol: An Account of Experiences in Education and Community Development in Trinidad and Tobago, West Indies*. The Hague: Bernard Van Leer Foundation.

———. 1984. *The Servol Village: A Caribbean Experience in Education and Community*. The Hague: Bernard Van Leer Foundation.

Parker, Ashley. 2013. "House Renews Violence against Women Measure." *New York Times,* February 28.

Parker, Robert Nash. 1989. "Poverty, Subculture of Violence, and Type of Homicide." *Social Forces* 67 (4): 983-1007.

Pascale, Richard, Jerry Sternin, and Monique Sternin. 2010. *The Power of Positive Deviance: How Unlikely Innovators Solve the World's Toughest Problems*. Boston, MA: Harvard Business Press.

Pereda, Noemi, Georgina Guilera, Maria Forns, and Juana Gómez-Benito. 2009. "The International Epidemiology of Child Sexual Abuse: A Continuation of Finkelhor (1994)." *Child Abuse & Neglect* 33 (6): 331-42.

Perry, Bruce D. 2002a. "Childhood Experience and the Expression of Genetic Potential: What Childhood Neglect Tells Us About Nature and Nurture." *Brain and Mind* 3 (1): 79-100.

Perry, Bruce D. 2002b. Youth Violence: Neurodevelopmental Impact of Violence in Childhood. In *Principles and Practice of Child and Adolescent Forensic Psychiatry,* edited by Diane H. Schetky, and Elissa P. Benedek. Washington, DC: American Psychiatric Pub.

Pianalto, Matthew. 2010. "In Defense of Intolerance." *Philosophy Now* 79: 13-15.

Pinheiro, Paola Sérgio. 2006. *The United Nations Secretary General's Study on Violence Against Children*. New York: United Nations.

Pinker, Steven. 2011. *The Better Angels of our Nature: Why Violence has Declined*. New York: Viking.

Polanyi, Karl. 1944. *The Great Transformation*. Boston: Beacon Press.

Pollack, William. 1998. Real Boys: Rescuing Our Sons from the Myths of Boyhood. New York: Henry Holt and Company, LLC.

Posner, Eric, and Kenneth Roth 2014. "Have Human Rights Treaties Failed?" *The New York Times,* December 29.

Povrzanović, Maya. 1993. "New ethnography" in The Situation of Radical Cultural Change: Croatia 1991-1992." *Journal of Area Studies* 1 (3): 161-68.

Prasad, V. Kanti, and Lois J. Smith. 1994. "Television Commercials in Violent Programming: An Experimental Evaluation of Their Effects on Children." *Journal of the Academy of Marketing Science* 22 (4): 340-351.

"Pregnancy Problem in Primary Schools". 2011. *Trinidad and Tobago Express,* January 18.

"Pregnant Woman Killed in Accident." 2011. *Trinidad and Tobago Express,* January 27.

Quainton, Anthony. 1983. Terrorism and Political Violence: A Permanent Challenge to Governments. In *Terrorism, Legitimacy, and Power: The Consequences of Political Violence,* edited bt Martha Crenshaw. Middletown, CT: Wesleyan University Press.

Ragoonath, Reshma. 2011. "Accused in Midnight Slaughter in Dow in Court Today." *Trinidad and Tobago Guardian,* January 14.

———. 2013. "Injured Mom Begs to See Body of Child Killed in Accident." *Trinidad and Tobago Guardian,* February 11.

Rawlins, Joan M. 2000. "Domestic Violence in Trinidad: A Family and Public Health Problem." *Caribbean Journal of Criminology and Social Psychology* 5 (1 & 2): 165-80.

Reardon, Betty A. 1997. *Tolerance: The Threshold of Peace*. Paris: Unesco Pub.

Reich, Wilhelm. 1970. *The Mass Psychology of Fascism*. New York: Albion.

Ring, Kathy. 2001. Young Children Drawing: The Significance of the Context. Paper presented at the *British Educational Research Association Annual Conference, University of Leeds, 13-15 September*.

Rist, Gilbert. 1997. *The History of Development: From Western Origins to Global Faith*. London: Zed Books.

Robinson, Harold, Karoline Schmid, and Monica Paul-McLean. 2007. "United Nations Launches Study on Violence against Children." *ICPD in Action in the Caribbean* 1 (1): 1-2.

Romero, Simon, and William Neuman. 2013. "Sweeping Protests in Brazil Pull in an Array of Grievances." *The New York Times,* June 20.

Rosling, Hans. 2006. "The Best Stats You've Ever Seen." *TED*. Filmed February 2006. Accessed December 22, 2012, ttp://www.ted.com/talks/hans_rosling_shows_the_best_stats_you_ve_ever_seen/transcript?language=en.

Rossman, B. B. Robbie, and Joyce Ho. 2000. "Posttraumatic Response and Children Exposed To Parental Violence." *Journal of Aggression, Maltreatment & Trauma* 3 (1): 85-106.

Russo, Nancy Felipe, and Angela Pirlott. 2006. "Gender-Based Violence: Concepts, Methods, and Findings." *Annals of the New York Academy of Sciences* 1087: 178-205.

Ryan, Selwyn. 2013. "Prison Reform: Beyond the Pail." *Trinidad and Tobago Express,* May 15.

Said, Edward W. 1978. *Orientalism*. London: Penguin Books.

Sanders, William B., and Thomas K. Pinhey. 1983. *The Conduct of Social Research*. New York, NY: Holt, Rinehart and Winston.

Santos, Boaventura de Sousa. 2005. "The Future of the World Social Forum: The Work of Translation." *Development* 48 (2): 15-22.

Sapers, Howard. 2013. "Aboriginal Corrections Report Finds 'Systemic Discrimination.'". *CBC News,* March 7. http://www.cbc.ca/news/politics/aboriginal-corrections-report-finds-systemic-discrimination-1.1338498.

Saxena, Shobhan. 2011. "India's Invisible Children: Swallowed By The Streets." *Times of India,* November 6.

Scaff, Lawrence A. 1984. "Weber before Weberian Sociology." *British Journal of Sociology* 35 (2): 190-215.

Schmid, Alex P., and Janny de Graaf. 1982. *Violence as Communication: Insurgent Terrorism and the Western News Media.* London: Sage.

Scott Ms. 2011. "Our Children Aren't Racehorses" [letter to the editor]. *Trinidad and Tobago Express,* February 6.

Sefa Dei, George J., and Alireza Asgharzadeh. 2001. "The Power of Social Theory: The Anti-Colonial Discursive Framework." *Journal of Educational Thought* 35 (3): 297-323.

Selvam, Saeed. 2013. "Canadian Values Can Thwart Terror." *Toronto Star,* April 24.

Sen, Amartya. 2006. *Identity and Violence: The Illusion of Destiny.* New York, NY: W. W. Norton & Co.

Sérgio Pinheiro, Paulo. 2006. *World Report on Violence against Children.* Geneva: The United Nations Secretary-General's Study on Violence against Children.

Shapiro, Jeremy P., Rebekah L. Dorman, Carolyn J. Welker, and Joseph B. Clough. 1998. "Youth Attitudes toward Guns and Violence: Relations with Sex, Age, Ethnic Group, and Firearm Exposure." *Journal of Clinical Child Psychology* 27 (1): 98-108.

Sharpe, Jacqueline. 1997. "Mental Health Issues and Family Socialization in the Caribbean." In *Caribbean Families: Diversity among Ethnic Groups,* edited by Jaipaul L. Roopnarine, and Janet Brown, 259-74. Advances in Applied Developmental Psychology, 14. Greenwich, CT: Ablex Publishing.

Shen, F., and T. Prinsen. 1999. Audience Responses to TV Commercials Embedded in Violent Programs. *Proceedings of the Conference of the American Academy of Advertising*: 100-106.

Sheppard, Suzanne. 2011. "Helping Others Heal." *Trinidad and Tobago Guardian,* January 30.

Shihadeh, Edward S., and Darrell J. Steffensmeier. 1994. "Economic Inequality, Family Disruption, and Urban Black Violence: Cities as Units of Stratification and Social Control." *Social Forces* 73 (2): 729-51.

Shiva, Vandana. 2002. *Water Wars: Privatization, Pollution and Profit.* New Delhi: Indian Research Press.

Silver, Beverly J., and Giovanni Arrighi. 2003. "Polanyi's "Double Movement": The Belle Époques of British and U.S. Hegemony Compared." *Politics & Society* 31 (2): 325-55.

Sim, Stuart, and Borin Van Loon. 2001. *Introducing Critical Theory: A Graphic Guide.* Cambridge: Icon Books Ltd.

Simmons, Catherine A., Peter Lehmann, Norman Cobb, and Carol R. Fowler. 2005. Personality Profiles of Women and Men Arrested for Domestic Violence: An Analysis of Similarities and Differences. *Journal of Offender Rehabilitation* 41 (4): 63-81.

Simon, Akile. 2011a. "Not Enough Daddies: John Sandy Plans Rally Promoting Father-Son Ties." *Trinidad and Tobago Express,* January 9.

———. 2011b. "Schoolgirls Taken to Hospital after Fight." *Trinidad and Tobago Express,* January 10.

Singh, Rickey. 2013. "The Domestic Violence Challenges for Caricom." *Trinidad and Tobago Express,* August 24.

Slaby, Ronald G. and Nancy Guerra. 1988. Cognitive Mediators of Aggression in Adolescent Offenders, I Assessment. Developmental Psychology. 74 (4): 580-588.

Smith, Lisa Anne, and Barbara Rogers. 2012. *Our Friend Joe: The Joe Fortes Story*. Vancouver: Ronsdale Press.

Smith, M. G. 1965. *The Plural Society in the British West Indies*. Berkeley, CA: Univeristy of California Press.

Spreitzer, Gretchen M., and Scott Sonenshein. 2004. "Toward the Construct Definition of Positive Deviance." *American Behavioral Scientist* 47 (6): 828-47.

St. Bernard, Godfrey C. 2010. "Demographics, Youth Victims and Prospective Measures for Prevention: The Case of Homicide in Trinidad and Tobago." *Caribbean Journal of Criminology and Public Safety* 15 (1-2): 1-34.

Stiglitz, Joseph E. 2012. *The Price of Inequality: How Today's Divided Society Endangers our Future*. New York: W. W. Norton & Company, Inc.

Straus, Murray A. 1999. The Controversy over Domestic Violence by Women: A Methodological, Theoretical, and Sociology of Science Analysis. In *Violence in Intimate Relationships,* edited by Ximena B. Arriaga, and Stuart Oskamp, 17-44. Thousand Oaks, CA: Sage Publications.

Straus, Murray A., Richard J. Gelles, and Suzanne K. Steinmetz. 1980. *Behind Closed Doors: Violence in the American Family*. New York: Anchor.

Streefkerk, Hein. 1985. *Industrial Transition in Rural India: Artisans, Traders and Tribals in South Gujarat*. Bombay: Popular Prakashan.

Surette, Ray, Derek Chadee, Linda Heath, and Jason R. Young. 2011. "Preventive and Punitive Criminal Justice Policy Support in Trinidad: The Media's Role." *Crime Media Culture* 7 (1): 31-48.

Swamber, Keino. 2012. "Tim: Teen Pregnancy a Big Headache." *Trinidad and Tobago Express,* April 13.

T&T Association of Psychologists. 2012. "Abundance of Violence in Media Harming our Children" [letter to the Editor]. *Trinidad and Tobago Guardian,* April 10.

Teeple, Elissa. 2004. "Transitions from Violence to Peace: A Cultural Change Model". In *(Re) Constructing Cultures of Violence and Peace,* edited by Richard Jackson, 123-36. New York: Editions Rodopi B. V.

Theodore, Karl, Althea La Foucade, Kimberly-Ann Gittens-Baynes, Edwards-Wescott, Roger McLean, and Christine Laptiste. 2012. *Situation Analysis of Children and Women in Trinidad and Tobago*, edited by Lynette Taylor. Christ Church: United Nations Children's Fund Office for the Eastern Caribbean Area.

Thomas de Benítez, Sarah. 2007. *State of the World's Street Children: Violence*. London: Consortium for Street Children.

———. 2011. *State of the World's Street Children: Research*. London: Consortium for Street Children.

Thompson, Richard, and Jiyoung K. Tabone. 2010. "The Impact of Early Alleged Maltreatment on Behavioral Trajectories." *Child Abuse & Neglect* 34 (12): 907-16.

Trinidad and Tobago. 2012. Children's Act. Act No. 12 of 2012.

Trouillot, Michel-Rolph. 2003. *Global Transformations: Anthropology and the Modern World*. New York, NY: Palgrave Macmillan.

Tylor, Edward Burnett. 1871. *Primitive Culture: Researches into the Development of Mythology, Philosophy, Religion, Art, and Custom*. London: John Murray.

UNICEF, Regional Office for Latin America and the Caribbean. 2005. *Investing in Children and Adolescents: Arguments and Approaches for Advocacy*. Panama City: UNICEF, Regional Office for Latin America and the Caribbean.

―――――. 2013. Global Report Card on Adolescents. New York: UNICEF.

United Nations Development Program. Regional Project RLA/97/014. 1999. *National Report Trinidad and Tobago*. National Reports on the Situation of Gender Violence against Women. http://freeofviolence.org/trintobbigfile.pdf: Inter-Agency Campaign on Violence against Women and Girls.

United Nations Development Programme. 2010. *Human Development Report 2010: The Real Wealth of Nations: Pathways to Human Development*. New York: Palgrave Macmillan.

United Nations Office on Drugs and Crime. 2014. *Global Study on Homicide 2013: Trends, Contexts, Data*. Vienna: UNODC.

United Nations Office on Drugs and Crime, and World Bank, Latin America and the Caribbean Regional Office. 2007. *Crime, Violence, and Development: Trends, Costs, and Policy Options in the Caribbean*. World Bank Report, 37820. New York, NY; Washington, DC: United Nations; World Bank.

Van Dijk, Teun A. 1997. "Discourse as Interaction in Society." In *Discourse as Social Interaction*, edited by Teun A. van Dijk, 1-38. Discourse Studies, 2. London: Sage Publication.

Van Oudenhoven, Nico. 2007. Growing Up in Institutions, strength in vulnerability: Lessons from Bulgarian Children. In *Lessons for Children and Adults,* edited by Valentina Simeonova, and Georgi Simeonov. Sofia: Free and Democratic Bulgaria Foundation.

Van Oudenhoven, Nico, and Rekha Wazir. 2006. *Newly Emerging Needs of Children: An Exploration*. Antwerp/Apeldoorn: Garant.

Verobej, Mark 2008. Structural Violence. *The Canadian Journal of Peace Research and Conflict Studies*. Volume 40, Number 2, 84-89.

Vertigans, Stephen. 2011. *The Sociology of Terrorism: Peoples, Places and Processes*. London: Routledge.

Violence against Children in the Caribbean Region: A Desk Review. 2005. http://www.UNICEF.org/barbados/spmapping/Implementation/CP/Regional/Violence_deskreview_2005.pdf: [UNICEF].

Violent Crime Down by 17% in Scotland. 2012. *BBC News,* June 26, http://www.bbc.co.uk/news/uk-scotland-18592130.

Wakin, Daniel J. 2012. "Venerated High Priest and Humble Servant of Music Education." *The New York Times,* March 1.

Walker, Julian S., and Gisli H. Gudjonsson. 2006. "The Maudsley Violence Questionnaire: Relationship to Personality and Self-Reported Offending." *Personality and Individual Differences* 40 (4): 795-806.

Wallerstein, Immanuel. 1974. *The Modern World-System I: Capitalist Agriculture and the Origins of the European World Economy in the Sixteenth Century*. New York, NY: Academic Press Inc.

Wallerstein, Immanuel Maurice. 1998. *Utopistics: Or Historical Choices of the Twenty-First Century*. New York, NY: New Press.

Walters, Glenn D. 2003. "Predicting Institutional Adjustment and Recidivism with the Psychopathy Checklist Factor Scores: A Meta-Analysis." *Law and Human Behavior* 27 (5): 541-58.

Weber, Max. 2000. *The Protestant Ethic and The Spirit of Capitalism*. London: Routledge.

Williams, Raymond. 1973. "Base and Superstructure in Marxist Cultural Theory." *New Left Review* (82): 1-16.

Wilson, Sascha. 2013. "Mom of Slain Student Pleads: Stop Violence in Schools." *Trinidad and Tobago Guardian,* June 1.

Winter, Yves. 2012. "Violence and Visibility". *New Political Science* 34(2): 195–202.

Winterman, Denise. 2005. "Table Manners." *BBC News,* May 18, http://news.bbc.co.uk/2/hi/uk_news/magazine/4551727.stm.

Wolfgang, Marvin E. 1958. *Patterns in Criminal Homicide*. Philadelphia, PA: University of Pennsylvania Press.

Wolfgang, Marvin E., and Franco Ferracuti. 1967. *The Subculture of Violence: Towards an Integrated Theory in Criminology*. London: Tavistock Publications.

World Health Organization. 2002. "Collective Violence". *Facts*. Geneva: World Health Organisation.

⎯⎯⎯⎯⎯. 2013. *Female Genital Mutilation*. Fact Sheet, 241, updated February 2013. http://www.who.int/mediacentre/factsheets/fs241/en/: World Health Organization.

Youssef, Valerie. 2010a. "The Culture of Violence in Trinidad and Tobago: A Case Study". *Caribbean Review of Gender Studies* (4): 1-9.

Youssef, Valerie. 2010b. "Sociolinguistics of the Caribbean." In *The Routledge Handbook of Sociolinguistics around the World,* edited by Martin J. Ball, 52-64. New York, NY: Routldege.

Zabludovsky, Karla. 2013. "Official Corruption in Mexico, Once Rarely Exposed, Is Starting to Come to Light." *The New York Times,* June 23.

Zaleski, Pawel. 208. "Tocqueville on Civilian Society. A Romantic Vision of the Dichotomic Structure of Social Reality." *Archiv Für Begriffsgeschichte* 50: 260-266.

Appendices

Appendix I

Violence against children I

This questionnaire is part of a research project on Violence against Children (VAC). Your input is highly valued and appreciated. For information kindly contact Rona Jualla van Oudenhoven, rjualla@yahoo.ca. Thanks for your help in this. Absolutely no personal information regarding your identity re: name, gender, race, religious affiliation is required.

| Date .... | Group .... | No. .... |

1. How would you define violence?

   ....
   ....

2. What do you see as the most common forms of violence in T&T?

   ....
   ....

3. What do you consider to be the worst forms of VAC?

   ....
   ....

4. What do you think are the 'causes' of violence?

   ....
   ....

5. *What are your main sources of information?*

....

6. *What do you think could be done to combat violence against children?*

....

....

7. *Do you think there a difference in violence against girls and violence against boys?*

....

....

8. *How can we protect girls against violence?*

....

....

9. *How can we protect boys against violence?*

....

....

10. *Do you think that physical punishment is (i) okay or (ii) not okay?*

....

....

11. *What would you do if you suspect an incidence of abuse or domestic violence?*

....

....

12. *What kind of violence do you see street children faced with in T&T?*

....

....

13. *Who are the main perpetrators of violence against street children?*

....

....

14. What can be done to lower the violence against street children?

 ....

 ....

15. What situations do you think help lessen violence?

 ....

 ....

16. In comparison with the outside world would you say in T&T we are:
    (a) More violent   (b) Less violent   (c) Same as

17. In T&T we:
    (a) Tolerate violence   (b) Stand up against violence

18. What are some things that you can do as an individual to stop the cycle of violence against children?

 ....

 ....

19. What role should the government play in fighting VAC?

 ....

 ....

20. Which do you think makes for a less violent T&T?
    (a) T&T 20 years ago   (b) T&T now   (c) T&T 20 years from now.

Appendix II

Violence against children II

| Date .... | Age Cohort .... | Group .... |

1. *How would you define violence?*
    1. Direct Violence: Physical harm; Physical and mental harm; Neglect; Bullying; Hurting vulnerable persons
    2. Structural Violence: Against the Law; Abuse of Power; Systemic
    3. Cultural Violence: Zero tolerance; Against Rights of the Child

2. *What do you see as the most common forms of violence against children in T&T?*
    1. Direct Violence: Crime; Drug abuse; Violence against animals; Violence against the Elderly; Robberies & Thefts; Murders & Shootings; Gang-related Violence; Suicide; Teenage Pregnancy; Neglect; Kidnapping; Violence in schools; Violence against children; Domestic Violence; Sexual Abuse; Mental Abuse; Verbal Abuse; Physical Violence
    2. Structural Violence: Abuse of power; Exploitation at Work; Child Labour;
    3. Cultural Violence: early marriages

3. *What do you consider to be the worst forms of VAC?*
    1. Direct Violence: Sexual Abuse; Physical Abuse; Psychological Abuse; Verbal Abuse; Murder and Shootings; Domestic Violence;
    2. Structural Violence
    3. Cultural Violence

4. *What do you think are the 'causes' of violence?*
    1. Direct Violence:
        - Substance abuse (alcohol abuse; drug abuse; smoking; disagreements and fights)
        - Media violence (music; TV/movies; electronic games; print media)
        - Poverty (unemployment; financial problems/stress)
    2. Structural Violence:
        - Education (lack of education/knowledge; illiteracy)
        - Power/control (abuse of power; need to control; need to feel superior; loss of power; sadism)
        - Environment (bad examples/role models; rough/run-down neighbourhood; growing up on the streets; crime; gangs and gangsters; easy access to guns
        - Political system (lack of formal support systems; under-utilisation of services; no commitment by the government; lack of punishment of violent acts; no law enforcement;

political tactics; governmental indifference; no communication with government; police violence)
- Home situation (poor parenting; poor upbringing — "no brought-upsy but dragged-up" —; family breakdown; single parenting; lack of love, care and attention; no proper supervision/guidance; "bad siblings"; exposure to domestic violence; unplanned, unwanted pregnancies

3. Cultural Violence:
    - Psycho-social make up (Insecurity/low self-esteem; feelings of hopelessness; depression/post-partum; poor anger management; inability to cope; lack of self-control/impulse control; revenge, jealousy, hatred; (sexual) frustration)
    - Morals and values (lack of empathy/compassion; disrespect of others; lack of spiritual development)
    - Social factors (poor communication skills; peer pressure; life styles; rivalry; arguments, desire and greed; poor social upbringing; the company one keeps
    - Culturally-sanctioned acts
    - Cyclical nature of violence -"violence breeds violence" — (cycle of abuse; cycle of violence; cycle of poor education; cycle of bad childhood; cycle of bullying)

5. *What are your main sources of information?*
    - Television ; Internet; Radio; Newspapers; Observations; Experience; On the job/In school; Education/Training; Ministries; NGOs; Libraries -Books/Pamphlets; Community; Common sense

6. *What could be done to combat violence against children?*
    - Legislative/Legal Reforms; Education/Training/Research; Improve Accountability/Monitoring/Evaluation; Engage Media; Poverty Alleviation Strategies; Strengthen Social/Family Services; Punitive Measures; Community-based Initiatives; Engage Children/Educate/Values; Counseling/Therapy; Break the Silence

7. *Is there a difference in violence against girls and violence against boys?* Yes   No

8. *How can we protect girls against violence?*

9. *How can we protect boys against violence? (same as above)*

10. *Do you think physical punishment is (i) Okay or (ii) Not okay*

11. *What would you do if you suspect an incidence of abuse or domestic violence?*
    1. Stay out of It (2) Inform/Involve Police/Social Services/Media (c) Intervene personally

12. *What kind of violence do you see street children faced with in T&T?*

- Emotional/Mental Abuse; Physical Abuse; Sexual Abuse; Verbal Abuse; Substance Abuse; Being away from home; Gang-related violence; Exploitation; Kidnapping; Murder

13. *Who are the main perpetrators of violence against street children?*
    - Drug Traffickers/ Addicts; Parents/Guardians/Friends & Relatives; Police; Street People; Caregivers; Unknown Adults; Sex Offenders; Gangs; Government/State

14. *What can be done to lower the violence against street children?*
    - Family Support; Foster Care; Homes/Institutions; Community/Engagement; Education; Training of Professionals; Legislative reform/Law enforcement

15. *What situations do you think help lessen violence?*
    - Family Support ; Education; Community-based; Religious/ Spiritual/Moral guidance; Social Support; Security; Punitive Approaches; Government Intervention

16. *In comparison with the outside world would you say in T&T we are:*
    a. More violent   b. Less violent   c. Same as

17. *What do you do as a citizen of T&T?*
    a. Tolerate violence   b. Stand up against violence

18. *What are some things that you can do as an individual to stop the cycle of violence against children?*

19. *What role should the government play in fighting VAC?*

20. *Which do you think makes for a better T&T? a. T&T 20 years ago b. T&T now c. T&T 20 years from now.*

Appendix III

Violence against children: institutions

This questionnaire is part of a research work being conducted on Violence against Children (VAC). Your input is highly valued and appreciated. *All information is anonymous and strictly confidential.* Please feel free to contact me, Rona Jualla van Oudenhoven, rjualla@gmail.com for any information you may require. Thank you for your help in this.

Age......................................	Religion	Gender ....

1. What do you think of when you think of violence? (sentences, words or images that come to your mind)

   ....

   ....

2. Which of the following do you think is an example of violence?
    a. A parent hitting a child for no good reason?   Y/N
    b. A parent hitting a child for misbehaving?   Y/N
    c. A teacher hitting a student for no 'clear' reason?   Y/N
    d. A teacher hitting a student for misbehaving?   Y/N
    e. A boy hits a girl?   Y/N
    f. A girl hits a boy?   Y/N
    g. Someone shouting bad and hurtful words at another person?   Y/N
    h. A husband /boyfriend hitting his wife/girlfriend?   Y/N
    i. A wife /girlfriend hitting her husband /boyfriend?   Y/N
    j. A child not being allowed to go to school and get an education?   Y/N
    k. A child not getting help in the hospital?   Y/N

3. Do you think physical punishment is necessary when a child does wrong?   Y/N

4. Do you think physical punishment is necessary when an adult does wrong?   Y/N

5. Do you see any of the following as bad forms of punishment?
    a. Beating with the hands   Y/N
    b. Beating with a stick or strap   Y/N
    c. Locking child in closet   Y/N
    d. Locking child in room   Y/N
    e. Taking away food from child   Y/N

    f. Tying up the child   Y/N
    g. Cursing the child (using bad words)   Y/N

6. *Have you ever heard about the Rights of the Child?*   Y/N

7. *Do you think children in T&T have rights?*   Y/N

8. *Can you name one (1) Right of the Child?*   Y/N

....

9. *Have you ever experienced any violence in your life?*   Y/N

10. *Do you think it is normal?*   Y/N

11. *Do you think some children never experience violence in their life?*   Y/N

12. *How do you feel about violence?*
    a. Badly   Y/N
    b. Sad   Y/N
    c. Angry   Y/N
    d. Helpless   Y/N
    e. Normal   Y/N
    f. Wrong   Y/N

13. *Who do you think can help stop violence?*

....

....

14. *Any ideas on how this can be done?*

....

....

Appendix IV

Violence against children: evaluation tool

This questionnaire is part of a research work being conducted in Violence against Children (VAC). Your input is highly valued and appreciated. All information is anonymous and confidential. Please feel free to contact Rona Jualla van Oudenhoven, rjualla@yahoo.ca for any information you may require. Thank you for your help in this.

1. What role does your Ministry/Organization/Department play in the fight against VAC?

   ....

   To the best of your knowledge, have plans to address the situation of VAC in T&T been adopted in the National Agenda? Y/N

2. Is there a specific department in your organisation responsible for the implementation and the systematic monitoring of matters related to children's issues and the CRC? Y/N

3. If yes, can you identify some of the tasks of this Unit?

   ....

4. What are some of the hiccups faced in achieving these tasks?

   ....

5. Have you witnessed any law reforms in recent years re: VAC in T&T? Y/N

6. Do you see the involvement of civil society in the discourse on VAC? Y/N

7. If yes, how?

   ....

8. Does the organization involve children in the discourse on VAC? Y/N

9. If yes, please say how?

   ....

10. How has T&T allowed for its children to experience their rights as outlined by the CRC?

....

11. Do you think that the political, economic, and social structures of T&T are connected to violence?   Y/N

12. If yes, how so?

....

13. Would you say that Trinbagonians are tolerant of violence in our daily lives?   Y/N

14. Would you say that Trinbagonians are less tolerant of VAC than violence against adults?   Y/N

15. If yes, why do you say this?

....

16. Do you think that there is more to violence than the direct violence we witness?   Y/N

17. If yes, what do you consider to be violence?

....

18. What do you see as the role of the State in this battle against VAC?

....

19. Are State Parties ensuring compatibility of existing and new legislation and judicial practice with the CRC?   Y/N

20. How is this?

....

21. Are there comprehensive reviews of CRC legislations?   Y/N

22. Are children's rights included in the Constitution?   Y/N

23. How is the State responding to "new" issues related to children's rights?

....

24. Has specific laws been developed to reflect the CRC principles and provisions?   Y/N

25. Are systems in place for children/ their representatives if children's rights are breached?   Y/N

26. *Are independent institutions for children's rights being developed — children's Ombudsman office, child's rights commissioners and focal points within national human rights institutions?*
                                                                                                        Y/N

27. *If yes, please identify a few*

....

28. *Do you experience cooperation amongst the various children's rights-focussed institutions?* Y/N

29. *Do they share similar agendas re: implementation of the CRC?*   Y/N

30. *Are resources being allocated by the State to children programmes?*   Y/N

31. *Is systematic monitoring conducted through effective child-related data collection, analysis, evaluation and dissemination?*
                                                                                                        Y/N

32. *Is education, training, awareness-raising on Children's Rights steadily promoted?*   Y/N

33. *Is there much collaboration between the various Ministries to discuss issues relating to VAC?*
                                                                                                        Y/N

34. *Is there much collaboration with the university (UWI, UTT) and the Government ministries on issues relating to violence?*
                                                                                                        Y/N

Appendix VI

Researcher's field experience that contributed to this Study[44]

Workshops, Seminars, Missions and Committees
- Conducted Evaluation Sizanani Children's Home, South Africa. October, 2014.
- Conducted Workshop in collaboration with Roma Education Fund (REF) and International Child Development Initiatives (ICDI) in Vienna, Austria. June 2014.
- Spoke at Seminar on Violence against Women. TRUST Programme, Jerusalem. November 2013.
- Conducted Programme Evaluation AMISTAD Nicaragua. March 2013.
- Conducted Evaluation and Needs Assessment OSI Tajikistan. March 2012.
- Attended Seminar Global Children Issues. Tokyo, Japan. March 2012.
- Conducted Evaluation and Needs Assessment OSI Pakistan. January 2012.
- Conducted Workshop on Positive Deviance, Istanbul, Turkey. September 2012.
- Held discussions on Evaluation Tool for Assessment of Pre-Schools. Moscow, Russia. December 2012.
- Keynote address 'Violence against children and families', Paramaribo, Suriname. June 2011.
- Conducted Workshop on Early Childhood Education. The World Bank/Yakutia Ministry of Education, Yakutsk. May, 2011.
- Conducted Workshops on 'Positive Deviance and Violence against Children, Kwale and Nairobi, Plan International, Kenya. March 2011.
- Participated in Workshop and lectures on 'Violence against children and families', Anton de Kom University, Paramaribo, Suriname. December 2010.
- Conducted Workshop 'Domestic Violence', Trust for Early Childhood, Family and Community Education, Jerusalem. November 2010.
- Presented on Children's Issues in International Perspective, Council of the Bar of The Hague Assembly of the International Legal Network, The Hague, the Netherlands, October, 2010.
- Conducted Evaluation mission 'Migrant Children', VSO-UBS Optimus, Thailand. 2010
- Conducted National Workshop on Violence against Children, Paramaribo. 2010.
- Attended various missions on Early Childhood Education. Siberia. 2008-9.
- Presented Paper Childs Rights Research Conference. Jamaica. October 2009
- Spoke on Multicultural Integration in International Perspective, International Conference on Multicultural Integration, Tilburg, Netherlands. May 2008.
- Wrote Policy Paper on the culture of violence tolerance in Nicaragua and Trinidad and Tobago- PLAN Nederland. May 2008.
- Conducted Workshop on Corporal Punishment in Bucharest, Romania. May 2008.
- Attended United Nations Conference on Violence against Children- Paolo Pinheiro-Amsterdam, Netherlands. November 2007.

---

44. The following represents the researcher's involvement in the field in the capacity of Ph. D Research Candidate and Independent Educational Consultant with ICDI.

- Presented Paper on corporal punishment at Childs Rights Research Conference, Jamaica. July 2007
- Conducted Field Research on violence against children (slum areas, the street, schools) Nicaragua. January 2008.
- Developed and Presented Violence-testing Instrument for European Foundation for Street Children (EFSC) — Naples, Italy. November 2007.
- Member of the National Mental Health Committee of Trinidad and Tobago. 2004-2007
- Chairman of the Children in Need of Special Protection(CNSP) Committee)- 2005-2007
- Attended National AIDS Coordinating Committee Annual Research Symposium. March, 2007
- Social Assessment Training Workshop. Unit for Social Problem Analysis and Social Policy Development. University of the West Indies. March 2007.
- Participated in:
  - Participatory Methodology Training, U.W.I. Trinidad and Tobago, December 2006
  - Child Rights Research Conference. Hosted jointly by SALISES Jamaica and UNICEF Jamaica. October 2006.
  - TOR Training University of the West Indies. September 2006.
  - Conference on Violence against Children Trinidad Hilton. August 2006.
  - Conference on Latin American Issues, Trinidad Hilton. March 2006.
  - SAS Training. SALISES, University of the West Indies. Trinidad, January 2006.
  - Monitoring and Evaluation Capacity Building Workshop. World Bank, Ministry of Public Administration and Information. Trinidad and Tobago. September 2005
  - Workshop "Road mapping the Future". U.W.I. Mona, Jamaica. September 2005.
  - Effective Management Training. DAH Consulting, Inc. Ministry of Social Development. August 2005.
  - Technical Consultation on "Overcoming Hunger and Malnutrition for an Equitable Social Development in the ACS Countries". Hosted by World Health Organization (WHO).Panama. May 2005.

Papers and Recent publications
- (2015) 'A Rights-Based Approach to Understanding Violence-Tolerance and its Implications: A Bangladesh Example'. *Amity Journal of Human Behaviour and Development Issues,* Volume 2, No. 1, August. Amity University, Lucknow Campus: India.
- (2014), *Culturised Early Childhood Development: the well-being and healthy development of young boys and girls*, Antwerp/Apeldoorn: Garant. (Russian translation).*
- (2014),'The not-so-soft power of culture and diversity' *Amity Journal of Human Behaviour and Development Issues*, Spring, Amity University, Lucknow Campus, India.
- (2013), 'There's more to ECD than teaching the '3-Rs' at ever earlier ages', *An Leanbh Óg* (OMEP), Volume 7.*
- (2012), 'ECD QUAT', Quality Assessment Tools of services for young boys and girls. ICDI, Leiden, The Netherlands.

---

* With Nico van Oudenhoven.

- (2012), 'Girls' QUAT', Quality Assessment Tools of services for girls and young women. ICDI, Leiden, The Netherlands.
- (2012), 'Boys QUAT', Quality Assessment Tools of services for boys and young men, an instrument to measure the quality of ECD services, ICDI, Leiden, The Netherlands.
- (2011), 'The Positive Deviance Approach to Worrisome Children and Youth Issues: Pointers for Policy Action and Training', ICDI, Leiden.*
- (2010), 'Community-based Early Years Services: the Golden Triangle of Informal, Nonformal and Formal Approaches', *Psychological Science and Education,* #3/2010, Pages 22-31.*
- (2009), 'Early Childhood Education and its Golden Triangle of Informal, Nonformal and Formal Approaches', The World Bank Moscow, Russia.
- (2008), Lowering the Tolerance towards Violence against Children: Lessons from Nicaragua and Trinidad and Tobago, PLAN International, Amsterdam, the Netherlands.
- (2008), Lowering the Tolerance towards Violence against Children: Lessons from Nicaragua and Trinidad and Tobago, University of the West Indies, Mona Campus, Jamaica.
- (2008), Diagnostic Toolkit on Street Children. EFSC, Brussels, Belgium.
- (2007), 'Explaining Corporal Punishment: The Jamaican and T&T Contexts'. Conference: University of the West Indies, Mona Campus, Jamaica.
- (2007), 'A Culture of Violence: A Rights-based Analysis of Child Abuse in Trinidad & Tobago'. CYD 2007, ICCYS, Leiden and The Hague, the Netherlands.
- (2005), Various papers on Socially Displaced Persons in Trinidad and Tobago, June, 2005
- (2003), 'Corporal punishment in Trinidad and Tobago: an insight into teacher-training and teacher type', University of the West Indies Trinidad and Tobago.